BEGINNINGS

WALKER FAMILY SERIES ~ BOOK EIGHT

BERNADETTE MARIE

5 PRINCE PUBLISHING

BEGINNINGS

BERNADETTE MARIE

5 PRINCE PUBLISHING & BOOKS, LLC

PO Box 971

Golden, CO 80402-0971

www.5PrinceBooks.com

Digital 978-1-63112-221-7 Print 978-1-63112-222-4

BEGINNINGS Bernadette Marie

Copyright BERNADETTE MARIE 2018

Published by 5 Prince Publishing

Cover Credit: Bernadette Soehner

First Edition 2018

5 PRINCE PUBLISHING AND BOOKS, LLC.

To Stan,
I have loved you from the very beginning.
Yes, I mean that day I met you under the
window of my dorm room.
Forever and a day started then.

To Dad,
Thank you for supporting all of
the crazy dreams I chased from the very beginning.
I will miss you every day until I, too,
start a new beginning in heaven with you.
Until then, I will continue to work to make you proud.

ACKNOWLEDGMENTS

To My 5 Amazing Princes: Every beginning you make is a journey and a lesson learned. Keep making new beginnings.

To Mom and Anni: Beginnings are hard because there is no path set. It's time for us to set that new path and enjoy our journey down it.

To Cate: Thank you! Thank you! Thank you! From the beginning you've always kept me organized and on task. That warrants another thank you.

To My Tribe: You know what's fun? Beginning new traditions with all of you! Whether it's business related, fitness related, or family related, my tribe keeps my heart so happy.

To My Readers: Thank you for your support since the beginning of my journey. I love to write for you all.

Beginnings

THE MATCHMAKER SERIES

Matchmakers

Encore

Finding Hope

THE THREE MRS. MONROES TRILOGY

Amelia

Penelope

Vivian

THE ASPEN CREEK SERIES

First Kiss

Unexpected Admirer

On Thin Ice

Indomitable Spirit

THE DENVER BRIDE SERIES

Cart Before the Horse

Never Saw it Coming

Candy Kisses

ROMANTIC SUSPENSE by BERNADETTE MARIE

Chasing Shadows

PARANORMAL ROMANCE by BERNADETTE MARIE

The Tea Shop

BEGINNINGS

BERNADETTE MARIE

1

─────

*I*t wasn't as if the wedding of his cousin to the movie star had been a surprise. The invitation had been sitting on Ben's kitchen counter for nearly a month. Then again, everything had been on the counter since he was taking his sweet time unpacking after his move into the modular home he'd had dropped on his piece of the Walker Ranch land.

He'd have liked to have built his own home from the ground up, but where would he get the time?

A lot more responsibility had fallen on him since his brother Eric had become a father. It wasn't as if Eric completely blew off his duties, but he'd rather spend time with his daughter.

Ben understood that. After all, one day he would like to have children, too. He didn't see that happening anytime soon. It was hard to meet women when you lived forty-five minutes away from the nearest city. Besides, he'd never been good with women, anyway.

His mother had been trying to persuade him to take a date to his cousin's wedding. In his head, he'd made a list of five or six women he could ask, but when it came down to it, he knew he'd show up solo.

The reflection in the mirror caught his attention as he checked the traffic behind him. His hair was a mess, and one more thing for his mother to harp on. He could hear her voice rattling his head. *You need a haircut before Audrey takes time off for her wedding.*

Ben blew out a long, ragged breath. She'd been saying that for two weeks. Now, he was enroute to Audrey's new salon in the hopes that one of her employees could sneak him in for a necessary haircut, because of course, Audrey had already taken time off for her wedding.

He pulled up in front of the *Bridal Mecca*, the strip-mall his cousin Pearl and her sister-in-law Lydia owned. Nearly all the businesses were bridal related, except for his sister-in-law Gia's Italian gift shop. There was no denying he was extremely proud of his family for what they had built. Sometimes he wished he had it in him to do something as big, but the truth was he would much rather be around his family and the animals. Working with the public didn't seem like an advantage in his book.

Ben parked his truck and climbed out. The lights in the salon were still on, and he figured that was a good sign. His mother would probably kill him if he showed up to the wedding tomorrow looking like he did.

Just as he opened the front door, a small remote-controlled car jumped over the toe of his boot.

"Whoa! Did you see that?" The young, excited voice came from a boy who darted from the back room and ran to the car. He picked it up and looked up at Ben. "Who are you?"

"Ben. Who are you?"

The boy stood straight as if he'd been trained to do so when meeting someone. "Zane. Did you come to get your hair cut?" he asked as he looked up at the mess atop Ben's head.

"Yeah."

Zane stood there studying him for another moment before he yelled, "Mom, there's a man out here who needs a haircut!"

Ben stood there, the door still opened behind him, while he waited for the anonymous mom to appear.

The moment that Nichole, Audrey's first employee, came from the back room, Ben's heart rate kicked up. On her hip, she carried a little girl with hair color that matched her own dark brown.

"Hey, Ben. What's up? We were just packing up," she said as she let the little girl down and she ran off after Zane.

Ben shut the door behind him. "I didn't realize it was this late. I came to see if somebody could sneak me in for a haircut. The wedding is tomorrow and..."

A smile formed on her beautiful lips, and she pushed up her designer pink and black framed glasses. "The wedding is tomorrow, and you forgot to get your hair cut?"

"Yeah, it's not looking too good."

Nichole laughed, and his stomach knotted. "Let me settle these guys down, and then I'll get you in. We don't want some tabloid to accidentally get a picture of you tomorrow if you don't look your very best," she teased.

The very thought that there would be photographers there to put the pictures into tabloids made Ben a bit uneasy. His cousin Bethany had been a movie star. Of course, he didn't see her that way anymore, but he supposed—had she been around more often—the entire family would have been exposed to such things as tabloids and reporters. But she hadn't come back home until she had given up her movie career. It was her sister, Audrey, who was marrying Gregory Bishop, one of Hollywood's most sought-after leading men. He thought it was interesting how a family who owned a ranch outside of Macon, Georgia had that many connections to the movie industry.

The noise around him drew him out of his thoughts. Nichole

gathered toys and set children in waiting room chairs. It was then he noticed there was one more boy, Zane's twin obviously, who must have just come out of hiding.

The three of them settled down with an iPad between them and the unmistakable sound of SpongeBob SquarePants.

Nichole let out a breath. "Okay. Are you ready?"

"Are these your kids?"

She gave them all three a look. "Nah, I get lonely, so I rent them."

The other little boy, whom he had yet to be introduced to, looked up at her. "Mom, why do you tell people that?"

She gave him a wink and laughed. "Because my sense of humor is horrible and I think it's funny."

The little boy shook his head and looked back down at the iPad.

Nichole gave Ben a nod toward the shampoo bowl. "Yeah, they are mine. They're my whole world."

Ben sat down in the chair and reclined backward, his head resting in the divot in the bowl. "I forgot you had three kids. I've seen the pictures on your station, but I didn't know if those were nieces and nephews," he said as she turned on the water.

"I don't usually ever have them here. But tonight, I was working late. You are not the only Walker man who was not prepared for this wedding tomorrow."

"Who else?"

She laughed again, and it sent a warmth through him that had him swallowing hard. "Sworn to secrecy," she whispered.

Ben had his own thoughts on it, and at the top of his list was Jake—yes, he assumed his cousin was equally behind in his grooming as Ben was.

He sat there quietly while the warm water ran over his head, and Nichole massaged shampoo into his hair. He was sure he could fall asleep under the touch of her fingers.

Once she was done, she dried off his hair with the towel and led him to her station, then looked back at the kids quietly watching their iPad.

"They're pretty good," Ben said as he sat down in her chair.

Nichole draped the cape around him and fastened it in the back. She rested her hands on his shoulders and looked at him in the mirror. "They are good kids. They had to do a lot of sitting around the last year waiting for me to get done working. I try to make it up to them."

"Well, if you ever need any help..."

Nichole laughed loudly, as she picked up a comb and ran it through his wet hair. "I'm sorry. I should never laugh when a man offers his help. Are you good with children?"

Ben let his shoulders drop. "Honestly, I don't know. My brother's stepson is five now, I think. I get along with him. I also have two new nieces."

"I know. I've been around them, remember?"

That was right. How could he possibly have forgotten? Probably the same way he'd forgotten he'd seen her with her children at various weddings and parties over the last six months. That was his own fault. He seemed to get nervous and tongue-tied whenever she was around. Most of the time, he found himself hiding in the kitchen or outside with the stragglers at wedding receptions.

He watched her in the mirror as she began to comb and cut his hair. He figured they weren't too far apart in age, though she might have a few years on him. It was funny to think this beautiful woman had three well-behaved children. Ben, on the other hand, had only recently moved out of his parents' home. No wonder he didn't have a woman who would want to go to the wedding with him. When he thought of it, he sounded like a loser.

Nichole kept the conversation going as she cut his hair, and Ben wondered if he'd ever learn to loosen up around her.

"So, who are you taking to the wedding?" she asked as she pulled her small set of clippers from a drawer.

"I'm going by myself."

"That surprises me. You're a good-looking guy."

Ben clasped his hands in his lap underneath the cape. "How about you? Who are you going with?"

Nichole turned around and looked at three children sitting with their heads pressed together. "Those are my gorgeous dates. But maybe you'll save me a dance?"

Ben wasn't sure he answered, as she took off the cape and brushed the hair from his neck.

"You look perfect," she said as she gave him a wink. "I'll see you tomorrow then."

Standing, he pulled his wallet from his back pocket. "How much do I owe you?"

She rested her hand on his which held his wallet. "Just save me that dance."

While he stood there, more than likely with his mouth open, she folded up the cape, cleaned up her station, and began to gather up her children.

Ben slid his wallet back into his pocket. "Thanks. I'll make sure to save that dance, maybe a couple of extras too," he said without really thinking it through first.

He let himself out of the salon and looked back inside as he closed the door. Nichole looked up at him, smiled, and gave him a wave as she tucked items into a bag while kids tugged at her, redirecting her attention.

Ben wondered if his heart rate would slow down before he saw her tomorrow. He seemed to be a bit infatuated with her. What was he thinking? She was a beautiful woman, one with three kids and a missing husband. Chances were, all he'd ever get was a promised dance.

As he climbed into his truck and drove away, he realized that's all he had in him anyway. It all went back to the reason he didn't have a date for the wedding. He wasn't very good with women.

2

The suit and tie were stiff, Ben thought, as he tugged at the collar of his shirt. He calculated in his head how many more cousins and brothers were left to get married. Then he'd have a long reprieve from wearing suits until they all started to die.

He kicked his boots against the tire of his truck, out of habit, then cursed himself for scuffing up the bright shine. Well, who would notice a scuff on a boot out in the country? If you didn't want scuffed boots at the wedding, then have it in town.

Ben opened the back door to his parents' home and stepped into the chaos in the kitchen. Okay, maybe it wasn't chaos, as his sister-in-law, Susan, seemed to have everything under control and everyone doing exactly what she asked. She was efficient that way.

At the sight of the brownie tray, his mouth began to water. He didn't dare move in and take one though. He feared Susan enough to respect the rule of no eating before the party.

The part Ben didn't understand was why Susan was catering a pre-wedding brunch, where everyone was all dressed up, and then a reception after as well in town. He supposed he'd never really understand why women did what they did for weddings after all. But he wouldn't argue that. The women in his family knew weddings. They'd built an entire empire around it.

For a moment he thought he'd sneak through the kitchen and into the living room unnoticed, until his nephew Lucas ran through the organized chaos and hid behind him. A second later, a well-dressed Zane, or was that his twin, ran after Lucas and both boys erupted in hysterical laughter.

Ben caught the hint of annoyance at Susan's glance, and he knew that the boys and men weren't quite welcome in the kitchen.

"Lucas, where's your mom?" Ben asked as Lucas moved back and forth behind him to hide from the single twin boy, whom he wasn't sure was Zane.

"Getting her hair done," he said, gripping Ben's pants.

About that time, the other twin came toward them, this one at a much slower pace. Was that the secret? He'd met Zane in a full out race with a car. His brother, however, had been quieter, he remembered.

"Mom wants us to go outside," the other boy said. "And don't get dirty."

The boy which Ben had decided was Zane, halted his pursuit of Lucas with a grunt. "Fine," he scoffed. "Can he come too?"

Nichole moved through the kitchen, and again Ben found that when he looked at her, he was speechless. She was dressed in a dark dress with those little straps that went over well-sculpted shoulders. Her dark hair was done up, and he could swear it glistened. Today, she didn't have on her pink and black glasses, and when she looked at him with dark eyes, he felt that hitch in his chest that he often got when he saw her.

"Ben, can you keep the boys occupied for a bit. I don't have anyone to watch them while I finish Audrey's hair. Chelsea could use a friend for Lucas, too, if you don't mind."

He wanted to groan as Zane had earlier, but he refrained. "Sure. We'll go find something to do outside."

Nichole reached her hand to his and squeezed it. "You're a lifesaver. I owe you one." Then she turned her focus to the boys with matching eyes and haircuts. "If you cause Mr. Walker any problems you're going to have to answer to me, and you don't want to do that, do you?"

Both boys shook their heads.

"Good." Nichole then tilted her head to look at Lucas. "You too. You do what your uncle says and be good. Or you'll have to deal with me, too."

A stunned Lucas simply stared at her.

"You don't want to see her mad face," Zane's twin said.

"Wyatt, you set the example. Show him what I expect."

Wyatt! The kid had a name.

Wyatt nodded in agreement, and Nichole gave them all one more smile before she hurried away.

Once she was out of sight, Ben felt the stare of three sets of eyes on him. What had he gotten himself into? He was a young boy once. What would he do to stay out of trouble?

"Ben." He heard his father call from the other room.

With the three boys nearly attached to him, he walked out into the living room where his brothers Eric and Russell each sat with their daughters in their arms, feeding them bottles. What a sight, he thought.

"These two have their hands full, and your mother wants me to load up the truck with the gifts people brought." He pointed to the stack in the corner of the room. "Get them in the Escalade. Have them help you," he directed the comment to the boys.

Ben figured that would keep them all out of trouble for five more minutes. He glanced at the grandfather clock in the corner. They'd need to kill another half hour before the wedding out in his mother's garden. Whatever happened to churches, he wondered, as Lucas nudged him toward the gifts.

Ben walked over to the pile that had amassed in the corner. He picked up each gift and decided if it was too heavy, or perhaps breakable, then handed it to a boy. His father had taken one box and headed out the front door with it. Each boy followed, and Ben at the back. They repeated the process until all the gifts had been stacked in the truck and the door shut.

"Well, that killed five minutes. Now, what do I do with them?" Ben asked his father as he watched them run in circles around the truck. Lucas seemed to enjoy the two older boys' attention. Ben figured he'd been that way with his brothers at one time. Eric was too much older to enjoy a good chase around a car, but he'd done it with his other brothers. Maybe he'd find some joy in it now if he wasn't too worried about what Nichole would think if she saw him chasing her sons around.

As if the thought of her magically made her appear, she stood in the doorway watching her sons. When he caught her eye, she smiled at him. She sure had a way of turning his insides to goo.

"Boys, come on in now. We're going to wash up before the wedding."

Zane and Wyatt grumbled, but dutifully headed toward their mother with Lucas in tow.

"She has a lot of baggage," his father said as he crossed his arms in front of him and leaned back against the truck.

"Yeah, so?"

"So, you have an eye for her."

"She's a good-looking woman. And nice, too," he added because he felt that the first comment made him sound like a sexist pig. "The kids are nice, too," he continued, to give her the credit she deserved.

"Hey, I'm not one to balk at a woman with kids. Your mom took Eric on, and me."

That was true, he thought, though he often forgot that Eric was only his half-brother. "She's just a nice person, Dad. I don't have any plans other than friends. She did give me a haircut in exchange for a dance."

The comment had his father slapping him on the shoulder with a laugh as he stepped away from the truck. "Well, maybe you don't have eyes for her, but maybe she has them for you."

As his father headed back to the house, Ben contemplated what he said. There was no way a single mother of three could have an interest in him. He was nothing. But she needed friends. He understood that. He guessed he was as good a pick for a friend as anyone.

He watched as his brother Russell walked out the front door with Lucas and headed toward their truck to grab the diaper bag from the back seat. Russell had taken on a kid too, and to watch them, no one would ever know Lucas wasn't his.

Ben shook the thought from his head. He could hardly take care of himself. He wasn't even going to think about taking on Nichole's kids. Besides, they weren't a thing. She was a beautiful woman who made her customers feel good about themselves. That meant she was good at her job.

As his mother began calling out to everyone to gather in the garden, Ben thought about the dance he'd promised Nichole. It was just a dance. He'd survive it and go on with his life tomorrow.

3

*W*ith her daughter on her lap and a son on each side of her, Nichole watched as Audrey's family was seated in the chairs in the garden. The groom, such a stunning man, stood at the altar with the minister. His brother Scott and Audrey's brothers Jake and Todd stood to his side.

Audrey's dearest friend, and the owner of the building in which she'd opened her salon, Lydia walked down the aisle first. Nichole had been in town enough to know that when the beautiful and strong Lydia was present, that meant Officer Phillip Smythe was nearby. She spotted him two rows in front of her. His eyes were affixed to the woman, who never sent a look his way. It was sad, she thought. Their dynamic was interesting, to say the least. The man pined for her, and she wanted nothing to do with him.

Next down the aisle was Gregory's sister Kate. Gregory had been blessed with the looks of a god, and it must have run through the family, Nichole thought, as she watched Kate walk down the aisle with such confidence. Perhaps that was what the military gave her, and it resonated with everyone around her.

Pearl, Audrey's sister, the bridal shop owner, was next to

walk down the aisle. Her name fit her, Nichole considered. She was as elegant as the pearls that adorned her neck. Nichole had never known someone who exuded such class.

The music changed, and the guests stood. Zane moved around Nichole to get a better look at Audrey who walked, on the arm of her father, toward her husband-to-be.

Audrey had been adamant that she wouldn't have him walk her down the aisle. He wasn't someone Audrey particularly cared for, and Nichole had learned very quickly that the man escorting her wasn't the best father material. However, he must have had a change of heart a month ago, because he'd asked Audrey to be part of her wedding. She hadn't given in right away, in fact, she'd made him wait nearly three weeks before giving him an answer. She wasn't about to make the wrong decision for her wedding day. In the end, she gave in to his request.

Nichole smiled at Audrey as she passed by them, and Laura, whom Nichole had stood on the chair, waved. Audrey glowed as she neared the man of her dreams. She was truly happy, and it showed.

Nichole felt the sinking sensation that she'd been warding off all day hit her stomach. Once she had been that glowing bride. She'd been full of optimism and hope. That was all shattered now.

No, she wasn't going to think that way. Not today. Today belonged to Audrey.

Nichole looked at her children all dressed in their suits and dress that her mother had sent them for the occasion. Even though things hadn't worked out as she thought they would, she had her children, and they were her life. That was all she had to remember to make the joy in her heart return.

As the minister spoke, she noticed Ben turn his head from the front row. He caught her eye and panic struck his expression. But he smiled and turned back. What was it that she did to him, she wondered. She'd been nothing but nice to him, but he always had that look of fear in his eyes when he looked at her. Oh, she knew she was a strong woman with an intimidating personality. No one walked over Nichole Lewis. No one made her feel inferior either. Sometimes that came across as bitchy. Was that what he thought?

He looked back again, and this time he smiled when she caught his eye. Okay, now she was staring, but she couldn't help it. There was something about Ben Walker that attracted her to him.

Maybe she'd feel that out when she danced with him, because he'd promised her a dance.

The thought brought a smile to her lips as she picked up Laura and they all sat back down as the minister instructed them to.

For the next hour, she wouldn't think about the marriage she missed out on, or on why she made Ben Walker so nervous. She would enjoy watching Audrey marry the sexy movie star who was head over heels in love with her. There was no doubt in Nichole's mind that this was a marriage that would withstand anything. But even though she tried to push the thought out of her mind, she couldn't help but wish for that for herself someday.

BEN DIDN'T DARE to turn around again. Each time he had looked at Nichole during the ceremony, she was looking at him. Obviously a coincidence, but nevertheless, nerve-wracking.

As his cousin kissed her new husband, Ben felt the hairs on the back of his neck rise. He rubbed his hand over them and shook off the feeling that something was about to happen. This wasn't his wedding. He wasn't the one locked into forever, so why was he bugging out?

Then, as Audrey and Gregory passed him walking back down the aisle hand in hand, he realized the wedding was over, and the reception would commence. A party at Lydia's reception hall was always a good time, but this time, he had to dance. There would be no standing in the dark corner, or sneaking out the side door. He had a debt to pay and that had him itching.

His father's hand clamped down on his shoulder as the guests began to move from their chairs and wander back toward the house.

"This is a great garden for a wedding," his father said as if he were making a note of it to Ben. "All the Walker girls are married off. Just a few more Walker men to go."

When his father laughed as they exited the garden, Ben could feel the tie around his neck begin to choke him. He unbuttoned the top button of his shirt and loosened the tie.

"I think you'd better not make too many plans, Dad. Todd, Gerald, and I don't have any aspirations to follow in anyone's footsteps. You have grandkids to worry about now," he offered. "No need to think we all need to hurry off and get married."

His father laughed. "You need to get out more. You're almost thirty."

"And Eric was forty before he got married and had a kid. I'll be fine."

God must have felt his discomfort with the conversation, as someone called for his father and drew him away.

Ben ran his hand over his newly-cut hair. He thought women were the only ones who got stupid over weddings. Every female he knew wanted to be the next bride, but men didn't think that way. A man knew that a wedding had a reception, and that meant a nice cold beer. And he happened to know for a fact that Lydia carried his favorite kind.

He could hear the first cars driving away and down the long dirt road that led back to town. If he could manage his way out the front door before getting stopped by someone who wanted to talk, he'd be having that beer sooner.

As he managed his way out the door unnoticed, he saw Nichole buckling her daughter into her seat as the two boys ran in circles around the car.

How did she remain calm while they did that? It was making him anxious just to watch. A moment later, he heard the calm snap, and the boys came to attention, then climbed into the car.

As she lifted her head from the back, she caught his glance, and her eyes glazed over with a panic. Why was that? She'd smiled earlier.

A smile formed on her lips and he could tell she was putting on that calm for everyone around, but irritation shook underneath. She raised her hand and gave him a wave before she slid into her car and drove off without a word.

Perhaps she wasn't the only one rattled over being at a wedding. It was then he appreciated his cousin Pearl's approach to weddings. Pearl, the bridal shop owner, had eloped. There was no pressure on anyone to attend a wedding. During her reception, which was held after they returned from their elopement/honeymoon, they'd had beer, too.

That thought shifted his focus, and he hurried to his truck to head to town and get that beer that was calling his name.

4

_____

The parking lot at the reception hall was already filled. Nichole let out a grumble as she turned the corner to find a parking space. She was going to have to walk at least two blocks. Normally, that wouldn't faze her at all, but with all three kids, it was annoying her. Not to mention that it would be dark when they walked back to their car. And, if the past were any indicator, she'd be carrying at least two of them.

Their behavior during the wedding had pleased her. If she had been able to find a sitter, she would have gone alone. But that wasn't her life. And as she took a slow calming breath, she reminded herself this was the life she chose.

She noticed a spot just down the street from the salon. Managing to parallel park, just as her grandfather had taught her to do, she slid the car into the space. It was then she realized her mind must have been a million miles away, as Laura's scream pierced her ears.

Nichole quickly turned in her seat to see the three children in the back. The scream had been from delight, as Wyatt pulled a toy from Zane's hands. The boys were laughing. Laura was laughing. But Nichole felt the surge of irritation burst into her chest as she screamed, "Stop it! Stop it this minute!"

All three of her children stared at her wide-eyed. She knew she had crossed the line, but she couldn't help herself. She saw the hint of tears welling in Wyatt's eyes. Zane, the coolest of all three of them, handed the toy back to Wyatt and looked his mother square in the eye.

"We were just messing around," he said calmly. "We didn't mean to make you mad, Mom. We promise to be good at the party."

Nichole squeezed her eyes shut and let the calm from her son take over her own body. Someday, she knew he'd be a negotiator for something.

She opened her eyes and looked back at her children. "I'm sorry I yelled. I'm a little emotional."

Zane tucked the toy next to him in the seat. "Are you sad because Miss Audrey is getting married?"

Nichole chuckled and shook her head. "No, I'm very happy for her. Weddings are wonderful things. Marriages are wonderful, too." And that was the part that stung. She did believe in marriage. Well, she wanted to believe in marriage. It was no one else's fault that hers hadn't worked—or so her ex always reminded her. A good wife would work through the hard times. Obviously, she was a horrible wife. However, she was a fantastic mother. That's all that mattered.

She took another deep cleansing breath, then smiled at her children. "You may each have one soda, and one slice of cake. Mrs. Susan has prepared a wonderful dinner, and each of you are going to eat it."

"Yes ma'am," the answer came back to her in unison.

"And if I haven't told you already, you look mighty nice."

Zane wiggled in his seat. "When can we take these off?" he asked as he fidgeted with his tie and then yanked on his jacket.

"When we go home, before bath time."

He groaned. "We took a bath last night."

"And you will take another tonight," she demanded with her calm mother voice now intact.

Wyatt straightened his tie. "I like our clothes. Grandma is going to love the picture we took of all of us."

Oh, he knew how to win her over. "She sure will. Now, let's all go inside and find a table. There's going to be music, so you can dance all night long."

Zane unbuckled his seatbelt and leaned in toward her. "Are you going to dance, Mom?"

Nichole could feel the heat rise in her cheeks. "Of course, because you're going to dance with me."

"No way," Zane protested. "Maybe that Ben guy will dance with you."

"Why him?"

Zane shrugged. "Because he hung out with us. He seemed cool."

Nichole chuckled to herself as she opened her door and climbed out of the car. Yeah, he did seem cool.

BEN FIGURED Lydia was eager to buy the building behind the reception hall. Though she usually filled any vacancy with a new business, she seriously needed more parking.

He had parked two blocks over, and more cars were arriving. There were a few fancy cars and a few limos that had arrived as well. Sometimes he forgot that his cousin had married one of Hollywood's elite. The thought crossed his mind as he walked down the street, who might be at this reception? Was he about to rub elbows with famous actors and actresses? That might make the afternoon worthwhile, he decided.

As he turned the corner, he saw Nichole unloading her chil-

dren from the car. Something inside of him made him want to
stand and watch the whole process. One of the boys noticed him
and waved. Ben smiled and waved back. He wasn't sure which
one it was, so he didn't call out a name.

Nichole noticed the boy waving, so she turned to see him
walking toward them.

Ben tucked his hands into his front pockets. "Lydia could
invest in more parking."

"I've heard it mentioned."

The boy that had waved stepped toward him. "Are you going
to dance with our mother?"

He felt the surprise of the question hit him in the chest with
a jolt, and then he heard Nichole's gasp.

"Zane Parker Lewis, please mind your manners," she scolded.

"It's okay," Ben assured her. He studied the boy briefly. Zane
had a mole on his cheek, and Wyatt did not. " I did plan to dance
with your mother if that's okay with you. I owe her for my
haircut."

They nodded. "That's cool."

Nichole picked up Laura and rested her on her hip. Ben
wondered what kind of sight they made. walking down the
street; three kids, a man, and a woman.

"It's interesting, that I've been here for six months and have
already attended a couple of Walker weddings," Nichole said as
they rounded the building toward the reception hall.

"Who knew everyone would get married in such a short span
of time?"

"It happens. I see it all the time. Usually, it's when there's a
lot of women in a family. One girl gets married, and another girl
wants to get married. Weddings are addictive."

"Weddings are just a party. It's the marriage that matters,"
Ben said, and noticed that her back stiffened.

"Agreed." Her voice shook. "It seems as though your parents have a good marriage."

The smile that came to his lips was genuine. "They do. My mom's a saint. She married my dad and took Eric as her own after his mother died."

Nichole's eyes had gone wide. "Eric is your half-brother?"

"Yeah. I don't remember him being a pain in..." He stopped before he said another word. "Just a pain. But I think he gave her a run for her money. Mom just loved him. She introduced him to his wife. That seemed to work out well. Now they have a kid."

"It sounds like marriage is important to your entire family."

He thought about it. It did seem that way. His uncle Byron was the only one that didn't seem to fit the Walker standard. He'd been married multiple times, had never married Bethany's mother, and was living with yet another woman. But his cousins had seemed to learn the importance of marriage. Pearl and Tyson were happy. Jake and Missy were still newlyweds, but as far as Ben could see, they too had what it took to make it. He had no doubt Audrey and Gregory would have a happy life.

Music flowed from the reception hall as they approached. Ben couldn't swear by it, but he was sure he had just seen someone who had played an action hero walk into the building. By the look on Wyatt's face, he might have seen the same person.

It was then that Ben decided he needed to get out more. The sight of that many people was giving him anxiety.

"Are you expected to sit at a certain table?" Nichole asked.

Ben shook his head. "No. I don't think so."

"I see a table across the dance floor. I'll snag it. Maybe you can get us some drinks?"

"Sure. I can do that. Is anything off the table?"

Nichole looked at her children. "I promised them each one soda. I'll take whatever you have."

Ben nodded and headed toward the bar as Nichole and her children hurried toward the empty table.

Officer Phillip Smythe was waiting for his drink. "Lydia sure knows how to throw a party, doesn't she?" he offered as Ben moved in next to him.

"She sure does." Ben ordered three Shirley Temples and two beers.

"Does she have you serving tonight?" Phillip nodded toward the drinks.

"Oh, no. I was getting these for Nichole and her kids. Well, not the beer. The beer is for me and Nichole," he explained as if Phillip would've thought differently.

Phillip took a pull from his beer. "So, you seeing the new stylist?"

"No. No. Just walked in with her. She's nice."

"Has her hands full."

"Yeah. I don't know much about that. The kids are nice though."

Phillip took the two beers as the bartender put them on the counter. "I'll carry these. You carry those."

Ben picked up the three glasses and followed Phillip across the dance floor toward the table where Nichole settled her kids in.

"Officer Smythe, it's nice to see you," Nichole greeted him.

"Nice to see you." He handed her one of the beers and set the other on the table. "I haven't had the chance to meet your kids yet."

"That's right. You haven't met. This is my daughter, Laura, she's two," Nichole said as Laura buried her head into her shoulder. "And these are my boys, Wyatt and Zane."

Phillip gave them a nod. "It's nice to meet you. Well, I think I'm going to go find Lydia and see if I can get in some trouble."

Ben watched as Nichole's lips pursed. "Let me know how that goes."

Phillip gave her a wink and tilted his beer toward her in a salute before he walked away.

"Lydia has to know the man is in love with her, right?" Nichole asked as Ben set the drinks in front of the kids.

"He's just always been around. I don't think it's love."

Nichole laughed as she picked up her beer. "I've only been around a few months, and I know it's love."

Ben sat down next to Laura and picked up his beer to take a sip. If that was true, that Phillip was in love with Lydia, it was apparent that Ben knew nothing about love. But he did under-stand attraction. And as he looked at Nichole, who was deep in conversation with Wyatt and Zane, he realized he was under the spell of that attraction. Taking a sip of his beer, he promised himself he would only let it go that far. He knew deep down inside this was not the right situation for him.

5

*T*he kids occupied themselves watching a video on Nichole's phone. Ben had nursed his beer until it was warm, and Nichole had managed to tear the label off her bottle. The DJ played background music while the guests arrived. Ben would never understand why it took so long for the bride and groom to arrive at receptions.

"I think it's funny which traditions stay intact," Nichole said drawing his attention to her. "Most couples live together before they even get married. So why is it so important not to see each other before the wedding? I mean, taking pictures after the wedding, it could all be done before."

Ben chuckled as he took a swig from his warm beer and then pushed it away. "Did I say that out loud? I was just thinking that."

Nichole laughed, and he found that it warmed his skin to hear it. "I'm pretty sure everyone here is thinking that."

The server walked to the table, a silver tray in her hands. "Can I offer you some hors d'oeuvres?"

Nichole looked up at the woman. "Hi, Patty. I didn't know you were working for Lydia."

"Oh, hey. Actually, I'm working for Susan. It's a good side job."

Patty handed them a napkin. Nichole took an appetizer for each of them, and Ben took some pastry and set it on his napkin. He watched the kids fumble with theirs. Laura went right to biting into hers while Wyatt carefully watched Zane dissect his.

"Don't play with it," Nichole warned. "Just eat it."

Zane winced. "I don't know what it is."

"It's the only food you're going to get for another hour, so eat it," she demanded.

Ben noticed both boys looked at him. He didn't know what it was either, but he felt under pressure to make sure he didn't get in trouble with Nichole.

He lifted pastry to his mouth and took a bite. "I think it's chicken. But it's really good. Susan makes the best food."

Neither of the boys took his word until he had eaten the second bite.

Then he watched as each of them took a bite and chewed slowly. Obviously, by the looks on their faces, it was edible for all.

Zane pushed his plate toward the center of the table. "Is all the food going to be like this?"

Nichole shook her head. "This just keeps the crowd calm," she said with a wink.

"Why didn't you cook the food? You're the best cook ever," Zane told her, and she smiled widely.

She shifted a glance toward Ben. "Don't let them fool you. I'm great with boxed mac and cheese. Anything beyond that is iffy."

"You have me beat in that department," Ben admitted. "I try to walk into the kitchen of my parents' house right at dinnertime every night. My mother would never turn me away."

The comment lit humor in her eyes. "No mother could turn her son away."

And at that moment he knew Nichole was just like his mother. Her children were her world, and nothing could ever alter that.

NICHOLE HAD MANAGED to finish her warm beer and caved in letting the kids have a second Shirley Temple before the bride and groom arrived. She'd heard word that the wedding had been leaked to the press, and there was a helicopter flying overhead. In the past six months, she'd spent quite a bit of time with Gregory Bishop, Audrey's new husband. Though his face was in every magazine she saw in the grocery store, and he'd been on TV promoting the new film he was in, she saw him as an ordinary guy.

Phillip had been prepared for the disruption and had police presence at each entrance and around the block. But as the helicopter circled, their presence was more noticeable.

"Why are the cops here?" Wyatt asked.

"Gregory is very famous. They just want to keep him safe."

Wyatt took another sip from his drink and wiped his mouth on his jacket sleeve. "If he's so famous, why did he play baseball with us?"

Nichole chuckled. "Because he's a normal nice guy. His job just puts him out in front of a lot of people."

"Like when I'm a professional baseball player?" he asked and Zane elbowed him in the arm.

"You're not going to be a professional baseball player. You suck."

"Hey." Nichole's voice didn't rise, but she focused her tone directly on the boys, and they each eased back. "Mind your manners and cool your mouth."

It didn't go unnoticed that Ben was growing more uncomfortable around her little family by the second. She was sure when she scolded the kids he'd flinched.

"You don't have to just sit and keep us company. I'm sure your family would like you to mingle," she offered, hoping to free him if that's what he was looking for. The confused look on his face wasn't what she expected though.

"I'm perfectly happy sitting here. I have to admit I'm not much of one for working a room. Besides, it's my cousin's wedding. If it were one of my brothers..." He adjusted his tie. "Well, I didn't like doing it then either."

Nichole laughed and eased back in her chair. "You like your quiet life, don't you?"

He nodded quickly. "My little house out on the ranch is perfect for me. I see who I want when I want. Luckily I see Susan often, and she always has food with her."

She laughed again. "I like my quiet time, but I suppose I got into my profession because I liked to be with people. Different people."

"I'd have an anxiety attack," he admitted.

Nichole lifted her beer toward him in salute. "Here's to opposites. It's what makes the world go round."

He tapped his bottle to hers and then took a long, thoughtful sip.

It was then she noticed the police in the room readjust their positions. Even though they were in civilian clothing, nothing hid the fact that they were packing under their jackets.

A moment later Gregory carried his laughing bride into the room to the rousing cheers from the guests.

"Now can we eat real food?" Zane whined, and Nichole held up a finger to her lips to quiet him.

The truth was, she didn't want to talk to anyone for a few moments. The sight of Audrey's enormous smile and Gregory's matching one were wreaking havoc with her heart. Even when she'd married her ex-husband, they'd never looked that happy. Everyone deserved to find happiness, and she couldn't help but feel the twisting in her gut, wondering if she'd missed her chance.

But when she watched Zane help Laura up on her chair to see the bride and groom, and he held her hand to steady her, Nichole knew that her happiness wasn't justified in what her marriage had been. Her children brought that to her. It was enough, she promised herself. It was enough.

6

*B*en had never been so happy to see two people enter a room and sit down to eat. God, he was starving.

Seriously, why did wedding parties have to take their sweet time arriving? And why didn't they serve the food while the guests waited?

He watched as the staff that Susan had amassed began to carry out trays of food. Ben didn't know how she did it. He couldn't cook anything that wasn't frozen and tossed into the microwave, but Susan could cook for hundreds—and plate it.

"I sampled the menu," Nichole leaned toward him. "Susan brought in lunch one day. She's a genius."

"She is. I'm sure that's why Eric married her." He thought better of his comment and then waved his hand in front of him as if to erase it. "I mean it was a bonus. He married her because he loves her."

Nichole's smile widened. "I know."

Her attention was diverted back to her children as they were served their plates. Laura grabbed her fork, sat up on her knees, and dug in. Zane took his knife and pushed anything green to the far side. Wyatt patiently waited to see everyone else's reactions before he took a bite of anything.

Ben thought back to when he was a young boy. His mother went through a phase where she wanted them to try new foods. She wasn't a horrible cook, but she enjoyed experimenting. That didn't always turn out in their favor.

Gerald was always a bit better about trying things. Ben and Russell, on the other hand, had more than once given their dinner to the dog. His other brother, Dane, had a way of getting meals he wanted to eat. Ben wasn't sure what kind of voodoo that was, but now that he thought about it, Dane was always putting things in his mother's head. Perhaps that was a lesson, he thought. If you wanted something, you asked for it.

Knowing that anything Susan made was perfect, Ben began to dig into his meal. Marinated chicken breast, asparagus, fingerling potatoes, and a beautiful salad adorned his plate. As soon as he took his first bite, he realized just how hungry he was. Nichole must've realized it too, as his stomach growled and she turned and smiled. What a lovely way to make an impression.

Once the meal had been completed, Susan's staff began to clear the plates, and the DJ called for the bride and groom to meet out on the dance floor.

Laura crawled up into her mother's lap. "They going to dance?"

Nichole smoothed her hand over her daughter's head. "Yes. This is their first dance."

Ben gave that some thought. Didn't it start with the bride and groom's first dance, followed by a dance with the parents, and then what? When did they get to the part of the night when they got to eat cake, dance, and drink more beer? He noticed Wyatt scratching at something on the tablecloth and Zane tugging at his tie. It was then he realized he was no better off than a seven-year-old boy. He also was bored and wanted to run.

"Would you mind if I took the boys outside for a few minutes to stretch our legs?" he asked.

Both boys raised their heads simultaneously. At first, there was a slight sense of fear in their eyes, but a moment later they turned toward their mother and pleaded.

Zane fixed his tie again. "Please, Mom. I'm bored to death," he said with a strangling voice.

Wyatt nodded in agreement.

Ben set his napkin on the table. "I promise no more than five minutes. Just a walk around the block and we'll be back."

He could see the trepidation on her face, and he couldn't blame her. After all, he was a stranger, and these were her children.

"Just around the block?"

"Just around the block," he promised. "No walking through mud puddles or sliding in the dirt."

She thought for another moment and then nodded. "Okay. I suppose this is boring for young men. Hurry back."

All three of them stood from the table. Both boys moved to her and kissed her on the cheek while Laura watched with great interest. "You stay with me, and we will watch the bride and groom," Nichole informed Laura.

BEN FOLLOWED the boys out of the hall. They waited until they were outside before they let out a grateful whoop.

"Thanks, Ben," Wyatt said. "That is boring."

"Food was good though," Zane said, as he studied the water feature in the small courtyard at the entrance.

"It was good. C'mon, let's stroll," Ben offered as he tucked his hands into his pockets and started around the building that would take them in front of the shops his cousins and his sister-in-law owned.

"Did you go to school here?" Wyatt asked as he fell into step with Ben, and Zane continued at a faster pace down the sidewalk.

"I went to a school here. There are a few of them."

"Did you like it?"

"No," Ben answered honestly and saw that it shocked his young inquisitor. "I lived forty-five minutes from town, so getting to school was a big chore."

"That would suck."

Ben shrugged. "I don't know. Now that I look back on it, I guess it wasn't that bad. My mom always packed me a snack for the bus. My friends and I would play games, and when I was old enough, I'd hold hands with girls."

That made for a less than happy response from Zane who stopped in front of Gia's gift shop.

"Are all the girls who own the stores your sister? Zane asked.

"No. My cousin owns the bridal shop and hair salon. My other cousin works in the flower shop, and my sister-in-law owns the gift store."

"What's a sister-in-law?"

"Well, Gia is married to my brother," he explained. "Do you have any aunts?"

"Ya. Aunt Pattie," Zane said. "Uncle Doug is mom's brother."

"Then your Aunt Pattie is your mom's sister-in-law. See how that works?"

Zane shrugged as if the conversation didn't matter anymore.

When they turned the corner, Wyatt stopped in front of the salon. "Mom likes working here," he said as he cupped his hands around his eyes and looked inside as if he'd never seen it before. "She didn't like the old salon she worked at where we used to live."

"Audrey is easy to get along with," Ben assured them, though he'd had his tussles with her and she'd often won.

"Do you like my mom?" Wyatt turned from the window and looked at Ben.

He could feel the heat rise in his cheeks. "I ... well ... of course. She's very nice."

"No. Do you like her as a girl?" he pressed, and Zane moved in to stand next to his brother.

Both sets of identical eyes stared up at him.

Ben swallowed hard. "Of course I like her. And as a girl, she's great."

"She needs a new husband."

Now he could feel the air in his lungs grow thicker. "Did she tell you that?"

The boys exchanged looks. Zane shook his head. "No, but moms should be married."

"Not all of them have to be," Ben assured them. "But when the right guy comes around, I'm sure your mother will be happy with him."

The boys exchanged glances again and then headed down the street with Ben lagging behind.

Did the boys expect him to marry their mother? Hell, he could hardly talk to her. The whole situation was uncomfortable.

This was just one more reason he couldn't wait until the wedding was over and he was back home, alone, in his little house where no one questioned him.

7

When Ben and the boys returned to the reception, they found Nichole and Laura on the dance floor. He figured they'd been gone long enough, all of the traditional stuff seemed to be over.

When Laura saw her brothers, she ran to them and grabbed each of their hands. Her idea of dancing looked like a rendition of Ring Around the Rosie to him.

His mouth went dry when he noticed Nichole's eyes raised to his. This was it. He had promised her to dance, and his mother would still come after him if he didn't follow up on that.

Ben walked to her as guests and family gathered on the dance floor. The kids continued to giggle and dance.

"It seems as good a time as any to collect on that dance I promised," he said as he reached his hand out to her.

Even in the dim light, he was sure her cheeks flushed.

Nichole took his hand and rested the other on his shoulder, as he placed his on the small of her back. He was a horrible dancer. Back and forth, and back and forth. Surely she wouldn't want to do this too many times.

Nichole chuckled. "I've never been very good at this. If I step on your feet, I'm very sorry."

That made him laugh. "I was just thinking I'm a horrible dancer. I guess they'll ask us to leave the floor if we cause too much harm to the other dancers."

The laugh that erupted from Nichole warmed his heart. She was a lovely woman. Her laugh was as infectious as was her smile.

The kids bumped into them, and Ben noticed it had caused Nichole to step in closer to him. He adjusted his hand behind her and kept her close.

All three of the kids laughed as they danced in circles and other young children joined them. Ben's family laughed, and it all became infectious, just as Nichole's had been.

Soon the other dancers moved to the outside of the dance floor, and the children took over. There were at least ten of them of all ages and sizes. They danced to the music and spun in circles until they fell. The DJ took that as his cue and started the chicken dance.

Just as Ben was going to comment, Nichole let out a groan. "I love weddings. I really do love weddings. But I hate this dance."

"So do I."

"I'll buy you a beer," she offered with a smile since he knew it was an open bar. "Let's get out of here."

How can you turn down that offer?

They each waved at the kids and walked across the dance floor to the other side. His father gave him a pat on the back as he gathered his drink from the bar and turned to greet another guest. Ben ordered them each a beer and then handed Nichole hers.

She tipped the neck of the beer toward him. "Here's to avoiding that stupid dance."

"Back at you." He tapped his bottle to hers and then took a long pull. "Your kids don't seem to mind that song."

"If it's a silly song that will get stuck in your head, Zane is the first one to sing it until I think my head is going to explode." She smiled behind her beer and then took a sip. "If he hears a song once he knows all the words. Considering the music my ex-husband used to listen to, that wasn't always a good thing."

"Repeated everything he heard?"

"Remember how parents used to wash your mouth out with soap when you said something?"

Ben gave her a shrug. "I heard that it was done. But my mother only threatened."

"Let's say that if I did it to that child, he'd still have soap coming out between his teeth."

The comment made him chuckle. He couldn't imagine someone as sweet as Nichole shoving soap in a child's mouth.

They managed their way back to the table, and the children followed as the garter was taken from his cousin's leg. This was another tradition he didn't understand. But because his brother Gerald pulled him from his chair, he went out on the dance floor, and when Gregory flung the garter into the crowd, it landed right in his hand which hung at his side.

There was an omen that went with the garter, and he wasn't a fan. The slaps on his back in the comments whispered in his ear were congratulations. It was old wives' tales as far as he was concerned.

He put the garter on his arm and went back to the table. All three of the kids wanted to see it, and Wyatt was quick to ask what it was all about. Nichole gave him an easy explanation which seemed to satisfy him. "Legend says that Ben will be the next man to get married."

When Audrey went to the dance floor with her bouquet, and

the women moved in a bunch toward the center of the room, Wyatt focused on Nichole.

"Are you supposed to catch a stretchy thing, too?"

"No, the bride throws her bouquet."

"Why?"

"Tradition says the single woman who catches it is the next one to get married."

Wyatt and Zane exchange glances. "Then you're supposed to be out there."

"I have no intention of getting remarried," she said clearly. "I'm fine sitting here."

The countdown from the floor began. Three... Two... One.

Audrey gave the bouquet a grand fling behind her. It soared over the hands reaching into the air, and squeals and moans from all of the single women could be heard at a deafening pitch.

The bouquet flew over the crowd and into the tables and landed right in front of Nichole. Everyone in the room applauded, and even Zane and Wyatt squealed with delight.

He saw the horror cross Nichole's face, though she tried to plaster a smile on her lips. Then, Audrey and Gregory hurried to the table, taking each of them by the hand.

"Now you have to dance," Audrey instructed. "Together."

"But we've already danced together," Nichole argued as she was pulled to the dance floor.

"Ah, but that was before you were destined." Audrey kissed her on the cheek and hurried back toward her table with her husband in tow.

Ben had thought their first dance was nerve-wracking, but now the spotlight was on them, literally. When Nichole took his offered hand, he felt it shake, and her pulse had quickened. The smile was still pressed to her lips, but as he pulled her closer, he could feel her tremble.

"It'll be over in a moment," he whispered in her ear.

"When you promised me a dance, I didn't expect to have an audience."

Neither had he.

"Your kids have the strangest grins on their faces."

Nichole turned to look at them as Laura bounded out to them. The ah's resonated around the room as Nichole picked her up and Laura turned to put her arms around Ben's neck. He shifted to support her. He wasn't sure he'd ever held a two-year-old before.

"I guess she didn't want to be left out," Nichole said as she motioned for her boys to join them. She held hands with both of them as the music continued and Ben danced with Laura clinging to him as if he were hers.

Something washed over him, through him, as he thought of the little family enjoying the very uncomfortable moment. It was a warmth he'd never quite known. He was extremely close to his family, but this was different. This was seeing the unity of a family as an adult, and from the inside.

He swallowed hard as the song changed and others took to the dance floor, but Laura kept her arms wrapped tightly around his neck.

Well, hell. He'd been attracted to their mother, but now he found he was taken by the kids too.

Ben could be a good friend to them. That much he knew.

8

*I*t was hard to get back to work Tuesday morning. The boys had talked about Ben all weekend, and Monday night at dinner they asked when he was coming around again. Laura had even gone and renamed one of her favorite stuffed dogs Ben.

Nichole had managed to give them an answer, with a smile, which satisfied them, though she had no idea when he'd come back around. She tried to explain he lived out in the country and didn't come to town that often, but that didn't seem to faze them. He'd won them over somehow. She only hoped they'd soon forget about him. Ben Walker, though easy on the eyes, wasn't one to get mixed up with a single mother. Or she had to assume. Nervous energy resonated off of him each time she was near him.

Nichole folded towels in the back room before her first client. Coffee brewed in the pot, and her music played through the speakers. It was a good way to start each morning, she thought.

The bell above the front door startled her. With a towel still in her hand, she walked toward the front to see Lydia, her large leather messenger bag strapped across her.

"Oh, good. You have coffee. Can I help myself?" she asked as she walked toward the pot.

"Of course," Nichole said with a laugh as she went back to her pile of towels. Lydia poured herself a mug full of coffee.

Setting her coffee on the small table in the center of the room, and then following it with her bag, Lydia pulled out a chair and plopped down into it. She shook her short crop of chestnut hair and picked up her mug. "What a weekend, huh?"

"It was wonderful. Have you heard from the newlyweds?" she asked as she took her first sip from her mug.

"No. Pearl says they flew out Sunday afternoon to California. They were going to stay at Gregory's house out there for a few days and then head to Cabo."

Nichole heard her own sigh before she realized she'd even let one out. Forcing a smile back to her lips, she reached for another towel. "I'm happy for them. I'm happier that they're going to settle here. I was a little afraid they'd move to California, and she'd close the shop."

Lydia laughed. "She could never leave her family. And I don't think she could leave this either," she said, looking around the room. "She's awfully proud of what she built here."

Nichole was proud of it too, and knew just how damn lucky she was to be part of it. "So, what's with the business case?" she asked, nodding at Lydia's messenger bag.

With eyes wide, Lydia pulled a notebook from the bag and set it on the table. "We're having a spring open house for the *Bridal Mecca*." She opened the notebook. "Actually, it'll be for the whole street when I'm done. I have meetings with the barber shop, the deli, and the antique store today."

Nichole set down the towel she was folding and sat down at the table across from Lydia. "This looks like a whole carnival," she said, looking at the concept drawing Lydia had pushed toward her.

"We're going to close down the street on a Saturday afternoon. All of the businesses will stay open, offer a gift or something. We will have the restaurants offer the food and drink. I'll have some games and music at the reception hall, but I want it to be a community event. I'm going to line the street with tables from the hall and Susan is going to make cupcakes." She took out another list and looked it over. "Audrey was going to have shampoo samples and things like that. I'm sure she'll talk to you about that when she gets back."

"I'm sure she will." Nichole looked at the drawings again. "Jake and Missy are going to have their race cars here?"

Lydia laughed. "They repainted them. His and Hers. It's a riot. But they are looking for some additional sponsorship and thought it would be a good time to show them off."

Nichole knew that Lydia sponsored Jake's car, so she could only assume it would boost Lydia's other businesses too. She had to admire her business sense.

Lydia closed up the book. "I'd better get to my first meeting. The printer will have the banners done today for the street lights and posters for every business."

"I can help pass those out if you'd like."

Lydia placed a hand on Nichole's. "I'd like that," she said as she placed her book back into the messenger bag and took another long sip of coffee before she stood to leave. "Oh, hey, how are things going with you and Ben?"

"Me and Ben?"

"Ya." Lydia swung the bag over her head and rested it across her. "You guys looked cozy at the wedding, not to mention you caught the flowers and he caught the garter."

Nichole let out a laugh. "We had a nice time and the kids like him. He's a sweet guy. But there's nothing going on between Ben Walker and me."

Lydia let out a deflated sigh. "That's too bad. You two would be cute together."

"Why not you and Ben then?"

Now Lydia laughed. "He's like a brother to me. No thank you. Okay, I'm off. I'll bring the posters by when I get them."

She left the salon with a little wave, and Nichole was sure she was whistling, too. Lydia Morgan was a wonder to Nichole. Her go-go attitude and her savvy business sense was something she couldn't help but envy. Nichole thought there was a bit of sadness to Lydia too, though it never showed through that peppy exterior. It lingered in her eyes and hinted in the crease of her smile. Perhaps she was lonely. Most of her friends were getting married and having families. Nichole knew how that felt. She knew what it was like to have that marriage crumble around her, too, and to wonder why everyone else got to have a happily ever after.

She shook her head and stood from the table as the bell above the door chimed. Enough wallowing in her self-pity brought on by the curiosity of a friend.

It was time to get to work.

"Hey, Marshall," Nichole called as she saw a man with a scraggly head of hair walk through the door.

"Hey."

"Have a seat in my chair. I'll be right with you."

Marshall Collins was one of her first clients when she'd moved to Georgia. His mother had set up the appointment when Nichole was still cutting in her kitchen. Nichole wasn't foolish enough to think his mother was simply helping Nichole build a clientele. No, she was matchmaking. Lucky for Nichole, Marshall had no interest in her at all. None. For a while, she figured she was the wrong gender. But after she'd gotten to know him, he just wasn't made for socializing. He liked working from home, a software designer of some kind. There was an online social aspect he could deal with, and he never had to leave his home office. Marshall could hold a conversation for a few minutes, but then she knew he got nervous. Perhaps she should be honored that he came in each month, or two, or three, to see her.

She walked to him, placed her hand on his shoulder, and looked at him in the mirror. "It's nice to see you, Marshall. How's your mom?"

That began the conversation as Nichole got to work, forgetting about the weekend and that Lydia had images of her and Ben in her head, just as her children did, too.

9

*B*en stood looking out the window over his sink at the vast, sprawling land outside his front door. They'd moved the cattle into the pasture just to the south, and there was some comfort in the noise and the movement.

Knowing Susan was going to stop by, Ben had gotten busy cleaning the pile of dishes in his sink. He figured his mother made her drop by, fully announced, so that he would clean his house. Well, it worked.

Just as he set the last plate in the drying rack, Susan's car bounced over the hill, a plume of dust following.

Ben dried his hands and headed out to meet her. As Susan stepped out of the car, he heard his niece wailing from the back seat.

"She's not happy," he offered.

"She's hungry. Hate to do it to you, but I need twenty minutes on your couch."

It took everything he had not to wince. The thought of Susan sitting in his house with her breast out made him a bit uncomfortable. This was his brother's wife. It wasn't something he should see.

"No problem. I'll get the stuff out of the back. What did you bring?"

"I had a bridal shower in town yesterday, and they over-ordered. And because I didn't like the mother of the bride and her snippy ways, I brought all the leftovers back. You should have lunch for the rest of the week."

Susan lifted the baby from the car and cradled her against her shoulder. "Bring it in and then come sit with me. I could use the conversation," she said as she turned, not giving him a chance to argue.

He watched his sister-in-law slip through the front door as she consoled her daughter. It was as natural to see Susan with a baby as it was for him to want to hide in the kitchen, or out in the barn when she was feeding her.

On a curse, Ben pulled the two boxes from the back seat and carried them into the house.

He caught a glimpse of Susan on the couch, a sheer blanket covering her chest and most of the baby. Ben quickly moved to the kitchen and set the boxes on the counter.

There was nothing wrong with breastfeeding a baby, and Ben would be on the front line to make sure all women had the right to do so. But he had to admit he was grateful that she covered up for his sanity.

Taking his time, he put the leftovers in his bare fridge. Yes, he was grateful for his sister-in-law.

"Don't tell me you're avoiding me," Susan called from the other room. "When you come out here can you bring me a glass of water?"

Ben let out a long breath. "Yeah. I'll be there in a moment."

He pulled a glass from the cupboard and filled it with ice and water, then he gave himself a little pep talk, and walked out to the living room.

He could hear the baby grunting from under the blanket. "She's hungry, huh?"

Susan laughed as she took the glass he offered. "She has an appetite like her father."

Ben managed to sit in the chair furthest from Susan and eased back. He should be comfortable, after all, it was his home.

"Are you ever going to decorate in here?" Susan asked as she looked around.

Ben shrugged. "Don't see the need. It's just me."

"Oh, you still deserve something nice to come home to. Put some paint on the walls. Hang some pictures."

"Of what?"

"Family. The land. Gia has some nice things in her store."

Ben had grown up in a family of boys. And even though Susan and Eric had been married for years now, he often forgot that he had sisters now, too. Sure, his brother Dane's wife would have plenty of things to spruce up the place. Victoria, his brother Russell's wife, had a knack for putting furniture in places that made a room look right. His cousin Bethany, she was a whiz with flower arrangements.

"I'll look into it."

Susan grinned at him as she set the glass he'd handed her on the table next to her. Carefully, she maneuvered the baby out from under the blanket and held her out.

"Here, hold her."

Ben stared at her for a moment before he stood and moved to her.

"Put her high on your shoulder and pat her back."

"Why?"

"She'll have some air and needs to burp. You're not going to break her, Uncle Ben."

Hesitantly, he took Caroline from her mother and did as

Susan said, consciously turning his back to her as she buttoned her shirt.

"I'm going to use your restroom," Susan said as she left him alone with his niece.

For a moment, the thought of dancing with Laura crossed his mind, and he began to sway back and forth, just as he had with the two-year-old.

Caroline let out a little burp and rested her head on his shoulder as he swayed and patted. He had to admit the act was soothing. As they swayed, and she made little noises in his ear, he thought about how drab the house looked. White bare walls and simple wood floors, yeah, he could certainly make it homier. He most certainly deserved that. After all, he worked hard, and it was nice to come home each day, sit on the couch, kick his feet up, and drink a beer as he watched some TV on the enormous centerpiece of his living room. The thought had him chuckling to himself as Susan came back into the room.

"Oh, you put her right to sleep. See, I told you she wouldn't break."

"We're bonding," he said as Susan took back her seat on the couch and picked up the glass of water again.

"So, how are things?"

Just because Caroline was being good, he wasn't sure he wanted to keep holding her. At some point, she was going to wake up and begin fussing. He wasn't quite ready for that. But he kept swaying as Susan looked up at him.

"Good. We just moved the cattle out this way, so that keeps me busy."

"Haven't been into town in a few weeks. It looks like you're due."

"Why?"

"Hair is shaggy," she said with a grin before sipping her water.

"No one out here minds."

She shrugged. "I just thought you and Nichole had hit it off. I wondered why you hadn't been back to see her?"

The swaying became harder to do as he thought of a reason. "She's nice. Her kids are nice."

"That's not what I mean. I mean I thought you *hit it off*."

Caroline stirred on his shoulder, so he moved toward Susan to hand her off.

Susan gathered the sleeping baby and cradled her in her arms, but it didn't work as a hint for her visit to be over. Instead, she eased back on the couch and gently tapped Caroline's bottom with her hand.

Ben raked his fingers through his hair, which she was right, it had gotten long in the past three weeks. "Why would you think that?"

"Because I'm a woman. You sat with them all night, and you danced—a lot."

"I promised her a dance, but I hadn't meant to dance more than one dance. I think we got wrangled into it with that garter and the bouquet."

Susan laughed. "It was fate, Ben. That bouquet was headed in Lydia's direction. Somehow it caught a breeze and ended up in front of Nichole."

"Strange."

"Certainly was. And I swear Phillip Smythe had that garter in his hand when it snapped off and landed in your hand."

"I didn't steal it if you're saying that."

"Nope," she offered. "I watched the whole thing. It was legit."

"Makes more sense that it would have gone to Phillip and Lydia."

Susan shrugged. "Maybe that was fate, too. They can't even have a civil conversation with each other."

"I fault Lydia for that."

On a sigh, she nodded in agreement.

"I'd better get back home. Maybe she'll sleep long enough I can get dinner started before Eric comes home." Careful not to wake Caroline, Susan stood still cradling her in her arms. She moved to kiss Ben on the cheek. "They're having an open house this weekend. They're blocking off the street and having food and music. You should support your sisters-in-law," she said with a wink.

"I'll be there. Gia already texted me to make sure of it."

"Good. I'll see you then. Enjoy the leftovers," she called over her shoulder as she walked down the steps and to her car.

Ben watched as she loaded the sleeping baby into her seat, and then gave him another wave before she drove off down the dirt path that would lead to her own house a mile over the crest of the hill.

He took a moment to appreciate the serene and quiet moment. The cattle moved in the field, and their noises soothed him. Thinking about the open space, he thought about the tree-house they'd had, the days by the creek, and all the running space any boy would want, growing up. Oh, the miles and miles he'd put on his bike riding from the house to the barn and back.

It made him wonder if Nichole's boys had bikes. Would they spend their summer exploring?

Raking his fingers through his hair, he let out a breath. He didn't want to be thinking about those kinds of things, but he was.

Turning back in toward the living room he decided to finish up what chores he had to tend to. It looked like he was spending his Saturday in town, and not because his sister-in-law had invited him, but because he was settling with the fact he did want to see Nichole again.

10

*S*amples of shampoos and hair products had been meticulously set up on the table in front of the salon. Nichole had swatted Wyatt's hand away from the small dish of candy more than once, and she was glad when Katie Brown offered to take the kids for the day. Katie had a genuine motherly instinct at nineteen, and she'd become a lifesaver on many occasions. When she moved back home to Oklahoma City after college, Nichole was going to be devastated. But she figured she had three years to worry about that. Katie had already told her she was staying in Macon for the summer and working with Lydia, whose own schedule seemed to be filled.

Audrey had been busy walking up and down the street passing out business cards for discounted haircuts, and two of their stylists were waiting for new customers to walk in the door.

Nichole watched as the street grew full of people. They ate, drank, and ducked in and out of the stores. Lydia was a genius when it came to organizing events and getting people to attend. Nichole didn't know how she did it. After all, the last time she'd hosted a party, only her mother showed up. She'd be happy to leave these kinds of things to Lydia.

As she watched a family stroll past the barbershop across the street, and they handed each child a balloon, she noticed Ben Walker making his way down the street in a slow stroll.

His hat was tipped back on his head, and sunglasses shielded his eyes. But when he caught her looking at him, she knew it.

With a small wave, he acknowledged her, and she gave him a nod. No need to get worked up over seeing him. They'd danced at the wedding, and she hadn't seen him again until now. She'd lost count of how many weeks ago Audrey had gotten married.

It was obvious he wasn't interested in her in the least, and she wasn't sure why she'd expected him to be. They didn't have much in common, and she had kids. Nichole understood that. But she'd hoped maybe he'd come around more often than he had.

When he said hello, Nichole realized that while she had been having a conversation in her head, Ben had walked over to her and removed his glasses. Now those bright blue eyes stared at her.

"Hi, Ben. Haven't seen you around much."

He hooked his glasses over the collar of his T-shirt. "Ya, I don't get into town much."

That should have been what turned her off of him. She knew that, yet he twisted her up a bit.

"I'll bet you're due for a haircut again."

Ben pulled off his hat and dragged his fingers through the sandy blond mess on his head. "Yeah, I suppose you're right. Would you have time this week? Or should I go back to having Audrey do it?"

Of course, he would think of family. If Nichole had learned anything in the months that she'd been there, it was that the Walkers took care of each other.

"I'm sure she wouldn't mind. I could do it now if you'd like."

His eyes went wide. "You're working today? I thought it was just a celebration."

"It is. But I can sneak you in."

Then she heard her kids calling to her as they raced toward them, their faces covered in paint.

"Oh, my. I see that you've been to the bakery. I heard that Tonya Adams is painting faces."

Laura laughed. "I'm a clown, Mommy."

Nichole picked her up but held her out as to not get the paint on her. "You sure are. Are you being good for Katie?"

As Katie walked up to them, she noticed the long slow look she took at Ben and Nichole thought it was funny that a surge of jealousy zipped right through her.

"They're perfect," Katie offered, shifting her attention to Nichole. "I hope you don't mind the face paint. Tonya said it washes right off."

"It's fine. Do you know Ben Walker?" Nichole asked and watched as Katie's eyes shifted.

"I've never met you," she said, holding her hand out. "I've met Gerald, your brother, right?"

Ben shook her hand. "Yeah."

"Well, it's nice to meet you. Okay, kiddos," Katie captured their attention. "Mr. Lanzo said he was making our pizza, so let's head back to the pizza parlor."

Without even saying goodbye, Zane started running toward the restaurant with his brother in tow. Laura grabbed Katie's hand, and they were off.

"I guess we know where we rank." Nichole laughed.

"Is that your babysitter?"

She didn't like that he asked, but it was innocent enough. She was foolish to be put off by it.

"Yes. She's a gem. She's a college student and she's been a huge help with us moving here. So, what about that haircut?"

Before he could answer, Lydia was running their way. "Ben, I need your help. Will you help my brother unload the truck in the parking lot? I ordered some new decor for the reception hall, and of all days they delivered it today."

Nichole watched as relief seemed to wash over Ben's face. "Sure." He turned back to her. "I'll stop back by."

Nichole smiled at him and watched as Lydia hurried off with Ben.

"I'm sorry, Ben. I didn't mean to drag you away from Nichole," Lydia apologized as they rounded the building.

"No worries. She said she could get me in today for a haircut."

Lydia shifted him a side glance. "She's working today? I thought that was why the other girls were there."

Ben shrugged. "That's what she said."

As they approached the truck where Tyson Morgan began pulling boxes out of a truck, Lydia placed a hand on Ben's arm. "I promise this won't take long and you can get back over there. In fact, I'll tell Lanzo to make you two up a pizza."

"You don't have to do that. I should be getting..."

"Consider it done," she said before turning back toward the street and disappearing into a sea of people.

"You can't reason with her," Tyson said. "If she has a plan, *consider it done*," he mimicked his sister.

"I guess I'll stay for pizza then," he agreed and took the box that Tyson handed him.

"I have some new stout beer in the bar. Interested? It's a microbrew with coffee and cherry."

That had piqued Ben's interest. "I do like a microbrew."

"I knew that." Tyson jumped out of the truck and carried a box with him. He led them through the side door of the reception hall. "When we were younger, and my sister told me that one day she was going to own the town, I thought she was kidding. I had no idea she was going to seriously own most of the businesses in it."

Tyson set his box against the wall and Ben followed. "I'm guessing she has something to do with that microbrew too?"

"For now. It's a startup, so they're looking for investors. But I heard Phillip Smythe was investing too."

Ben laughed. "Then they can kiss her support goodbye."

Tyson agreed with a nod. "If they're smart, they keep their investors' names under wraps."

When the two men were finished unloading the truck, Tyson pulled two beers from the fridge under the bar in the reception hall. He handed one to Ben, then opened the top of his own. He took a long pull, studied its label for a moment before swallowing, then let out a refreshed sigh. "It's good."

Ben opened his bottle and took his first sip. "I like it. She should keep her money in it."

"He told you I invested?" Lydia's voice came from behind him. "They have a solid project. The pizza is on the table by the salon. Take Nichole one of those beers too. And, Tyson, Pearl needs you at the bridal store. She's had a great day. She sold six of those sample dresses she had on sale and booked four appointments for just this week. Love is in the air, and everyone is getting married," Lydia sang with a smile before heading back out the door.

Tyson pulled another beer from the fridge and handed it to Ben. "Good luck."

"Why?"

"Lydia wants to see you and that Nichole girl together. She usually gets what she wants."

Ben assumed his shock registered on his face when Tyson laughed. With that, he gave him a nod and headed back out to the street.

11

*N*ichole watched as Katie carried Laura on her hip and followed the boys from street game to street game. Lydia had brought a pizza and told her to sit down for a few moments. Audrey had walked by, taken a slice from the box, and headed inside to take a call from her husband, who was in Hawaii shooting retakes for a movie.

Ben caught her eye as he walked out of the reception hall and headed toward her. He had two bottles of beer in his hands.

He stopped at the table. "Lydia thought you might enjoy one of these with your pizza," he offered, handing her one of the beers.

"Thanks. Will you join me?" she asked, and a grin formed on his lips.

"I think that was the plan. Lydia is taking care of everyone and running this whole thing," he offered as he twisted the top from his bottle and sipped his beer. He pulled out the chair next to her and sat down. "Looks like they're having fun."

She watched Wyatt throw a ball at a pyramid of bottles, and one fell from the top. "They are having fun. Lydia is genius with this stuff."

"She is. I heard Pearl sold six dresses today, or something like that," he said.

"We've cut thirty clients today that were walk-ins," she boasted as she'd talked each of them into walking through the door. "It's good for business."

Ben lifted his beer in salute. "Here's to that."

She tapped her beer to his and took a long sip. She studied it for a moment. "Coffee and cherry?"

"See, I can't taste the cherry too much. But I like it." He took another thoughtful sip. "Yeah, I like it."

"Lydia investment?"

"You're catching on quick. What did she put on our pizza?"

"Sausage. Only sausage." She pursed her lips.

"My favorite."

"Lydia knew that, I guess."

"Lydia knows everything," he said as he opened the box and took out a slice. "She's a wizard that way. You don't like sausage pizza?" He held the piece to his lips as if waiting for an answer.

"It's fine. Don't you like veggies on it?"

"Veggies go in a bowl and get covered in dressing," he teased before he took the bite. "Nope, this is perfect."

Simple, Nichole thought to herself. He was a simple man. The pleasure of life came easy to him. No wonder he didn't come into town often, he probably enjoyed the peace and quiet where he lived. She hadn't seen his house, but she knew he lived on the family land. She'd only ever been out there for the wedding, but it was beautiful and tranquil.

Taking a slice from the box, she slid it onto one of the paper plates that Lydia had brought. She sipped again from her beer and then took a bite of her pizza. It wasn't something she was going to admit aloud, but he was right. Sausage was perfect. There was nothing to throw off the flavor, like an uncooked bit of green pepper, which she always added to her pizzas.

"Good huh?" he asked.

"I've only had their subs. I've never had one of their pizzas."

"If there is anything I miss about the city, it's pizza. No one delivers out as far as the ranch," he joked, and Nichole covered her mouth as she laughed.

"I guess you have to trade pizza and convenience for beauty and peace."

The glow that lit from his eyes said she'd hit the nail on the head. When she gave it a little more thought, as she took another bite of the pizza, she supposed she understood that. When she'd gotten divorced, she'd moved from the only home she'd ever known. There was no one to run to when she was having a bad day. Her mother couldn't just drop by and have a cup of coffee, or watch the kids when she needed a few moments alone. She'd traded in all of those things to get away from a bad situation and to take her kids with her. And even after a year, it still was the best decision she'd ever made.

"The sunrise over the pastures in the morning is worth getting up for," he said as he settled back in his seat.

"I'll bet that's lovely."

"You should come and see it sometimes," he offered, and his eyes grew wide.

Nichole felt the warmth rise in her cheeks at the invitation.

"Maybe I'll make up breakfast burritos and bring the kids up for that some morning."

She watched as the panic on his face settled. "That sounds great."

Zane ran back toward the table. "Can I have some pizza?"

"Didn't you already have some?" Nichole asked as she brushed a wayward strand of hair from her son's brow.

"I'm starving, Mom," he whined, and it amused her.

"Yes, make sure Ben has enough to eat."

He held up his hand. "I'm good."

Zane took a piece and picked off all the pieces of sausage, which had Ben leaning in over the table. "Dude, you're taking all the good stuff off."

Zane looked up at him and winced. "Nope. Cheese is good."

Ben reached for the little balls of meat that Zane had discarded and put them on his half-eaten slice. "Now it's perfect."

Nichole realized that she watched the man sitting with her with great interest. He was still a boy at heart, she thought, as he carefully ate the slice of pizza while balancing the extra sausage on top.

"I'd be happy to get that haircut done for you when you're done eating," she offered.

He looked up at her mid-bite. "Are you sure?"

"The kids are having fun. The day is winding down. I'd be happy to."

"Thanks."

Nichole sat back and finished her beer while she watched her children play. It felt good to be happy. With a nonchalant glance toward Ben, she smiled from behind her bottle. What was it about this man in particular that made her happy? She wasn't sure he was interested in her. Well, it was always good to have one more friend in a new city.

BEN FOLLOWED Nichole to the salon after they had finished their pizza. She'd tried to offer him the leftovers, but he'd seen the look in Wyatt's eyes that said he was looking forward to a slice later. They'd agreed she would take it and store it in the refrigerator at the shop.

Outside, the vendors and stores began to pick up their wares, and the kids settled into the waiting area of the salon as the other stylists tidied up and headed home.

Nichole escorted him to the shampoo sink, and he leaned

back, careful not to make eye contact. She started the water and waited until it was just the right temperature before he felt the spray over his scalp. Then she massaged shampoo into his hair, and it took everything inside of him not to moan. Wouldn't that be embarrassing?

As she worked the lather through his hair, Ben felt every muscle in his body relax. He didn't remember that last time he'd felt nearly entranced. She massaged the tops of his ears, and down his neck. Seriously, she was going to expect him to stand after all of this?

She turned the water back on and gently rinsed the soap out of his hair, her fingers tunneling through the strands.

When the water turned off, he realized he'd closed his eyes. Crap! Had he moaned? It was completely possible since he didn't even know he'd closed his eyes.

Nichole ran the towel over his head pressing the water from his hair and then stepped back from the sink.

"Ready?" She smiled down at him waiting for him to follow.

Words eluded him now.

He followed her to her station and watched as she prepared for his haircut. Unfolding her cape, she pulled it up around his neck and fastened it. Her delicate fingers were grazing his skin.

It was then that words came to him, though he hadn't anticipated them until they'd been spoken.

"Would you like to have dinner with me next weekend?"

She had just taken the comb to his hair when she stopped and looked at him in the mirror.

There was a smile on her lips, and she didn't look too put out by the question that had blurted from his mouth.

"I would love to. I work on Saturday until four. I can have Katie watch the kids."

"Great. I'll come by then," he offered, and Nichole went on with her work.

Well, now he had a date. That hadn't been in his expecta-
tions when he'd headed into town that morning. He noticed the
kids behind him, and suddenly his stomach clenched. What
right did he have asking out their mother? She had enough on
her plate. The last thing she needed to worry about was him.

Maybe in the next seven days he could come up with an
excuse not to go through with the date. Yeah, maybe that's just
what he'd do.

12

When the last client of the day walked out of the salon, Nichole felt her stomach begin to flutter. It had been a long week waiting for Saturday to arrive, but it was here. Ben had asked her out to dinner, but she hadn't heard from him all week. Still, with a little bit of hope left in her, she'd called Katie and asked her to watch the kids.

Now she stood alone in the salon wondering if she'd been foolish to think he would show up. After all, if he'd been looking forward to the date, wouldn't he have called and finalized it?

She turned the sign in the window to read closed. Looking down the street, she didn't see his truck parked anywhere. Well, she'd close up, turn off the lights, and sit in the back room and have a glass of wine. Her kids were taken care of, so she might as well take a moment for herself. Maybe the wine would soften the blow when Ben didn't show.

Nichole pulled down a glass from the cupboard, took the bottle of wine from the refrigerator, and poured herself a generous glass. There was a bag of potato chips on the shelf. She'd consider it dinner out.

Sitting down at the table with her glass in one hand, and the bag of chips in the other, she took a long sip of wine and let it warm her as she reclined in the chair and propped her feet up on another. It had been stupid to get worked up over an offer for dinner. Ben Walker was a nice guy, but he was a bit of a loner. Nichole knew that, and Audrey had even backed up her thought of him. He liked his little house out on the ranch and away from town and people. That wasn't the kind of man Nichole could get involved with. She was a people person. She liked the bustle of town, and well, she had her kids to think about, too. When it came to them, there was no place for romance.

She took another long sip of wine, then pulled a few chips from the bag when she heard a tapping at the door. Standing, she looked around the wall, and she saw Ben standing at the front door of the salon, his hands cupped around his eyes looking in.

"Well, I'll be damned," she said to herself as she walked toward the door. Still, with her wine in one hand, she unlocked the lock and pulled open the door. "You came."

The expression on his face was one of pure shock. "We had a date, didn't we?"

Nichole smiled and nodded her head. "We sure did. Let me get my stuff. Would you like a glass of wine or a bottle of beer before we go? Lydia brought more of those microbrews you like."

Ben closed the door behind him. "No, I'm good."

"Okay, then let me get my purse, and I'm ready to go." Nichole took one last long sip of her wine before pouring out the last few sips and rinsing the glass. When she returned, she found Ben fixing his hair in the mirror. Oh, he was nervous, and it made him even cuter. "I'm ready," she said, and Ben's head shot up.

"Great. I'm sorry I'm later than we'd agreed on. I got a flat on the way here."

"It's no problem. That kind of stuff happens."

"Right. Well, I should have called, but I'm not used to calling people. I mean, it didn't cross my mind until I saw the lights off."

It would be a fun evening, no matter what, Nichole thought. Some adult conversation and a meal with a nice-looking man. But seriously, a man who didn't even consider calling his date to tell her he was going to be late? That was just self-centered.

They walked out of the salon and Nichole locked the door behind them. "Where are we going?"

"Do you like Mexican food? Juan's Cantina is not too far. We could even walk if you'd like."

A nice walk on a spring evening sounded delightful. "I'd like that," she said tucking her keys into her purse. "Do they have margaritas?"

"Of course," he offered, tucking his hands into the front pockets of his jeans. "They have regular ones, and then a big grand-daddy strawberry one rimmed with sugar."

The way he described it, Nichole found her mouth watering. "I think that's what I'm going to have. I could use it."

"Tough day?" Ben asked as they walked down the street past businesses she knew Lydia had her hand in.

"Not too bad. I just don't get out too often. But Katie has the kids, and I get to be free for a few hours."

"I guess it takes a lot of planning to have a night out. I didn't think too much about that. I'd be happy to pay for Katie's babysitting fees."

Now that was a gem of a man. "We're trading babysitting for hair services. For both of us, it's a win."

"That's good."

They walked in silence the rest of the way to Juan's. Nichole had never been there, but from the looks of the patio and the music coming from inside, it appeared to be quite popular. Ben walked straight to the hostess and then gave Nichole a nod to follow. They were seated out on the patio with a view of the river.

"There was a line at the door. Who do you know, to walk straight in?"

Only a beat later, Nichole's question was answered when Lydia hurried to the table and pulled Nichole up into a hug. "Oh, I'm so glad you guys got here. I was worried."

Ben stood and kissed Lydia on the cheek. "I got a flat."

"I thought Jake just got you new tires."

Ben laughed. "Yeah, they're still at his shop. Guess I'll be heading over there tomorrow to get them."

"I'm giving out samples of our newest beer. They're going to start carrying it on their menu. I'll bring you guys out some sample trays. Oh, and some chips and guac on the house. I've brought in enough business tonight by word of mouth they're giving my friends some perks," Lydia said with a wink as she hurried off.

Nichole laughed as she picked up a menu. "Where does she get the energy to do all of this stuff? How many businesses does she own? And how does she get involved in all of this?"

Ben's eyes went wide. "You've never met her mother, have you?"

"No."

"You'd understand then. She has the entrepreneurial blood running through her. Her grandfather owns the ranch adjacent from ours. We've been family rivals for longer than I've been alive."

"Your family and Lydia's family? Rivals? But your cousin is married to her brother."

Ben eased back in his chair. "That rivalry is what TV movies are made of. Our families never got along. Then a few years ago, about the time Eric and Susan got together, it came out that Eric's late mother was actually Tyson's mother too."

Nichole lifted her eyes from the menu to stare at him. "Your brother Eric is Tyson Morgan's brother?"

"Like a soap opera, right?"

"I'd say. And feuding families are now intertwined and married?"

"Yep."

"And Lydia is in business with a Walker, or many Walkers, actually."

"You got it."

"That's a lot to take in. I don't know if I'd ever have put all the pieces together. Does she have anything to do with her grandfather?"

Ben eased his arms to the table and leaned in. "He raised her. She doesn't see eye to eye with him, but she still talks to him."

She could feel the unease of it.

A moment later Lydia came back with a tray. She set down six small glasses of beer and a basket with the chips and a bowl of guacamole. "Here is a map of what beer is what. I'll come back by, and you tell me which one you like the best." She handed them the small printed menu of the beers. "Word of mouth got around quite well, I guess. Smythe just walked in with a date. I can't even believe it," she growled as she walked away.

Nichole watched Lydia move through the crowd. "Now that's a relationship I don't understand."

"No one does."

"Why does she hate Phillip so much? He's nothing but nice."

Ben shrugged his shoulder. "Eh, he wasn't always a fan of the Walkers, so I suppose maybe he wasn't a fan of the Morgans either. I'm not sure what happened there. I just know he's over the moon about her and she couldn't care if he's alive."

"He doesn't feel that way about the Walkers anymore, does he?"

Shaking his head and reaching for a chip, Ben lifted it to his lips. "Nah. Superficial dislike. I have to agree he's a great guy."

Nichole picked up the beer glass closest to her and took a sip. "Oh, this one is nice. It has some citrus to it."

She handed it across the table to Ben, who took it, but studied it long and hard before took a sip. The commitment would be hard for this man she thought watching him process what could have been construed as an intimate gesture.

"I do like that." He handed the glass back to her, and she moved right in to take a long sip from it. His eyes widened, and it humored her. Perhaps she could have a little fun seeing what pushed his buttons. After all, she might as well enjoy her night alone with a man. It was probably going to be a very long time before she got the opportunity again.

13

Upon recommendation from Lydia, Nichole had enjoyed the enchilada platter. After sampling the beers Lydia had brought to the table, Nichole decided against the margarita, but she thought she'd go back to Juan's again someday and have one. She'd seen the size of them when they'd been delivered to other tables. Surely it would give her a mini vacation just to drink one.

The sun was making its descent in the western sky as she and Ben began to walk back toward the salon.

"Thank you for a nice evening. That was a lot of fun," Nichole said as she let her arms swing freely at her sides.

"Lydia called me this morning to tell me about the gig she was working. I also think she wanted to make sure I didn't forget."

Nichole was going to have to thank Lydia for the push.

"Had you forgotten?"

Ben's pace slowed. "No. Of course not. Did you think I forgot?"

Easily, Nichole shrugged. "Oh, I just hadn't heard from you. I guess it crossed my mind. But I didn't mention it to anyone," she defended. "I was very happy that you showed. I've been looking forward to tonight all week."

His shoulders softened as he continued to walk by her side. "Admittedly, I'm not very good at this. Taking out women, that is. I tend to freeze up." Tucking his hands into his pockets, he bit down on his bottom lip.

"Well, I think you did a great job. I haven't been out with a man in quite some time. It was nice. Don't get me wrong. I like my girls' nights out, and with your cousins, I get a lot of those. They are sweet to include me. But just some one on one conversation with a handsome man, that was nice."

She caught the glance he'd shifted toward her. Turning her head, she saw that what she'd said seemed to have stunned him in some way. Seriously, she was worrying that she might in fact be the first woman he'd ever gone out with. Was that even possible?

The only thing she could do was to keep the conversation going.

"So, Ben Walker, what do you like to do for fun?"

He was silent long enough. This was the last outing she might have with the man. How could anyone be so timid?

Just as she was about to repeat the question, he raked his hand through his hair and blew out a breath. "I play guitar."

"No kidding?" The answer had honestly surprised her. "I didn't know that about you."

Ben shrugged it off. "It's no big thing."

"How long have you done that?"

"Since I was ten. I wanted to be the next Johnny Cash."

A bubble of amusement wanted to break through with a laugh, but Nichole stifled it. She gave him a playful nudge. "I'd like to hear you play sometime."

With that, his eyes opened wide. "Really?"

"Of course. You know my boys can strum a few songs, too."

"No kidding? Where'd they learn that?"

The happiness of the moment abruptly stalled. "Their father."

"We have something in common then. My dad taught me too."

The smile on his lips cured the momentary loss of enjoyment in her heart. "They'll love to know that."

"Do you like ice cream?"

The question humored her. "Who doesn't like ice cream?"

"Carla Burnston."

The answer came so quickly, Nichole burst out with a laugh. "Who is Carla Burnston?"

"Ex-girlfriend. Seriously, she hated ice cream. I mean I'm not some ice cream snob, but once in a while on a hot summer evening, ice cream is nice. She wouldn't have it. Obviously, it was a deal breaker."

The humor calmed her. "I agree. I don't think Carla Burnston and I can be friends either."

"C'mon, let's get some," he said reaching for her hand and tugging her along to the ice cream parlor at the end of the street from the salon.

BEN WATCHED Nichole study the menu. She was beautiful. Her dark hair lazily brushed her shoulders as she shook her head back and forth trying to decide on a flavor. And when she pushed up her glasses, it kicked him in the gut a little.

"I think I'm going to go with a bowl of that brownie fudge with sprinkle toppings."

When she turned to look at him, his stomach tightened. He'd been gazing. Not just looking—gazing. Christ, she must have thought he was demented the way he was studying her.

"That sounds sweet."

"The more sugar, the better. I'm not with my kids. I don't have to be the voice of reason," she said smiling. "What are you having?"

"Gotta go with a waffle cone if there is no voice of reason. I'll see your brownie and add a scoop of mint to that."

When her smile widened, he knew this wasn't the last time they'd share a moment. Now he wished his truck got better gas mileage because he was sure he'd be making more trips into town than usual.

They sat on a bench outside the ice cream parlor and watched the people pass by as they ate their decadent, sweet treats.

"I love to people watch," Nichole said as she lifted a spoonful of brownie ice cream to her mouth.

"Why?"

"It's fascinating. Don't you think?"

"Never gave it any thought."

"See those two people across the street?" She pointed, and he nodded when he'd located them. "They're newly married."

"How do you know?"

"They're cuddly. Not pawing on each other like a newly dating couple, but cuddly. The couple that is walking into that store," she said pointing again. "They've been married for a long time. He's walking a step behind her and following where she wants to go."

"So, men fall in line when they've been married a long time?"

"Good ones." She took another bite of her ice cream. "Okay, see the ones coming out of the pizza parlor? They're not happily married. He's leading the way, and she's got her attitude on."

He watched as the woman hurried to keep up with the man who was obviously paying her no attention. He could feel the tension in their mannerism, and it had him adjusting his own position on the bench to not seem so stiff.

"What about that man and woman looking in the window of Pearl's store?"

Nichole studied them for a moment. "Have been dating for a little bit. He's not too serious about the relationship, but she's trying to hint to him by looking in the window."

"Really?"

"Oh, I'd put money on it."

"This is a fun game," he agreed as he licked his ice cream and relaxed next to her. "Are you happy that you moved here?" he asked.

"I am. It's been a nice change for me and the kids."

"What about family? Don't you miss them?"

"Of course. That was a hard decision, but I knew it was the right one. They needed to start anew too, my kids that is."

"I take it your divorce wasn't very amicable."

He noticed that she stabbed at her ice cream now. His question had certainly raised the tension between them. Perhaps he'd crossed a line.

"I think amicable divorces are a load of crap, really. If your marriage were amicable, there would be no need for divorce." She bit the ice cream off of the spoon with a snap. "So, no. It wasn't pleasant."

"I didn't mean to..."

"I know. I know." Nichole let out a long sigh. "Sooner or later you'd ask, and I didn't handle that well."

"It's none of my business."

"Sure it is. We're friends. So you have the right to ask."

He licked his ice cream and watched as she formulated what she wanted to tell him—her friend.

"We got married young. I was twenty-one, and he was twenty-two. Life was just a big party to us. I worked full time at a salon and part-time as a waitress at a bar. We lived in a run-down apartment and never had enough money to, well, to live."

She took another bite of her ice cream. "It should have been my first clue that things weren't what he said they were. After a few months our money began disappearing, I realized he was gambling it all away. He was a blackjack dealer at a resort. He got sucked into it, and soon we were being evicted.

"We went our separate ways in year two. We couldn't afford a divorce, but we stayed apart for a year. But then one night we met up, and wouldn't you know it? I got pregnant with twins."

"Your boys are incredible," he said honestly and for the purpose of defusing the tension.

That brought a smile to her lips. "They are. We managed to work it out for five more years and then had Laura. That was nearly as much of a surprise as having twins, but even then, he wasn't around. He was gambling again, but this time we had bigger stakes. First, he lost his car, then his job, and then the lease on our house. I couldn't do it anymore."

"So you left?"

"I packed up my kids and just started driving. We ended up in Athens first. We lived there for six months or so before we made it here and I fell in love with the area. Luckily, Audrey was opening her salon, and I talked her into hiring me. End of story."

He was sure that wasn't the end, but he had a good grasp on what she'd gone through.

Nichole took another bite of her ice cream and then eased back against the bench. "My divorce was final the first month I was here. Lydia and I celebrated all weekend."

"I'm glad you're here." The words fell from his mouth, and he hoped he didn't look as terrified as he felt when she turned and studied him.

"So am I."

They silently finished their ice cream and then started back toward the salon.

The May evening was perfect, and as they walked past the

storefronts of the many businesses Lydia Morgan was a part of, their hands brushed, and instinct took over as he took her hand.

He caught the hitch in her breath and noticed the subtle smile that settled on her lips. No big deal was made about it, not outwardly, that was. His heart was hammering in his chest, and he was just holding a woman's hand. They walked the rest of the way, their fingers interlaced with one another's.

NICHOLE FOUND that the closer they got to the salon, the slower she wanted to walk. She hadn't been too sure about her evening with Ben Walker, but now she didn't want it to end.

When they reached the door, his hand slipped away from hers. She dug into her purse and pulled out the keys, then unlocked the door, and pushed it open.

"Can I interest you in a glass of wine or beer?" she offered, hoping for a few more moments.

"I have a long drive home."

"Right. Well, Thank you. I had a wonderful time. "

"So did I. Maybe I could drop by this week and take you all out for pizza or something."

Her chest swelled with the anticipation of his offer. "I think the kids would like that."

"Great. What night is best?"

"Wednesday? I'm done early on Wednesdays, so I can pick the kids up from school."

"I'll come by around five?"

"That works. We'll meet you here."

Ben nodded but stood in the doorway another moment, his hands tucked securely in his pockets. Nichole studied him. Was he waiting for something? She'd invited him in, and he didn't accept the offer. Was she supposed to...

There wasn't another moment to think about what Ben

Walker wanted to do when he moved in and took her mouth with his.

She felt the gasp in her throat, but it never surfaced—suffocated by his kiss.

For a moment they stood in the doorway, lips pressed together, but with an imaginary wall between them.

Oh, to hell with it, she thought, as she lifted her arms around his neck and sank fully into the kiss that had her head swimming.

Ben's hands came to her hips and pulled her in closer.

Once she was breathless and damn nearly faint, he pulled back. "I'll see you Wednesday," he said calmly, which surprised her more than the kiss.

Nichole could offer nothing but a gurgle of acceptance as she caught her breath.

Ben dropped his hands, gave her a wave, and disappeared into the night.

Nichole watched until he was out of sight. She shut the door and leaned up against it.

Her heart raced, her head spun, and her lips tingled. She could feel the enormous smile that tugged at the corners of her mouth. It had been so long since she'd been kissed like that, she thought maybe she was floating.

Pressing a hand to her chest, she stood a moment longer. Wednesday seemed so far away.

14

Weekends were made for recuperating, and Nichole had done just that. She and the kids had gone to the park on Sunday and played some basketball. She'd taken them to the ice cream parlor too, and she and Laura shared that decadent brownie ice cream. Maybe she was making memories with her family. Or maybe she'd been trying to keep that moment intact, the one where Ben had swept her off her feet.

Monday she took the boys to school, and as it was her day off, she and Laura did domestic things. They went to the grocery store, filled the car with gas, and cleaned the house. Luckily Laura was still young enough to think that pushing a vacuum cleaner around was fun. And though it was three times her size, and Nichole would have to do the job again, she let Laura have at it.

In fact, if she didn't get back around to it, it didn't matter. Nichole's head was so far in the clouds nothing seemed to matter.

How could a kiss from a timid man make her so deliriously happy? Then it hit her—because she was lonely.

By the end of the day, Nichole had dropped down on her bed after the boys had finally fallen asleep, and she wept.

A hollowness filled the void where the deliriously happy bubble had been since Ben had kissed her on Saturday night. When she realized she was a single mother of three, divorced, living far from home—the happiness fell out of her.

This wasn't what she'd wanted—this feeling of despair. Damnit, she deserved a life of happiness and kisses from men who were decent and family-centered. She deserved brownie ice cream any damn time she wanted it, and who the hell cared if she never did get back to that vacuum?

The more she wept, the more she realized she was still broken from the man who stole everything from her.

Wiping her tears away, she cursed herself for ever going back to him—but without him, she wouldn't have the three joys in her life that slumbered just down the hall.

She rolled over and punched the pillow. Why did it always have to circle around and hurt? Why couldn't her anger make his memory go away?

It wasn't as if the kids asked where he was. Okay, Zane did from time to time, but her ex hadn't been there for them anyway. He'd stolen from them too. He made their house disappear too.

Rolling back to stare up at the ceiling she made her mind go back to that kiss. That simple stupid kiss that Ben had laid on her.

That happy bubble percolated in her chest again. Maybe she should call him. Would he freak out? He was the one who asked her out, took her hand, and kissed her. Would he be receptive to her call?

Picking up her phone from the nightstand, she studied it. Ben Walker's phone number wasn't in her phone.

It was stupid really. She had more than a dozen contacts of

people that would happily give it to her, but she replaced the phone on the nightstand.

Wednesday. He'd invited them all out on a date.

She could wait until Wednesday.

Nichole turned off the bedside lamp and closed her eyes. She was going to have an aneurysm if she kept going back and forth like that. But it was the way it had been for so long she didn't know how not to doubt herself.

She'd work on that tomorrow. For now, she'd get some sleep and dream about that kiss again.

15

*B*ecause she worked later on Tuesdays, Nichole hadn't walked into the salon until one o'clock. Katie would pick up the boys from school, and help them with their homework until Nichole got home that night. It was routine.

When she opened the door to the salon, it didn't go unnoticed that Audrey and the other three stylists were seated in the waiting area, chairs facing the door all staring up at her.

"What's going on?" she asked as she let the door close behind her.

The four sets of eyes were wide, and stupid grins were on each of their faces.

Audrey sat back in her chair and crossed her legs. "No clients for the next half hour. Sit your butt in a chair and dish."

Nichole set her bag and her purse on one of the empty chairs. "Dish on what?"

"Oh, don't be smug. You had a date on Saturday, and we want every hot and torrid detail, even if it was my cousin. Sit."

A headache began to form behind Nichole's eyes. Were they kidding? Were they going to force her to talk about this? If

Audrey knew her cousin at all, she knew there weren't any details to share.

In the spirit of sisterhood, Nichole pulled up a chair and sat down.

"I can't believe you guys are doing this to me," she whined.

"Don't go there," Patty said. "You were right here in this circle when I went on that date with, oh what the hell was his name?"

"Bob," Darlene injected. "His name was Bob, and he was as dumb as a doorknob."

"Was not," Patty argued and then reconsidered. "Okay, he was. Maybe that's why I can't even remember his name."

They all shared a laugh, but then all eyes turned back to Nichole.

"Fine. We had a nice time. He came here and picked me up. Actually, I'd given up on him. But he showed."

"He got a flat," Audrey chimed in.

"So if you know that detail, why are you asking me for the rest."

"I know that detail because Missy was the one who told me. She said Jake had fixed Ben's tire and that he was all worked up over your date. And that's why I'm sitting here wanting all the juicy details."

Funny, Nichole thought. He'd been worked up over the date? Did that mean he'd been nervous or had had second thoughts?

"Lydia had tuned him in to the fact that she was serving samples from the craft brewery she's involved in at Juan's. So, we went there for dinner. We had a nice time. I had the enchilada platter as suggested by Lydia," she said with a laugh trying to draw out the story. "Then we took a walk back toward the salon. Of course, we stopped for dessert first."

"Damn," Darlene pushed back in her chair. "You had sex after dinner, just like that?"

Nichole bore a stare at her. "What? Did I say I had sex? I said we had dessert."

"Yeah, sex. First date sex."

Nichole shook her head. "Not in my book, sister. I mean we stopped for ice cream."

Beth clasped her hands together. "That's romantic," she said sweetly, as that was more her style, Nichole knew.

"Right. Romance, no sex after dinner," she reiterated. "We sat on the bench outside the ice cream parlor and enjoyed the nice night people watching."

"And that was it?" Darlene sat forward leaning her forearms on her knees. "Boring."

"We did walk back to the salon, and our hands brushed together. Then he subtly took my hand." She heard Beth sigh. "When we got back to the salon he said he'd like to see me again and take my whole family out for pizza on Wednesday."

She could nearly see Beth swooning in her seat.

Audrey mimicked Darlene's stance and leaned in on her forearms. "C'mon, C'mon. You're killing me here. Is my cousin good in bed or not?"

"What is wrong with you?" Nichole laughed. She was mortified at the question but fully understood that if one of the other girls were in the hot-seat, she'd be wanting lurid details too. "I didn't have sex with your cousin."

"What's wrong with him?"

"I didn't say I wouldn't have sex with your cousin. I just said I didn't."

"So that was all? Dinner, ice cream, and hand holding?" Audrey sat back in her chair. "What are we, in sixth grade?"

"You never let me finish. Before he left, he took me by surprise and laid the hottest kiss on me. Which proves we're up to eighth grade," she joked and received a laugh from each of them. "Well, it was the hottest kiss because it's been nearly a year since I've kissed anyone, but it made my knees weak."

"Eh," Darlene protested as she stood up and picked up her can of Coke from the coffee table. "I wanted hot details. Tell me when you're banging someone," she said as she went to the back room.

Beth's cheeks pinked, and Audrey laughed. "You're going out again, though?"

"With my kids."

"That's a big step," Audrey offered. "He's a good man, Nichole. You couldn't do better."

"I'm not looking for the real thing. I would be selfish to even think about it. I have three kids and an ex-husband. Who in their right mind wants that?"

"You can still have sex with the man even if you don't plan to keep him forever. Even if he's the boss' cousin," Darlene called from the back room, sending the women into a laughing fit that only ended when their next client walked in the door.

BEN WIPED his brow with the back of his hand. The sun was hot, and the work that was left to be done was plentiful. He'd thought Gerald was going to help him unload the hay from the trailer, but as he had yet to show up and Ben was halfway through the load. He'd given up.

This was what he loved to do, though. The physical labor involved in running the ranch, that made sense to him. He never could be a paper pusher. The Walker men were hands-on with whatever they did.

Taking a break, he sat on the edge of the trailer and took a long satisfying swig from his water bottle. When this day was done, he was going to sit on his front porch and have a nice cold beer and watch the sun go down over the fields. What better life was there than that?

With his next swig of water, he thought of how lonely it sounded. Oh, he didn't mind it, but he had a hard time concentrating on the things that were normal lately. A certain brunette kept creeping into his thoughts. And that kiss they'd shared, it had made an appearance in more than one dream over the past few nights.

He'd never dated anyone with kids before, and that brought a whole new level of thinking to any relationship. A laugh escaped his throat as he lifted his bottle for another drink. Relationship. A date and a kiss did not qualify as a relationship. However, the stupid garter that had landed in his lap, and sat on his nightstand, did justify obsession. He couldn't get the woman out of his mind, and his mind wandered a lot lately. Just as it was now when he had an entire half a trailer of hay to move.

When he heard the sound of a vehicle coming up on him, he twisted the lid back on his bottle and walked around the truck.

As Gerald parked his truck and stepped out, Ben moved toward him. "'Bout damn time."

"I was hoping you'd be done with this," he joked as he pulled on his gloves. "Eric had a rider go missing. We found her. She had gotten turned around and was heading the wrong way."

"I keep thinking someday someone is going to sue us when they get lost on our property."

"That's why we have that legal jargon they have to sign."

Gerald stepped up onto the trailer and began moving the next bale of hay. "Heard you had a date on Saturday."

"Yeah, so?"

"So no big deal. How did it go? Was this with that gal that works for Audrey?"

He tossed down the bale from the stack so that Ben could grab it. "Nichole. Yeah, she works for Audrey."

"And has a house full of kids, right?"

"Three," he specified.

"Any sparks?"

"Could be," Ben said reaching up for the next bale. "She's great actually, and so are the kids."

"That makes you nervous though, doesn't it?"

"Sure it does."

"Maybe you should talk to Russell about that. He took on Lucas."

"I'm not looking to take on anything," Ben assured him. "It's just nice to be in her company."

That seemed to pull a laugh from his brother. "Nice to be in her company. Oh, hell man. You're screwed. You've got it in big time for this gal. Why not just make a move on her?"

"I kissed her. That's a move, right?"

"Sure. An opening move."

An opening move, Ben kept that in his head as he and his brother continued to unload the trailer. What was the next move? Had he been out of the dating scene long enough that there was something new? He had no idea, but he had to assume then neither did Nichole. She'd be as new to the scene as he was.

He'd see how Wednesday went with the kids, and then he'd decide on how to make the next move.

16

*C*ould a single day get any more chaotic? Nichole had been called out of work to pick up Zane because he'd spiked a fever and complained of stomach pain.

Audrey had stepped in and taken over her clients for the day, and Nichole headed home to take care of her son. The day suddenly became a blur as she organized Katie to pick up Wyatt from school and take him to the park for an hour, just to keep him away from the house. But then Katie carried a sick Wyatt into the house.

"I'm so sorry," Katie apologized as she set Wyatt on the couch. "He was playing and having a great time. Then he just looked at me and ran to the trashcan and threw up."

"Oh, baby, how are you feeling now?" Nichole sat down beside him on the couch and pressed the back of her hand to his forehead. "Yep, you've got this crap too."

"How can I help you?" Katie asked.

"I don't know. Maybe you'd better get home so that you don't get this too."

"I hate to leave you with all of this. Is Laura sick as well?"

"Not yet," Nichole said gratefully. "I think I'll set her up with a movie and put these guys in my bed with a movie, too. That'll isolate them."

"Call me if you need my help. My immune system is pretty good."

Nichole smiled wearily at her. "I appreciate it. There is nothing worse than a springtime sick," she said sweetly to Wyatt whose cheeks were flushed.

Katie left, and Nichole arranged her little family to maximize the potential of the boys getting better and Laura not getting sick.

She settled Laura in the living room on the couch with Paw Patrol, a few snacks, and her favorite toys. The boys were both in her bed, a trash can on either side of the bed. Wyatt's fever had gone down once she'd given him some Tylenol, and Zane had finally fallen asleep. They'd asked for an Avengers movie, and she made that happen for them.

Deciding that they'd need to eat something, she hunted up a few cans of chicken noodle soup and some crackers. Laura had chanted something about wanting macaroni and cheese.

Nichole went about making it all happen in her tiny kitchen, all the while listening to the baby monitor she usually had in Laura's room but had carried in with the boys, just in case.

Just as the water began to boil, she poured in the noodles, and the doorbell rang.

Blowing the strand of hair from her eyes, she set the wooden spoon over the pot to keep it from boiling over and hurried to the door. Seriously, the solicitor on the other side was about to have a rude awakening.

As she passed through the living room, she gave Laura a stern look to keep her perched on the couch with her teddy bear.

BEN ROCKED BACK on his heels as he stood on the small porch of the cottage like house. He'd been by the house numerous times, but he hadn't known that Nichole lived there. The swing set in the small backyard gave him a flurry of happy memories. His father had built them a fortress in the backyard, and it had become one of the greatest childhood adventures of his life.

Just as he considered ringing the doorbell again, the front door flew open, and a wild-eyed Nichole stood there staring at him. Her hair was piled atop her head, with wisps that hung over her face. She had on a pair of sweatpants that said San Diego down the leg, and a T-shirt that looked as if it might have been used for painting at one time.

When she registered that it was him standing on the front porch, the wide eyes grew terrified. She pushed open the screen door and stood there looking at him.

"Ben, hi. What are you..." her words trailed off and her hand covered her mouth. "Oh, God. It's Wednesday."

"Yeah. Are you doing okay?"

She pulled the door behind, leaving it open just a crack. "I'm so sorry. Things kind of fell apart around here today. I don't think I'll be able to go for pizza. None of us. The boys came home sick. I'm making soup and macaroni and cheese. And look at me." She looked down at her shirt and brushed off something he didn't see. "Never mind. Don't look at me."

Ben chuckled. "You look fine. It sounds like you've had a hard day."

Nichole pursed her lips and batted her eyes. Then he watched as she quickly wiped a tear that had fallen. "Sorry," she said again. "I guess it just got the better of me. Maybe we could reschedule."

"Of course we can. But why don't you let me come in and help you."

She shook her head. "No. I don't want you to get sick."

"I'm not worried. So, the boys are sick?"

"I picked Zane up from school sick. Then Katie picked up Wyatt, and he got sick on the way home. They are isolated in my bedroom watching Avengers and Laura is on the couch watching Paw Patrol, staying away from her brothers."

"I happen to be an aficionado on the Avengers. I'd really hate to miss a showing," he joked. Then he raised his hand to her cheek, just needing to touch her and offer her comfort. "You're not alone, Nichole. Let me help you."

Her eyes damp, she reached up and covered his hand on her cheek. "Are you sure?"

"Yeah."

The door behind her opened, and Laura stood there looking up at them. "Water, Mommy."

"God! I left the noodles boiling."

Turning quickly, Nichole hurried into the house.

Laura stood there looking up at Ben. Now he was out of his element, but he decided it was the perfect time to get over that.

"Hey, Laura. What are you watching on TV?"

Laura took his hand and pulled him into the quaint little living room and walked him to the couch.

"Paw Patrol," she offered as she climbed up on the couch and sat down. Looking up at him, she handed him a stuffed puppy. "You sit there," she said pointing to the other end of the couch. "Hold puppy. He likes it. His name Ben, too."

The conversation about the puppy, that seemed to share his name, warmed him.

Ben did as instructed by Laura. He wasn't completely unfamiliar with Paw Patrol. It had been on when his nieces and nephew were around. His nieces were infants, but it seemed that regular TV was out of the question when they were in the room.

He could hear Nichole in the kitchen cursing at the noodles, and what a mess it had made. Then she muttered something about juice for one of the boys.

"I'm going to help your mommy for a minute," he told Laura. "Can puppy stay with you?"

Laura took the animal with a nod and then focused in on the animals on TV who were setting out to rescue someone. Hopefully, there wouldn't be a quiz on that, because he hadn't been paying that much attention.

Nichole was at the sink with steaming noodles in the strainer. She looked half mad with her hair pulled back and her glasses fogged over.

Ben took a moment to appreciate the raw moment before he spoke. "Where can I help you? And don't tell me you don't need it."

Nichole let out a breath. "Zane wants juice. I have the baby monitor in there with him, so I can hear him."

"Okay. What kind of juice and what kind of glass?"

She motioned with a nod of her head. "There are plastic sip cups in that cupboard with lids. And don't lecture me on giving my seven-year-old a cup with a lid. I can't afford to have my mattress cleaned if he spills it."

"I wouldn't judge you at all," he said reaching into the cupboard for the cup and lid. "Juice is in the fridge?"

"Yes. Apple juice."

"Got it," he announced with some triumph as he opened the door to the refrigerator, which was decorated with artwork and stickered homework. "Just one glass? Does Wyatt need one too?"

She smiled when he asked. "He's asleep."

Ben poured the juice, affixed the lid to the cup, and replaced the container in the refrigerator—not to impress her, but he could hear his mother say, "If you took it out, put it away."

He contemplated tapping on the door before walking in, but he didn't want to wake Wyatt. Slowly he opened the door and the unmistakable sound of Hulk yelling, "smash" filled his ears with joy. Who didn't like the Hulk?

"What are you doing here?" Zane looked up at him with hollow eyes and rosy cheeks.

"I was supposed to take you all out for pizza tonight. But it looks like you had different plans."

"Pizza?" His eyes lit for a small moment before they sank again. "I don't think I want pizza."

"No, but I have juice for you. I'll take you for pizza another time," he promised as he skirted the bed and handed Zane the juice.

"So Avengers, huh?"

"Yeah. You wanna watch?"

He did, but he wondered if Nichole needed more help. He decided on sitting for a few moments.

An upright chair sat in the corner of the room. Ben carried it to the side of the bed next to Zane.

"Do you like Bruce Banner or the Hulk?" Zane asked as Ben sat down.

Ben contemplated. "That's a hard one, bud. I wish I were as smart as Bruce Banner. But, do you know how much stuff I could get done at the ranch if I were as strong as the Hulk? Man, I could throw bales of hay out into the pastures from the truck instead of driving back and forth."

"Why do you have to do that?"

Nichole listened to the conversation that played out on the baby monitor. He'd sat down with her son and made conversation. They were having a full discussion on the Hulk and the kinds of damage he could do.

She covered her mouth when a sob wanted to escape. Ben was telling Zane about his brothers and how they would play superhero when they were younger. A laugh broke through the sob when he told him that even Eric would pretend with them once in a while, even though he was much older.

"Mommy," Laura's little voice startled her, and she realized she was leaned into the monitor listening to the conversation. "Noodles and cheese," she said, demanding.

"Yes, baby. I have it for you. Come climb up in your seat."

Laura walked to the table and did her best to climb up the chair and into the booster that was strapped to it, but not without Nichole's expertly positioned hand on her rear to give her the right direction should she need it.

Nichole pushed her up to the table and set the small plastic bowl and spoon in front of her. "Try not to make a mess, okay, princess?"

"Yup," she agreed as she took her first spoonful and most of the noodles fell to the table before she reached her mouth.

It was worth a shot Nichole thought as she tried to tidy the small kitchen which had seen its better days.

The conversation on the monitor continued, and soon there was another voice. A wide-awake Wyatt added his opinion on Ironman.

Nichole poured a cup of juice for Laura, who was making her way to the bottom of her bowl of noodles. Then she poured one for Wyatt. She would take it into him when she took Laura for her bath.

Once Laura had finished her dinner, she let her down from the table and cleaned up the mess she had made trying her hardest to be a big girl. Who was Nichole trying to fool? She was a big girl and getting bigger by the minute. What a thing to cherish—watching her daughter grow into a little girl. The thought only seemed to anger her. How could her ex not have wanted any part of that? His loss. He would regret the day he didn't see her spill four noodles for every one or two she got in her mouth. There was a lot riding on that.

She heard Wyatt ask for a drink on the monitor just moments before she heard the bedroom door creak open and Ben walked down the hall toward her.

Lifting the cup, she had filled earlier toward him she smiled. "This is for Wyatt."

His brows drew together in confusion. "Are you psychic?"

She gave a sideways nod with her head toward the speaker on the counter. "Baby monitor."

"So, you've been eavesdropping? Talks about superheroes are sacred male conversations. I don't know if you have what it takes to keep up."

Nichole pushed up her glasses and planted her fists on her hips. "Wonder Woman was no slouch, and I could keep up just fine on the superhero front. Don't make me show you all what I have under all this fine exterior." She fanned out her hands to encompass the messy shirt and sweatpants, which now had macaroni and cheese on them. "This is all a facade."

The smile that spread over Ben's mouth warmed her. "I had no doubt that was what was buried beneath the common exterior of a super mom. I stand corrected."

Nichole tucked a strand of hair behind her ear. "Thanks for the help, Ben. It means a lot."

"I haven't done much but keep two young men company. What else do you have to tend to tonight?"

"I need to give Laura her bath."

"I'll sit with the boys then. They're both awake, and not looking too bad. But I'm sure they'll be ready to go back to sleep by the time the movie is over. You take care of Laura. Do you put her to bed after?"

"Yes. I'll read her a little story first, but then she usually falls asleep."

"I'll stay and hold down the fort. When Laura is asleep, why don't you run yourself a nice warm bath. You could use one. You've worked extremely hard here today. I'll just be an ear to the ground in case the boys, or Laura needs something."

Nichole couldn't help but stare into those compassionate eyes. He'd stay—he had stayed. He'd driven that far to have plans changed on him, and he'd stayed to help nurse sick children. He was a blessing to her, and you never saw blessings coming. This was a beginning. Not just for her and her kids in Georgia. But a beginning for her heart, a chance for it to mend.

"I really appreciate all of this, Ben."

He reached his hand out to her arm and gently slid it from her shoulder to her hand where he grasped it in his. "It's a minute gesture. Your job here is ginormous. It's the least I can do. Now go. Get her that bath and story. Then you take one."

"I will."

"I'll go sit with the boys."

As she turned to walk to toward the bathroom with Laura, she gave his hand a squeeze. Seriously, how was she going to deal with the way her heart pulsed at that moment? A nice night out and a kiss at the end of it had been one thing, but this attention to family, that was another. It was just what she wanted, and she didn't want to be let down when he wasn't as strong as he seemed to be right at that moment.

17

*B*en moved to the bedroom where he could hear the boys chatting. There was an intense conversation brewing about Superman and Batman now, and it reminded him that he and Gerald would go rounds on which one was better. He had to hold to his opinion, when a superhero was super and didn't have actual powers, he was the more superb being.

Both sets of eyes looked up at him when he walked through the door and the conversation broke off. They looked so little in Nichole's big bed. It was then he took a moment to look around the room. How intimate it was to be standing in Nichole's bedroom, he realized. It wasn't just a sick ward, and the thought had him chuckling.

The boys were buried under a mass of tan sheets and a comforter that looked as if it had been purchased to match the paint on the walls. With the pile of small pillows on the floor, he decided, when made, the bed was feminine and beautiful, just like its owner.

"Where's Mom?" Zane asked.

"She's going to give Laura her bath and then take one too."

Wyatt sipped from his cup of juice. "We want to watch another movie," he said with a slight whine. "Can you ask her if we can watch Thor?"

"Thor? You have Thor?"

"The new one," Zane added. "It's funny too."

"It sure is," Ben agreed. "Let me ask."

NICHOLE HAD SET Ben and the boys up with Thor, and all three of them seemed to be satisfied with their choice.

She knelt down near the bathtub, as Laura splashed in the bubbles, and thought about what was happening in that other room. There was a bonding happening that she hadn't expected.

Ben had seemed easy when he'd arrived. And even though the kids were sick, the house was a mess, and she, having given herself a look in the mirror, was a complete wreck, he'd stayed to help and to comfort. Did men do that kind of thing? Did they step in when a woman and her children needed help? There was nothing he could gain from having stayed, and she wouldn't have faulted him had he turned to go either. With some resentment, she thought about the fact that her ex-husband had never taken care of the kids when they'd been sick before. No excuses or anything, he just disappeared into his own man-world. Ben hadn't done that.

As Laura captured bubbles between her hands, Nichole wiped a washcloth over her own face and removed the traces of makeup which had smeared her eyes.

She supposed if Ben stuck around, he'd see her worse off than she looked right at that moment. Sick kids and a chaotic house was nothing. He'd only seen her with clients or at the salon being professional. Even on their evening out, she'd been put together and managed to keep any personal angst at bay while she'd drunk craft beer, ate enchiladas and ice cream, and she'd kissed the man.

The thought of that kiss still made her head swim. She certainly wouldn't mind doing that again.

Laura called to her and she turned to see her daughter standing in the bubbles, her arms held up to signal she was finished.

"Let's get you rinsed off."

NICHOLE COULD STILL HEAR the movie playing in her bedroom when she'd tucked in Laura. Thor and Loki were having a brotherly battle, much like her sons would often. One of the reasons she liked Thor and Loki was because they had normal brother issues. Oh, sure, one would want to kill the other. One was defiantly good and the other evil, or the story would go. But how many times did she see one of them lend a hand to the other out of brotherly bond, even if they then went back to trying to expel one another out of some galaxy or something.

She hadn't gone into her room to get clothes or her robe. Instead, she'd tiptoed to the laundry room and pulled her yoga pants, a bra, and a loose T-shirt from the dryer. The towels she saved for special occasions, were pulled from the linen closet, and so was the special bath bomb that Audrey had given her in a gift basket for covering for her while she was on her honeymoon. On her birthday, the prior year, her mother had sent her candles which she'd always wanted to use around her tub. This was as good a time as any to set them up.

Ben was saving her day, and she wasn't sure he knew that. She'd owe him. Maybe she could take him out to dinner, or cook for him.

Watching the water fizz a pink foam, she stepped into the

warm water, and sank in. Oh, the glory of a few moments alone in the flicker of candlelight.

Easing back against the tub, Nichole closed her eyes and focused on the sounds around her. She was in absolute heaven.

THOR and his friends would go on to avenge another day, Ben thought as he turned off the TV and looked at the sleeping boys. They were sweet. He pulled the covers up over Zane. Nichole had done a good job with them, and no doubt all on her own.

Leaving the room, he pulled the door, leaving it open just a crack so he could hear them. A dim light shone from under the door of the bathroom, and he considered knocking to check on Nichole, as he thought she'd been in there a long time. But, she was a grown woman, and didn't his mother talk about how she adored her baths when she'd had a stressed day?

He could slip out and leave now that the kids were asleep, but he just didn't want to do that. He wanted to see her before he left—wanted to kiss her one more time too.

The thought of turning on the TV crossed his mind, but not knowing the system, as every TV setup was different, he decided against it as to not wake anyone up.

He picked up the few toys of Laura's that had been scattered around the living room and piled them into the large chair. He folded the quilt that had been draped over its arm and stacked the books and magazines on the coffee table.

On the top of the reading pile was a book he'd been hearing a lot about. Probably because there was a movie coming out about it. He didn't know much more than it was about gaming. Thumbing through it, he decided maybe he'd download a copy to his iPad when he got home. It had been a long time since he'd sat down and read for pleasure.

Replacing the book, Ben sat on the couch and rested his

head back for a moment, closing his eyes. Then he heard the door open to the bathroom and a moment later Nichole stood in front of him. Her hair was in a knot atop her head and she had on different clothes. It was the first time he'd seen her without her glasses.

"I fell asleep," she said on a hushed laugh. "I'm so sorry that you've been just hanging out here and obviously tidying up."

Ben sat up. "Just was helping out a little. Do you feel relaxed? You look relaxed."

Nichole moved to sit next to him, leaning back against the couch as he had earlier. "I'm mush."

He leaned back again. "Good. You needed it. I tucked the boys in. They'd both fallen asleep. They don't feel as warm."

Nichole took Ben's hand and gave it a squeeze. "It means a lot that you stayed tonight. I could have done it all myself, but having you here was nice."

Ben rolled his head to the side to look at her. "Why don't you bring the kids out to my house this weekend and I'll cook dinner. They could run and explore. We could go visit the animals at the barn. We'll make up for missing out on pizza."

"Are you sure?"

"Most certainly. I like them, Nichole. They're fun to be around. Even when they're sick."

She tucked in her lips and obviously considered his invitation. "I'm not expecting anything from you, Ben. I want you to know that."

"Not sure I follow."

"This is a lot to think about, dating a woman with kids. I have a lot to consider when it comes to them—to me."

"I would be disappointed if you didn't consider them first. And, I don't date, so you have a lot to consider too," he offered.

The comment had her lifting her head from the back of the couch. "Now I'm not sure I follow."

Lifting an arm up and over her shoulders, he pulled her in. "I'm interested in you." He heard his voice shake as he said it. "I'm not good with women, so I'm bound to make some mistakes. You have them to think about, so you're bound to be very sensitive to those mistakes. I'm okay with going nice and slow. But, I thought, since I'm not good at this kind of stuff, I should make it clear that I'm okay with making it go too."

Her lips curled into a sweet smile. "I'm interested too."

"Well, alright then." He lifted his free hand to her cheek. "I guess you're my girlfriend," he joked, deepening his southern drawl to make her laugh.

Nichole let out a breath. "May the adventure begin."

Lifting toward her, he pressed his mouth to hers and planted the kiss he'd been dying for. Her hand came to his shoulder and pulled him in closer as she opened to him, letting him taste her just as he'd been dreaming of since the last time they'd kissed.

Hot and heavy, just as if they were a pair of lustful teenagers, their teeth scraped, and tongues slid against the other as if they were in a hurry to race to the end. Reaching her hands around his neck, Nichole pulled Ben down on her and they stretched out on the couch, their lips still locked in a maddening kiss that was scorching his brain.

_____

18

*T*hey'd made out on the couch like a couple of randy teenagers, she thought as she watched Ben drive away. It was nearly midnight, and it was going to be a long night.

The boys were sound asleep, and so was Laura. Nichole had settled herself on the couch with a pillow and a blanket, but her body buzzed with an energy she'd forgotten was buried deep inside of her.

Things could have kept going, but one thing she was finding out was that not only was Ben Walker better with women than he thought he was, but he was a gentleman.

When the breath between them was hot, and inhibitions had all but melted away, he'd pulled back and stared down at her. Common sense, which had long eluded her the moment their mouths had come together, seemed to be still rooted in Ben.

He'd been right to leave when he did. The last thing she needed was him spending the night. Sure, her kids liked him, but Ben was their friend. Nothing led them to believe that he was more than that to her or them. Would it all change if she explained it to them?

Then again, they'd need time to explore this new relationship, she and Ben. When she thought about it, she wasn't even sure what she wanted. Her first commitment was to her kids. Nothing would ever get in the way of that, not even a man.

Pulling the blanket up under her chin, she told herself to stop thinking about it. At that moment, she was just his girlfriend.

When she thought about that, it made her laugh to herself. Oh, he was cute, and the fact that he made her feel silly, she appreciated him even more.

All of the thoughts keeping her up were thoughts for another day. For now, she needed to get some sleep, or there were going to be some very fussy customers the next day who were not satisfied with their hair service.

WHAT AMAZED Ben was how quickly word traveled in a tight-knit community.

He'd been tending to the chickens in his mother's yard when she approached him about having company on Saturday.

Through narrowed eyes, he looked at her over the top of his sunglasses. "How did you hear that?"

A sly smile formed on his mother's lips. "A mother knows everything. Besides, Katie, who babysits for Nichole? Her roommate's mother was in the salon the other day talking to Audrey about the kids going to the ranch on Saturday. Audrey told Lydia that Nichole hadn't mentioned it. Lydia told Gia about the date. Of course, your brother is going to talk to his wife, so this morning Dane asked me how I felt about it."

Ben rubbed his fingers over his temple, as his mother's account of getting the information had begun to give him a headache.

"Well, it wasn't a secret. But I guess next time I'll put out a press release."

"Honey, it would be easier," she joked, her humored eyes shaded by her large straw hat. "What are your plans?"

Ben shrugged. "I thought I'd grill something for dinner. I told her we'd take the kids to the barn to see the animals. Then, I don't know."

"You make sure you bring those sweeties by the house. I'll make some dessert, and we can sit in the garden while they run through the yard. I'd love to have some company too, and Nichole is a nice girl."

"I'll make sure we do that," he agreed.

His mother patted his cheek, then with her gardening tools in a bucket, she hurried off to dig in the dirt, he assumed.

Hopefully, his mother didn't have grand ideas about his relationship with Nichole. It was all so new. He didn't want anyone getting thoughts in their heads that weren't realistic.

He'd seen what happened in his family when people moved in and out of love. Not that he was in love with Nichole, just interested.

But once the talking started, there were a lot more involved parties than just the people involved in the relationship.

Maybe he should warn Nichole. Was she ready to be faced with that? She'd worked with Audrey long enough to know the process, he figured. Then again, perhaps he was the only one not in the loop. By the time Audrey, Pearl, Lydia, and Gia got their hands on Nichole, she'd be in full on relationship mode—or panic mode. He wasn't quite sure which way she'd fall yet. Obviously, it was much too late to give her warning.

Well, he figured that when she came out on Saturday, she'd either be panic-stricken, or she'd embrace the southern charm of chatty women. It was a crapshoot at this point.

Ben finished up in the coop and headed back out to his house.

Inviting a family over to eat meant he needed to plan a meal, and he had to go into town to get the groceries he would need. That hadn't been on his mind when he'd asked her. He might need to make sure he had enough dishes too. Seriously, he was out of his league.

WHEN THE FRIDAY afternoon rush had subsided, Nichole sat down in the back room, opened a Diet Coke, and kicked her feet up on the adjacent chair. Even though the boys had gone to school on Thursday, they'd had a restless night, and she was still exhausted.

The back door opened and Lydia walked into the room carrying a tray of bedding plants.

"Are you gardening?" she asked as Lydia set the tray on the table.

"I'm getting ready to do the beds around the reception hall, and word gets around, so Glenda asked me to get her a tray and have you take them out to her when you visit this weekend.

Nichole felt the heat rise in her cheeks. "She knows I'm going up there this weekend? You know?"

"Oh, hell, honey. Everyone knows."

And that tight community she grew to love now was knee deep in her business. "Didn't think I'd told anyone. But maybe I mumbled it in my sleep, and it was heard through the air."

Lydia laughed. "Don't get all bent out of shape. If it's any consolation, we all think it's pretty neat. Ben is a good man. I mean a good man. You deserve that."

"Yes, I do. I won't deny that. But aside from the fact that we are casually seeing each other, I don't need to have him spooked by all the gossip."

Lydia batted a hand through the air. "He's lived here his

whole life. He knows how the system works," she said with a slight laugh and then her face sobered. "You're not mad, are you?"

Nichole took a moment to collect her feelings and take inventory. "No. I'm not mad. Maybe concerned is more like it. I like him. But I have a lot of baggage for a single man. I don't want this spooking him."

"Ben doesn't spook that easily. Cut him some slack there. Anyone who isn't nervous about a woman with three kids doesn't have a heart. And I mean that. The only reason he'd be nervous is that he doesn't want to hurt them, not because of them."

And, when put that way, it gave Nichole a whole new perspective. "I'll take these to Mrs. Walker."

Lydia smiled. "Thanks." Lydia turned to exit through the door she'd come in through. Turning she said, "Do you have an opening tomorrow? Maybe something in the morning?"

Nichole gave it a quick thought. "Seems like I have a half hour about nine-thirty."

Lydia ran her fingers through her short mop of hair. "I could use a trim. Would you mind?"

"Not at all. I'll see you then."

Lydia disappeared out the back door, and Nichole rose to put her name on the schedule. As she stood, she looked down at the box of bedding plants. No doubt between Mrs. Walker's five sons and three daughters-in-law she could have gotten the plants picked up and delivered some other way.

This had been a mama's way of getting the woman her son was seeing to show up at her house. Nichole wasn't sure if she should be honored or mortified. The longer she looked at the plants she realized that the meter between the two didn't fall in favor of either emotion.

Well, she'd been grilled by mothers before, and having met Glenda Walker, she wasn't too terrified.

Letting out a sigh, she decided to be grateful that the woman wanted to visit with her—and no doubt her children. She'd make it a point to stop by her house first, tomorrow.

19

The ride out to the Walker ranch was loud. The boys had the evening with Ben all planned out, and it included a lot of Avengers talk. Zane had brought his Thor hammer and Wyatt his Hulk hands that now gave a muffled noise when smashed together. They'd been smashed together so many times that the sound effects were nearly gone.

Laura sat between her brothers in her car seat and watched as they bantered back and forth. She'd squeal in delight at their conversation from time to time, but Nichole was sure it was more from the delight of being between the two boys she loved so much.

They took good care of her, Nichole thought as she looked in the review mirror at the similar faces. The boys had their father's hair, but her eyes. Laura was her mini-me and that thrilled her. She bore very little resemblance to her father, and though that shouldn't be something that brought Nichole joy, it seemed to.

"How much longer?" Zane whined the question from the back seat.

"You've been out here. You know how far it is," she reminded him.

"Yeah, but how much longer?"

It was quite a drive. She would never begrudge Ben for not showing up unexpectedly. "About ten more minutes."

She heard the groan.

The thought of young Walker boys attending school crossed her mind. That would be one heck of a commute every day, but she knew they'd done it. Did their mom or dad take them into town, or were there stories of school bus shenanigans? She'd have to assume it was that latter of those options.

She was asked four more times if they were there yet, but she let the large wooden archway that read WALKER RANCH speak for itself as she drove beneath it.

Wyatt bounced up and down in his booster seat. "Finally!"

"Where is Ben's house?" Zane asked as he sat up tall in his seat to look out the window. "How much longer until we get to his house?"

"I don't know. I have to take those plants to his mother's house first."

The groan from the back seat mirrored her own thoughts. Not because she didn't want to see Glenda Walker, but because she wanted to get to Ben's house as quickly as the boys did. She missed him.

Perhaps that would benefit them in the end. If they didn't see each other every day, they'd long for the time they had. Though since the night they'd made out on her couch, she found she longed for him quite a bit.

She'd pushed the ache and need far down inside of her, but it churned there. Perhaps she was lonely for the attention of a man. No, she considered again. They'd been in Georgia for nearly a year, between Athens and Macon. She hadn't had that craving. Not like she did now. It was all Ben.

Tucking in her lips, she tried to mute the smile the thought of him brought to her. Oh, she might as well admit it, she was crazy infatuated with the man, and she couldn't wait until his mouth was on hers again.

As they turned the curve in the road, the Walker house came into view. There were actual cheers from the back seat, and even Laura let out a squeal.

Glenda appeared from around the side of the house, where Nichole knew there was a gate to the beautiful backyard, where Audrey and Gregory had gotten married.

Glenda waved as Nichole put the car in park.

Immediately, Glenda walked to the back doors of the car and opened the one next to Zane. "Hello, boys. Hello, Laura. It is so nice to see you."

"You live really far away," Wyatt told her, to his mother's anguish.

"I sure do," Glenda agreed. "That's why I'm so glad you came all the way out here to see me. I have some cookies in the kitchen. Would you like some?"

The invitation had both of the boys unbuckling their seatbelts and Laura protesting until Wyatt unbuckled her seat too. Nichole wanted to argue that they would be late to Ben's, but as there wasn't a set time to get to his house, and she was sure his mother knew that, she turned off the engine and climbed from the car.

"I'll get your plants from the back," she offered.

"Thank you, darling. Let's go through the back. Have you kids seen my chickens?"

Nichole laughed as her children followed Ben's mother to her backyard. Laura's hand in Glenda's. It was a sweet sight, she thought as she closed the hatch and followed.

Glenda already had them next to the chicken coop, and she was pointing out certain chickens she'd named.

Nichole set the tray of plants on the patio table and watched from afar as Glenda charmed her children. She was kind and gentle with how she managed them. Did that speak to the kind of mother she was, too?

She'd been so focused on them that she hadn't noticed Ben walk up behind her until she felt his arms come around her.

She jumped, nearly elbowing him in the side. "Christ, Ben, you scared me to death."

"Not my intent," he said softly as he pressed a quick kiss to her lips, and she knew he'd made sure all heads were turned away. "She couldn't wait to see the kids," he said looking out over the yard to where his mother knelt down next to Laura and pointed to the chickens that had come to the fence to greet them.

"Really? She wanted to see them?"

He nodded. "She loves kids. She and Russell's step-son Lucas are tight." He smiled. "I credit her for making Eric the fine man he is today, too. Though Susan had a lot to do with that as well. Marriage has taken the cranky old man out of him."

"Eric isn't that old."

"No, but he was cranky," he humored. "Give it some thought. My mom would like them to stay here while you and I go out to my place and have dinner. It's her thought, not mine, and it's up to you."

Panic lurched inside of her. "Oh, I don't know..."

"It's okay to tell her no. I'll just let her know they're going with us. I'd originally planned for them when..."

"I think it's a wonderful gesture. It'll be fine," she concluded, telling herself as much as she was telling him.

Wyatt came running toward them. "Mom, Mrs. Walker says we can stay and have pigs in blankets. She's going to make them and says we can help. Can we?"

A smile instantly formed on her mouth. "All of you would like that?"

He nodded. "Yeah. Zane asked if he could double wrap his pig and she said yes," he said with great enthusiasm.

Nichole exchanged glances with Ben, who gave her a nod.

"Okay. You can stay, but I'll be back in a little bit."

Glenda carried Laura on her hip and Zane followed. "You take your time. We'll be okay. I think Lucas is going to join us too. We will have a wonderful time. I think Lucas' granddaddy said something about a ride in the wagon with the tractor too."

Nichole watched as eyes lit up with anticipation. His family was sure accommodating when it came to easing her into a relationship with their son.

Considering the bitch she'd had for a mother-in-law before, watching Glenda Walker coo over her children was welcomed.

"The boys know my phone number," she told Glenda. "If you need anything, or they need anything..."

"You're not too far away. We're going to feed the chickens now, and then maybe plant those flowers before Lucas gets here and we make those pigs," she offered, and the boys laughed. "You two enjoy your dinner."

And with that, she carried Laura off and the boys followed, both chattering at the same time.

Nichole turned to Ben. "You're sure?"

"She's sure. This was her idea. They'll all be okay, but like I said, we can..."

"They'll be okay," she said with a wink and leaned in to kiss him.

———————

*a*t her suggestion, Nichole rode out to Ben's house in his truck. A bench seat in a pickup truck seemed romantic.

She'd slid over next to him, his arm draped around her, as they bounced along the dirt road to his home.

"There she is," he said as it came into view. "Tiny."

"It's quaint."

"It's a box with windows," he said as he pulled up in front of it and she noted he didn't even have a designated driveway. "It has potential, but I haven't taken too much time with it."

"Prefabricated?"

"Totally. Had it dropped here at the end of last summer. Seemed like the easiest way to get my house built," he mused. "And for the most part, it's been perfect."

"What's not perfect about it?"

He shrugged. "I'll let you make up your own mind."

Opening the door, Ben slid out of the truck and then reached for her hand. Nichole slid out behind the steering wheel too and into his waiting hands.

A moment later he had her pressed up against the truck, and his mouth was hot and fluid on hers.

God, she'd been longing for this since they'd been on her couch. She hadn't expected to have a moment to enjoy it, with the kids around. She owed Glenda a big thanks, and to think, she'd been hesitant to let her kids stay at the main house.

Ben's mouth moved from hers and trailed down her neck until he reached her collarbone. The intimacy of it nearly made her knees buckle beneath her. Oh, she'd missed the joy of this—the sensation that it sent through her.

"How pressed for time are we?" she asked as he feasted on her throat and she held herself up only by clinging to him.

"Don't know that we are," he mumbled against her skin as he worked his mouth back up to hers, skimming his tongue across her lips.

Her breath was labored and her heart hammered in her chest. As she lifted her arms around Ben's neck, the sides of her shirt rose, exposing her bare skin. Ben's hands found that tender, sensitive skin and touched her. Sizzling energy buzzed over her and through her. The need deepened until she thought it might steal her breath from her.

"Take me inside, Ben," she whispered against his throat as he explored her skin. "I need you."

He pulled back to look at her. Heat clouded his eyes, but she knew he was fully capable of understanding her need.

"Are you sure. I hadn't planned to..."

"I'm not some debutante you have to swoon, Ben."

The corner of his mouth curled into a sexy, devilish smile. He hoisted her up, her legs instinctively wrapping around his waist, and he carried her into his house.

She would be the first woman he took into his bedroom in this little house on his family's land. His home. His bed. That had to say something—something special.

Of course, he debated with himself. Should he set her back on her feet and give her a minute to reconsider what she was about to do? His moment of hesitation must have spoken louder than the words he was muttering in his own head.

Nichole eased her head back and looked at him. "Take me to your bed."

He studied her eyes for another moment. Heat and passion resonated from her. Pressing his lips to her throat, she threw back her head as he continued to walk towards his bedroom.

The glory of the little house, which sat out in the middle of acreage and with no one around, was that he didn't have to kick the door shut. He didn't have to lock it or draw the blinds. He could take this beautiful woman, basking in the glow of a gorgeous sunset.

With all intent to ease her down onto the bed, he hit his leg on the edge of the bed and flung them both to the mattress. Landing atop of her, he quickly moved to make sure she was okay. Laughter rolled from her, her chest heaving beneath him as she caught her breath.

"I have a feeling you'll only surprise me," she said in a laugh.

"I'd like to say I'm a little more stealth than this. Perhaps you just took me off guard."

The humor died in her eyes and they went dark with something else. When she licked her lips and her cheeks filled with color, he knew it was passion that flooded through her. "How about we take off that shirt instead," she offered as she began to tug the T-shirt up and over his head.

When his skin was bare, he found he was the one being surprised when she rolled him over and straddled him. "I feel as though I need to warn you, before you take off this dress, and before you see what's beneath it, it's not all glamorous."

Ben bit down on his bottom lip and considered his next words carefully. "I could sincerely be offended by that. This part of our relationship has nothing to do with how I feel about you. Nothing under that dress could surprise me, or deter me. Your body has done miraculous things, Nichole. Those three bright and shining lights that are your children, they came from this body. Don't be ashamed of that."

She studied him for another breath, and then lifted the dress from her body. Her eyes locked with his, and he left them there. He wasn't just making up words, not to just appease her. He wanted her. He wanted her body. He wanted her heart. He wanted everything she had to offer. In that very moment, he knew that was what he'd been feeling.

Nichole sat there as if she waited for him to scan his eyes over her and judge, even though he had said he wouldn't. Instead, he pulled her down on top of him, taking her mouth with his and he made love to her.

BREATHLESS, she lay beneath him. His breath labored. His damp skin pressed against her damp skin.

Ben was going to buy his mother something very nice for giving him this opportunity. It hadn't been in his plans. In fact, he figured if they ever did get to have sex, it would be months and months from now.

Rolling off of her, he took her hand and gave it a squeeze. He was afraid to talk. What would he say? Thanks for being the one to cave?

"Oh, I needed that," Nichole sighed as she lay there naked on his bed without remorse or need to cover. "Thank you."

The chuckle escaped him before he knew it. "You're thanking me? I've never had someone do that before."

Now she laughed as she rolled to her side and propped herself up on her elbow. "I'm no prude. Does that bother you?"

"Nope. Should it?"

She shrugged her shoulder. "Just making sure. I appreciate a good roll in the hay."

"I haven't gotten you to the hay, yet." That brought a laugh.

"I look forward to it."

Ben took her hand and pressed it to his chest. His heart raced beneath her touch. "Let me recover, and I'll start the steaks I bought."

"I'm ravenous. I'll help," she offered.

"I feel like you need to know, this wasn't in my plans."

"Mine either, but I'm glad it worked out." She rolled atop him and took his mouth.

The taste of her ignited him again, and his hands couldn't help but roam that soft and milky skin. Soon his body, exhausted and spent, was revving to go again.

BEN MANAGED to finally will himself away from Nichole's body long enough to pull on his pants and head to the kitchen. He'd start the grill and cook her the world's greatest steak. He did have some talents.

She'd gone to freshen up in his bathroom. At least he'd had the foresight to clean it before she'd come over.

He pulled the steaks he'd been marinating out of the refrigerator. Eyeing the pasta salad he'd made earlier, he thought he'd give it a little toss to make sure it was well coated. When he closed the refrigerator, he caught sight of Nichole leaning up against the doorjamb watching him. He thought she'd been sexy laying naked in his bed, but standing in his kitchen, bare footed, shirt ruffled, and her hair slightly mussed, she was more beautiful than he'd ever imagined.

The image of her standing there, in his home, stabbed at him. She was exactly the woman he'd always wanted in his home.

"Are you sure you know what you're doing?" Her voice was still sultry and soft.

"Seriously, I've got this part." He winked at her. "What can I offer you to drink? I have beer, wine, soda."

"Since I'll be eating before driving back to town, I'll take a glass of wine."

With a nod, Ben set the steaks on the counter and pulled a wine glass from the cupboard. He uncorked the wine, poured her a glass, and handed it to her. "You're beautiful," he offered as she took the glass.

"You already got me into bed. You don't have to charm me."

"All fact."

She took a sip of wine, her eyes locked on his. "Thank you. I don't know what to think of all of this, Ben Walker. Did your mother know what we were going to do when she took my kids?"

The very thought terrified him. "I'm going to say no because it creeps me out that she just might have orchestrated the best sex I've ever had."

"The best?"

It did sound like a line, but he certainly wouldn't have said it had it not been true. "The best." He moved back to the refrigerator and pulled out a beer.

He walked toward the back door and opened it. She followed as he moved to the grill, turned on the gas, and ignited it.

"The view is magnificent out here," she offered as she walked out onto the porch with her wine. "Nothing, as far as you can see."

"It's a prime spot, I think. Eric and Susan don't live too far, but you can't see the barn or their house from here."

"Is that why you chose it? It's secluded?"

Ben shrugged. "It called to me."

"And what are your plans for the house? I peeked. Your

bedroom is the only fully furnished room you have in the whole house. Minus a nice couch and a huge TV."

"Basics," he teased as he twisted the top from his beer. "Decorating my house hasn't been a big priority. I don't spend a lot of time here."

"You're not in town causing trouble, so where do you spend that time?"

He chuckled as he took a long pull from his beer. "I'm in the pastures tending to the cattle. Eric has me teaching riding once in a while when I'm not tending to the horses, too. The work never stops."

"So it's safe to say you'd be happy to live out here forever."

"No doubt," he rattled off as he sipped from his bottle again, but he didn't miss the clouding in her eyes. "You? Do you think you could see yourself living out of the city?"

He watched her carefully construct her answer as she sipped her wine. "I never gave it any thought. I've always lived where there was childcare and my job. Besides, If I had to drive that far to work each day, I can guarantee that I'd be late every day. I can't get out of the house on time on a normal day. Adjusting for travel time, that makes my head hurt thinking about it."

And just like that, the conversation seemed to stall. No matter how good the sex was or what kind of feelings were starting to form for the woman, he didn't know how they would get over this barrier.

It wasn't worth exploring right now anyway. He figured she'd be willing to give him maybe another hour before wanting to gather her little family and head back into town.

Ben walked over to Nichole and cupped her cheek in his hand. "I'm so glad you came out here," he said.

"So am I."

He pressed a soft kiss to her lips and lingered there. In every relationship he'd ever been in, there had been a point of disagreement. And though this particular one wasn't one they were even exploring yet, nor had it caused a rift between them, he'd never felt so compelled to keep a harmony between him and the other party. But this seemed urgent and important. This journey was just beginning, and everyone was right, she had a lot of baggage. But he was finding he was as enthralled with her "baggage" as he was with her.

He wasn't going to bow out of this. He wanted to feel it out, see what happened. The fallback was, if it didn't work out, he could hide in his little, undecorated house in the country. The hitch was if it did work out. Could he be man enough to understand that her needs, because of the kids, would have to come first?

21

The entire ride home was filled with non-stop conversation about Mr. and Mrs. Walker. Lucas had been dropped off, with his sister, and his parents had a date night, too.

They had fed the chickens, made their pigs in a blanket, rode in the wagon behind the tractor, and when Nichole had picked them up, they were having s'mores on the patio in the fire pit.

The smile on her face was permanent, she decided, as the words, "Oh, oh, and we..." kept being repeated.

Monday morning the Walkers were getting flowers delivered, or something sent to them since they did live so far away. They had gone above and beyond to make her night with their son wonderful, and luckily, they hadn't asked any questions.

When they returned home, Nichole unloaded a sleeping Laura and quieted the boys telling them to get ready for a bath. Once Laura was settled in bed, she got the bath ready for the two naked boys who were fighting with light-sabers in the hallway.

"Okay, you two. Get in here," she commanded as she turned off the water and arranged the mat on the floor.

She heard the distinct noise of the toys being dropped where they had stood.

Wyatt leaped right into the tub, water splashing all over her. "Hey, take it easy."

Zane followed his brother into the tub. "Get to washing. It's late, and you need to get to bed."

"Why?" Zane protested. "We don't have school tomorrow."

"No, but we need to go to bed. I'm tired."

She stood, and walked to the counter to begin taking off her makeup.

"Mom," Wyatt called to her.

"Hmmm?"

"What did you do when we were with Lucas' grandma and grandpa?"

She felt the flush move over her skin and prove itself in the mirror when she looked at herself. "He cooked me dinner."

"That's all?" Zane challenged. "We ate dinner and did all that fun stuff. What else did you do?"

Hiding her face with the washcloth, she scrubbed away her makeup. "We had a drink and sat on his porch. He showed me around the land."

"Boring," Wyatt groaned as he piled bubbles on top of his head. "We had more fun."

That seemed to conclude the question and answer phase of their evening, and she couldn't have been happier to see that come to an end.

When the boys were in bed, their eyes heavy despite protest, she went to her room and shut the door. She needed a shower, especially after the afternoon she'd had, but as she lifted her shirt over her head, she could still smell Ben. As she breathed in the scent, she thought about their afternoon, and her skin warmed just thinking about his touch. It would be hard to wait until they could do that again. Torture, she considered. It was going to be absolute torture.

Walking into the small bathroom off of her bedroom, she turned on the water to her shower, just as her cell phone rang on her dresser.

Hurrying back out to her room, she scooped up the phone, and her heart rate kicked up its pace when she saw Ben's name on the screen.

"Hey," she said, as she answered the call.

"Hey," his reply in return sent chills over her skin. "How did the kids enjoy their day?"

She moved to her bed to sit on the edge of it, naked and on the phone while her shower ran without her. "They couldn't stop talking about it. They had a delightful afternoon. I don't think I can thank your parents enough. And to think they did all of that with five kids of all ages. They are saints."

"It's the norm to them. Don't forget."

She let that ease her. "I never thought of that. Is that what kind of parents they were?"

"Hands on all the time. My uncle, on the other hand, uninvolved with all of his children. Mostly with Bethany, but yeah, with all of them."

She understood that too well. Her children would have a story like that, and didn't that just rip her up inside?

"I want to get your parents something as a thanks for tonight. Aside from having the most amazing time, they gave my children a night they won't soon forget."

"You don't have to get them anything. They enjoyed themselves as much as the kids did."

"Nope," she argued. "It's not how I work."

"Then come back out tomorrow. Bring some more flowers for her garden. I'll make sure the kids get to see my place. I can't let my parents outdo me when it comes to impressing your kids."

"Tomorrow?" She choked out the word.

"Unless you don't want to drive that far. I get it. If not, I'll come there, if you want to see me."

God, she hoped she didn't sound as if she didn't. She wanted that more than anything. "What time should we be there?"

The sigh he gave over the phone let her know he was worried she'd turn him down. "Anytime."

"We'll try to be there around eleven. That way I can stop by the nursery."

"Sounds perfect. Do the kids like hamburgers?"

"I've never seen them turn one down."

"Good. We'll have an impromptu barbecue. Susan brought me some potato salad, and some brownies from a catering gig."

"Sounds like she takes good care of you."

"It's because of her I don't starve."

"I'll see you tomorrow, then."

"Hey, Nichole," he called out before she said goodbye. "I had the most magnificent time today. I just wanted you to know."

She could feel tears stinging in her throat just thinking about how wonderful it had been, and it wasn't just because the sex was good. Did he feel as emotional as she did over it? "I did too."

"I'll see you tomorrow."

She sat there a moment longer, holding the phone in her hand and thinking of his voice now, the deep masculine tone. She knew she'd better think about what she was doing real hard, because in one fell swoop she could lose control of her common sense. Her little family came long before an affair with a man she couldn't shake from her mind. And even though she'd known him for six months, she didn't know him at all.

What she did know was how he made her feel, in her heart and in her body. It rocked her even as she sat there on her bed naked while the shower ran in the other room.

Nichole tossed the phone on the bed, and walked to the bathroom, shutting the door behind her. She stepped into the shower and let the warm water soothe her. She might not know Ben Walker very well, but she knew he was a family man. Walkers understood that family came first. She could buy into that.

She tipped her head under the spray of the shower head. She knew that she had fallen in with good people. If she was going to continue this relationship with Ben, there was going to have to be some give-and-take, but she knew he understood that. Ben's work was important to him, as hers was. At this point, the only thing standing in their way was the price of gas.

She laughed as she pumped shampoo into her hand. What a silly thing to hold back what might be an amazing relationship.

---

22

*B*en had been up since four o'clock. Most Sunday mornings he was able to sleep in just a little bit. There were enough people on the land that they could all take turns getting up early in the morning. But on this particular Sunday, he was wide awake.

As the sun came up and gave him the light he needed, he finished fixing the fence out in the pasture after turning off his headlights, which had been aiding him before the sun. After all, since he was up he might as well get a head start on some of the chores for the next week.

He supposed his restless night had something to do with the guests he was going to have today, and the guest he'd had yesterday. There was no way to get her out of his mind. When he'd gone to bed last night, he could smell her on his sheets. That alone, he figured, accounted for most of his restlessness.

He was looking forward to having the kids at his house. And that, too, was something he never thought he'd say. He didn't have any toys. He didn't have a swing set. Heck, he hardly had any trees around.

If they got bored and began to complain, he figured they'd

find something to do. After all, if his parents could entertain five little kids all day long, he could do it for a few hours.

Once the fence was fixed, Ben headed back home. He looked around the tiny little house. It certainly was less than homey. In fact, it was downright dull. Perhaps he should think about some paint for the walls, at least for now. Furniture and decor wasn't his forte, but he had enough women in his family that did that for a living. He was sure they'd come to help the cause when the time was right.

It was close to noon when he heard the sound of tires on the road. He walked out, in his bare feet, to his porch and watched as her car pulled up to his house.

The moment he saw her his heart began to flutter. He had never had that happen with another person.

She stepped out of the car in a yellow sundress. The color made her glow.

Nichole gave him a little wave and moved to open the back door. A moment later one of the boys jumped out, and he realized from that far he had no idea which one.

As she unbuckled the other two, the first boy walked up towards him and showed him an action figure. "Have you seen the new Spider-Man toy?" Wyatt asked.

Ben smiled as Wyatt walked up the steps toward him. "Nope. It's been a while since I've cruised through the toy aisle. Show me what he's got."

As Wyatt showed him all the features of the toy, he saw Zane running up behind his brother. "Mom let us each get one. I got Superman."

Zane shook his head. "Superman is a wuss."

"And Spider-Man is stupid," Wyatt retorted.

The argument made Ben chuckle, but he listened intently to what the boys had to say. He hadn't even noticed that Laura had climbed up the stairs all by herself and was pushing her way through the brothers.

She held out her toy to him and just smiled. "And you got Wonder Woman?" Ben asked as Laura nodded wide-eyed. "I think she's awesome."

Laura agreed again with a nod and turned around to bash Wonder Woman into Wyatt's Spider-Man.

"Hey," Wyatt whined.

Nichole set her hand on his shoulder. "She is just trying to play with you. That's how she sees you play. You guys bash things all the time."

Wyatt studied Wonder Woman very carefully for a moment. Then, Spider-Man seemed to snatch her up and take off with her. Laura squealed angrily for one moment, and then realized it was part of the game. She took off after Wyatt and Zane and Superman chased after them. The giggles began, and he noticed that Nichole eased.

Rising to meet her, he took her hand. He wanted to scoop her up and place a kiss on her lips, but not with the kids around. This was new to them.

"I'm glad you came out."

"So am I," she said. "We stopped by your parents' house first and took your mother the plants. Of course, she wanted the kids to help replant them. So that's why it took a little longer."

"Had I known that I would've met you down there."

"It was fine. But I will warn you, they're pretty hungry."

Keeping her hand tucked into his, he led her into the house to gather the items they would need to cook lunch.

The kids had run around the yard, and around the house, while he and Nichole grilled hamburgers. He'd found some Oreo cookies in the cupboard, and so they'd wrapped up their lunch with dessert.

Before they could clean up, the boys had announced that they were bored.

"How about we go on a scavenger hunt?" Ben suggested.

Wyatt's head bobbed up at the sound of it. "What kind of scavenger hunt?"

"We'll go on a walk, and I'll tell you things to find."

Wyatt considered for a moment. "Do we get to keep the things we find?"

Ben laughed. "I guess that'll be up to your mother."

Nichole shook her head more as a sigh than a no. "Let's see what you collect first."

Ben stood from his seat. "Okay, the first thing you have to find, are the three silver pails in the shed."

Without another word, all three of the kids started for the building just outback. Laura made some kind of squealing, that he assumed meant for them to wait for her, but the boys went on.

"I should go with them," Nichole said. "I don't want them to get hurt."

"I set it up so that the buckets were right in front of the door. They'll be okay for two seconds."

"I'm always going to worry."

"And so you should," he said as he moved toward her. "We'll go find the rest of the items with them, but I wanted two seconds to kiss you."

She smiled as he leaned in and touched his lips to hers. It wasn't enough, but he'd take it and be happy with it for now.

Just as he stepped back, he heard the distinct sound of buckets being carried.

"Found it," Laura said holding up her bucket.

"You sure did. Let's go for a walk."

NICHOLE WAS IMPRESSED. Ben had set up the entire scavenger hunt. He'd given them each items to find along their walk and to put in their pockets. They were simple items, things he probably dug out of that shed and hid on the trail.

But he taught them things as well. If it was a minute piece to some of the equipment on the ranch, he told what it was for. There were seeds for a garden, and he told him to take them home and plant them. Heck, he'd even had wrapped candies.

He loaded them all into the pickup, all five of them on the bench seat, and drove over the hill to the barn. They met the horses, and Wyatt was brave enough even to feed one. Laura was thrilled to find out that Eric and Susan had goats, so they went to visit the goats.

Now, as Nichole pulled into her driveway, she reminisced about what a wonderful day they had had. Some men might do this just to impress the kids, without actually liking them. But she knew better than that. Ben had a genuine interest in them. If he didn't, he wouldn't have stayed all night and helped her when they were sick. He wouldn't have taught them things along their walk. And he certainly wouldn't have driven all the way to Eric's house just so that Laura could see the goat when she found out they had one. No, he was taking his time with them because he cared.

As the evening progressed, all of the kids got showers after dinner. Any last-minute homework that they had forgotten to tell her about was handled. And because they seemed up to the task, the boys helped situate their lunch for the next morning.

She had tucked Laura into bed, read her a story, and kissed her on the cheek as she walked out. Zane and Wyatt were supposed to be reading in their beds, but she could hear the whispers.

"Okay, boys. Let's get settled down and go to sleep."

She picked up the dirty clothes that they had scattered on

the floor and a couple of toys that hadn't made it back to the box. However, she couldn't help but notice that whatever they had been chatting about was still in the air.

She pulled up a chair and set it between the beds, much like she used to do when she would read them bedtime stories. "What are you boys discussing?"

Neither seemed to want to be the first to say anything, so she sat there and eyed each of them carefully. "Wyatt, why don't you tell me what you guys are talking about."

His face grew tight, and she watched as he mulled around whatever it could be in his little mind. Seriously, were they worried about the peanut butter and jelly sandwiches she said she was going to make for lunch tomorrow?

"We want to know if you're going to marry Ben."

The comment knocked the wind right out of her. She hadn't expected that to be their thought at all.

"Why do you think that?"

"Because men and women who are friends get married."

Nichole nodded thoughtfully. "Well, men and women can be friends without getting married."

"Yeah, but at Miss Audrey's wedding you caught the flowers, and he caught that band thing."

Nichole nodded again, trying to keep her wits about her. "You're right. But that is just tradition, and it doesn't mean anything."

Zane sat up in his bed and crossed his arms in front of him. His brows drew together. "What's wrong with marrying Ben? Don't you like him?"

Nichole crossed her legs and clasped her hands in her lap. "Of course I like Ben. That's why we've been spending time with him. Don't you like him?"

"Yeah, we like him a lot," Zane told her. "So it's okay with us if you want to marry him."

Trying to keep her face looking calm, and her hand stilled because they were shaking, she smiled. "Well, that's not something we have talked about. But I will keep it in mind because it means a lot to me to have your blessing."

Now Wyatt sat up and swung his legs over the side of the bed. "If you haven't talked about marrying Ben, why did you kiss him?"

The calm exterior shattered and she knew she had to look mortified. "You saw me kiss Ben?"

Both boys nodded.

She drew in a deep breath. "It just so happens that Ben and I like each other a lot. We're friends, and we haven't talked about getting married."

"Why not?" Wyatt asked.

"Because all of this is new, sweetheart. I didn't know I liked him this way."

Zane moved to hang his legs over the side of his bed, too. "Does that mean Ben is your boyfriend?"

The thought about what they had done the day before definitely secured the boyfriend situation. And, hadn't he said she was his girlfriend when they'd made out on the couch? The very thought humored her.

"Yes, I would say he is my boyfriend."

The boys exchanged glances. "So, maybe if you keep liking him, you will get married?"

"Maybe," she said easily.

"So Ben could be our new dad?" Zane continued to ask questions.

"You have a daddy," she said, reminding them.

Wyatt fidgeted with his sheet. "I don't think he likes us. He doesn't want to be with us. So we just wanted to tell you that it's okay if we get a new daddy."

Still trying to keep the calm exterior, Nichole processed what they told her. "Okay, I'll remember that. And you'll be the first to know if things go that direction with Ben and me."

Both boys nodded and climbed back onto their sheets. Whatever she had said to them seemed to suffice their curiosity. She, on the other hand, was a mess now.

She replaced the chair in the corner and tucked each boy in leaving a loud, noisy kiss on each of their foreheads. As she walked out of the bedroom, she shut the door.

The moment she walked into her bedroom, she fell to her bed, pressing her hands to her jittery belly. Was this the direction all of this was going? Here she was afraid she would break her little kids' hearts by being involved with the man. Now she was afraid to break their hearts if she didn't follow through.

This was going to take a lot of thought. She had to decide if she should let Ben in on the secret.

23

*T*he decision had been not to tell Ben about the conversation with the boys. Nichole couldn't even imagine how she would bring it up.

"Oh hey, we just started dating, slept together once, and now my boys want us to get married. You don't mind, do you?" She played the situation in her head.

No, it wasn't worth talking about.

She pushed the grocery cart through the store, Laura happily kicking her legs into Nichole's belly from her perched seat. This was normal, Nichole wrapped her head around that. Mondays with Laura grocery shopping, washing the car, vacuuming the house, and normal things that people did on their day off.

It already saddened her to think that next year Laura would go to preschool. A few years later she would go to kindergarten. And then just like that she'd be in school all the time. She hadn't gone through withdrawals with the boys quite as much, because of Laura. But she was going to be devastated when her baby girl grew up.

For some reason, it surprised her when she ran into Lydia at the store. It never occurred to her that the woman would actually be in a grocery store. Wasn't she too busy to eat food? Or at least eat food that perhaps she prepared herself?

"Oh my goodness, look how big you are getting," Lydia said to Laura and Laura lit up. "I saw her at the street fair. How big has she gotten in those few weeks?"

And just like that, Nichole's fears were validated. "I don't know, but she's already outgrowing her 2T's and moving into the next size. And of course, I didn't keep many of the boys' hand-me-downs, because they were wild things," she said matter-of-factly.

"I think the best part about having a little girl would be dressing her. All those frilly dresses and hair accessories." Lydia raked her fingers through her short crop of hair. "Not that I ever had many hair accessories mind you. But I do think they're pretty."

"I'll let you come over when you're ready to dress little girls. We'll see in the end if you still find it as fun," Nichole joked, knowing that Laura would rather run around naked than put on a dress.

"I always figured I'd be better off with little boys if I ever had some. I seem to think that way. Though little girls are pretty," she said tapping Laura's nose and sending Laura into giggles. "So, you know, since I have you here alone, I have to ask how your date went with Ben at his house."

Oh, there was no way in hell she was going to share gossip with Lydia in the middle of the grocery store. And, for now, what they did on their date was going to be her secret. "On Saturday we all went out there, but his parents took the kids and Russell's kids and had a play date. They went on wagon rides, made s'mores, and learned how to make pigs in a blanket. Which reminds me, I need crescent rolls."

Lydia continued to stare. "Right, crescent rolls. Okay, so what did you and Ben do?"

"We had wine, he grilled steaks, we took a walk around his house, and had a very nice night." Nichole hoped she delivered that with the sincerity she wanted to show. "We all went out the next day, too," she told her. "He set up a scavenger hunt for the kids, and they found things in the fields while we took a little hike."

Lydia hummed out her consideration of the conversation. "I kinda thought things would move faster," she admitted. "But I guess that's okay. You can't just date him to ward off my curiosity."

"You're not interested in Ben, are you?" If Lydia was, Nichole had no idea.

"Oh, hell no." She waved her hand in the air as if to blow off that idea. "I'm just a curious kind of woman. Chances of me ever being in a relationship are near zero. So, I live vicariously through those of you who get in one. And, admittedly, any Walker man is a find. I say that now, after years of being forced not to even say the Walker name," she joked at her family's expense. "Ben's a good guy."

"I think he is too," Nichole added.

"Well, I guess I'd better get going. I have a marketing meeting with the beer people. If you're interested, I'll let you know when we're giving out samples next time."

"I would enjoy that."

"Alright. I'll see you two ladies around," Lydia said as she gave Laura's foot a little tug and then she waved goodbye.

Nichole continued through the store, but her conversation with Lydia seemed to have rattled her. She didn't want to be the focus of the town's gossip. Was that the way it always had to be? If you started dating someone, then everybody wanted to know about it? She supposed with a family like the Walkers, who were prominent in everything, that was the way it was. Hell, what was she worried about? Audrey Walker married a movie star, and their wedding was in the tabloids. Certainly, that wouldn't happen if she did get involved with Ben more than she was now.

If she was going to pursue a full-on relationship with Ben, at the request of her children, and her heart, the best thing to do would be to talk to him first. Did he want people to know they were seeing each other? She worked in a gossip-friendly environment, was that going to matter?

There was no doubt in her mind when she walked into work on Tuesday, that some of the girls would be sitting there in those chairs, tongues wagging and ears burning. What was she supposed to tell them?

Just as she pulled the cart into the checkout lane, her phone buzzed. There was absolutely no way to conceal her smile when she saw Ben's name pop up.

Susan just dropped off leftovers. Do you like lasagna? I could bring it over for dinner. Do the kids like blonde Oreos?

She found herself laughing out loud and Laura looking at her as if she'd gone mad and then reaching for her phone. Quickly, she snapped a picture of her and Laura as the line moved.

Sending the picture, she also said, *Laura and I love lasagna. And my boys have never met a cookie they didn't like.*

He sent back a picture of him with a thumbs-up and a cheesy grin, which had her laughing again. *I'll see you at six.*

The conversation ended there as she pushed her cart up and began to unload it onto the conveyor.

BEN LOOKED at the picture that Nichole had sent. Laura was the spitting image of Nichole, right down to her smile. He found that it was hard to put his phone away now. God, what was he doing?

It wasn't so much the kids anymore. He liked the kids. He was pretty sure they liked him too, though he'd never been in an authoritative position with them. It was seeming less like baggage, and more like a bonus, this pre-made family that Nichole came with.

With a few swipes of his finger, the picture of Laura and Nichole with the grocery shelves as their backdrop became his background image. Now he could stare at them all he wanted. And he was finding he wanted to do that a lot.

24

_N_ichole didn't tell the kids that Ben was coming. Instead, she let them whine and groan about having to pick up their toys and put on clean clothes.

She only laughed when she'd been asked six times, "what's for dinner?"

It shouldn't humor her, her poor kids, but it did.

At six o'clock, exactly, she sent the boys to the front door to answer it when the doorbell rang. Standing in the doorway of the kitchen, she watched as they squealed with delight seeing Ben standing there with a metal tray covered in tinfoil and paper bag in his other hand.

"Is anyone in this house hungry?" he asked, and was answered with squeals from the boys and a delighted Laura that turned circles until she fell over. "Okay then, if you want to eat the food, you have to help carry it in."

Wyatt took the bag, and Zane carried the tray.

Zane sniffed at the tinfoil. "What is this?"

"Lasagna," Ben said with a happy tune. "Do you like lasagna?"

Zane walked into the kitchen and set the tray on the counter. "I don't know. What is it?"

Ben gave that some thought. "Well, actually, it's spaghetti cake."

Wyatt set the bag on the counter next to the tray. He looked up at Ben speculatively. "Spaghetti cake?"

Ben nodded. "It has everything spaghetti has, including the meatball. The noodles are bigger. And instead of a sprinkle of cheese, it's ooey-gooey with cheese."

The boys exchanged looks with one another.

Nichole stepped over to the tray and pulled off the tinfoil. "This looks delightful. Let me stick it in the oven for a few minutes to warm it up." She turned on the oven and then turned to the boys. "Go get your backpacks. Come to the kitchen table. Let's get that homework done, and we will eat in a half hour."

She expected the grumbles, almost looked forward to them. What she hadn't expected was for them both to look at Ben and ask, "Will you help us with homework?"

The smile that formed on his lips was genuine, and it shot straight through Nichole's belly. "Sure. I'm pretty sure both of you are smarter than me. We might have to sound out words and figure out math problems. But we can do it."

The boys ran off to get their backpacks, and Nichole turned to look at him. "You're not just trying to impress me, right?" Her voice was awfully serious, even in her own ears.

"By bringing dinner? No, I was hungry, she brings a lot of food, and I wanted to see you."

"I mean with my boys. And with Laura. You're not just nice to them so that..."

Ben held up his hand to stop her. "Are you seriously asking me if I'm trying to get to you through your kids?" His voice was strained, and she seriously couldn't blame him for the anger that creased his eyes.

"Ben, I have to think about..."

"I get it," he whispered through gritted teeth, as the sound of the boys running down the hall filled the room before their approach.

She watched as his eyes lightened before he walked toward the table and took a chair. Without a missed step, he helped the boys unload their backpacks, go through the masses of crumpled papers, which they sorted out, and get down to work.

Nichole got busy prepping the lasagna and mixing a salad, noticing that even Laura chose to be with the boys at the table. When she walked over and tugged on Ben's arm, he picked her up and sat her on his lap. He continued to help with the math assignment that Wyatt was struggling with as Laura colored in her coloring book.

There was a well deep inside of her that was ready to break, she thought, as she turned her back to them all and washed the few dishes that had accumulated in the sink. At the slightest disagreement, her ex would have locked himself away in their bedroom or left the house completely. Wasn't it a sign of a true man that didn't back down, but didn't get angry or violent? Instead, he did what he'd promised to do—helped with homework.

Seriously, could he blame her for asking?

She turned to look over her shoulder and witnessed Zane taking a crayon and coloring with his sister while Wyatt squealed that he understood the problem Ben had just walked him through.

"Looks like dinner will be ready in about five more minutes. Will you all be ready?"

With a triumphant slam of the math book, Wyatt cheered. "Yup! All done, thanks to Ben."

When the words themselves could have cut through her, she let them simmer in her heart. He'd never try to step on her toes or take over the role as their father. But he was a good and decent man. Perhaps she just needed some time to decide where she wanted to go with this newfound relationship she had somehow become part of.

"Then get your backpacks put back together and set by the front door and then take your sister with you and everyone wash your hands," she instructed.

With as much noise as they'd rushed into the room with, they exited, with Laura squealing behind them in laughter. Ben took a moment to gather the remaining items on the table, including the crayons and the coloring book.

He set the items on the counter and moved to her as she gathered her pot holders from the drawer.

Taking her wrists, Ben turned her until she was facing him. She realized it was taking all the courage she could muster just to look up at him, but when she did, she saw nothing but softness in his eyes.

His thumbs brushed over her wrists as he looked down at her, his dark eyes searching hers. "I'm sorry that I upset you earlier. You have a lot to consider when it comes to your family. I was thinking maybe I should let you all have your evening and enjoy dinner."

Swallowing the lump that had lodged in her throat, Nichole shook her head. "I think that if you left the kids would be upset. They like you, Ben."

"And I like them." He lifted a hand to her cheek and brushed his thumb gently over her skin. "I like their mother too, but I don't want to rush anything."

Nichole tucked in her lips and forced the tears back as they began to sting her eyes. "I'm sorry I accused..."

He moved his hand to place a finger over her lips. "No apologies. I'd be disappointed if you didn't question every motive I might have. It just stung a little. I would never hurt you or your kids. And with that said, I wouldn't use them to get to you. I know you're a package deal."

Ben lowered his hand as they heard the kids race down the hall. He stepped away just as the boys jumped through the doorway to prove that their hands were clean.

"C'mon, help me set the table," Ben instructed, and they led him to the correct cupboards and drawers to retrieve the plates and silverware.

Nichole pulled the lasagna from the oven, all the while listening to the gentle commands Ben gave to her children, and they followed. There was respect in every word he used, followed by accolades for jobs well done.

She'd be an idiot to let this man out of her sight, she decided as she carried the lasagna to the table.

Wyatt eased himself up to the table. "I'm going to like this?" he asked with his nose already crinkled up.

Ben nodded. "I'll guarantee you that you will like anything Susan makes. In fact, you've eaten her food a lot of times."

Wyatt narrowed his eyes on Ben. "She cooked all the food for Audrey's wedding, right?"

"Yep. You liked those appetizers we had, didn't you?"

"Yeah."

"Give it a try. I think you'll like it. And," he leaned in toward Wyatt, "I have dessert in the truck, but you have to eat your dinner."

All eyes turned to get approval from Nichole, who carefully controlled the smile that wanted to surface.

"You have to eat dinner, just like Ben said," she offered. "Hand me your plate."

25

The only heartache from the entire night, and that included the misunderstanding with Nichole, was that Ben had only had a tiny slice of the cake that Susan had brought him. Laura had somehow scammed him out of the biggest piece and half of his piece.

He was still laughing about it as he pulled up in front of his house in the darkness. Really, was it too hard to remember to leave the porch light on?

Ben stepped out of his truck and listened to the sounds. Crickets, cows, the wind through the grass. Could anything else ever make him quite as happy?

He shut the truck door and leaned up against it. He supposed he knew the answer to that. Even though it didn't seem as though she trusted him, Nichole and her kids did make him happy.

Letting out a long breath, he started for the front door. Honestly, they came from two different worlds. She was a city girl, and he was a country mouse. They were still feeling it out. No need to worry that his little quiet life would be disturbed.

Ben pushed open his front door, just as his cell phone

buzzed in his pocket. The text message was from his brother Eric. *Gerald at ER. Accident during calf birthing assist. Mom says get your ass here.*

With his heart pounding in his chest, Ben raced back to his truck, jumped in, and sped back towards town.

Gerald did always seem to be unlucky, Ben thought as he hurried through the doors of the ER. Since none of his family were in the waiting room sobbing, he checked in at the desk. A few minutes later, he was escorted to the room where all of his brothers and his parents were.

Gerald lay on the bed, an ice pack covering half of his face. His clothes were covered in blood, but Ben heard his laugh come through first.

"You are always late to a party," Gerald mumbled as Ben walked through the door.

"Didn't realize this was going to be quite the gathering. What the hell happened to you?"

Ben's mother slapped him on the arm. "Watch your mouth."

Eric, who was leaned up against the wall, his ankles crossed and his arms folded in front of him gave Ben a nod with his head. "Dr. Gerald lost control of the forceps. Calf slid out, forceps let go, Gerald took it right in the eye."

He could see the smirk on Eric's face barely controlled. With a glance toward Russell, he knew that they'd had a good laugh over it.

"Black eye only or stitches too?" Ben asked.

"Six stitches and a black eye. Just missed my nose or that might've been flattened too," Gerald said with a laugh from under the bag of ice.

Ben looked around the room. His four brothers, sans wives and kids, and his parents surrounded Gerald, who wasn't going to die from his injuries.

His mother touched his arm. "As soon as they spring him,

we're all heading to Eric's. Susan is making dinner."

Ben took a breath to tell her that he'd eaten dinner with Nichole and her family nearly two hours ago, but he refrained. He didn't want to answer questions about that either. It would be easier to eat a second meal late at night than to be bombarded with questions.

NICHOLE WALKED through the door of the salon and got a wave from Gia, who was under the dryer with a head full of foils. She waved in return and continued to the back room to put her personal items in her locker.

Audrey stood next to the coffee pot watching the dark liquid drip into the pot.

"Good morning," Nichole said, noticing that Audrey hadn't acknowledged her.

When Audrey turned, she noticed the dark circles under her eyes. "Mornin'."

"You feeling okay?"

Audrey shrugged. "Greg is filming. I don't sleep well when he's not home."

"That's all?"

"Ya. I think I've caught a spring cold, too, and those are worse than winter colds."

Nichole would have to agree. "I can try to fit your schedule into mine. Maybe you should go home and get some sleep."

Audrey pulled a mug from the cupboard and filled it to the brim with steaming coffee. "I'll be better in a few minutes. Gia won't mind if it takes me a bit more time to get her hair done this morning. She's avoiding taking inventory." Audrey laughed as she took her first sip of coffee.

When the door opened again, Nichole knew her day was

about to begin. Mrs. Wilcox was due for her weekly set appointment. Though Nichole thought of herself as a hip and up to date stylist, setting the hair of an eighty-year-old woman each week kept her humble.

Mrs. Wilcox started her morning telling Nichole about her grandchildren, who were now in their thirties and had children of their own. Though Nichole felt as though she knew them all personally, she started her conversations each week as if she'd never told Nichole about her family. Once she had each curler in place and had helped Mrs. Wilcox to the dryer seat, she went to the back for her own cup of coffee.

As she walked back to her station, Audrey began sectioning Gia's hair to be cut.

"How are your kids doing?" Gia asked, and her warm Italian accent washed over Nichole.

"They're good. The boys hate school, and Laura loves her daycare provider. I guess all things are normal. How are you and Dane?"

Gia, holding her head still for Audrey, let out an exaggerated breath. "Oh, we are fine. Exhausted after last night. But everything is good."

Audrey stopped cutting and exchanged a look with Nichole. "What happened last night?" Audrey asked.

"You did not hear? Gerald was in the hospital."

Nichole set her mug on the station, and Audrey turned Gia around toward them.

"What happened? Is he okay?" Audrey asked.

Gia looked out from under the hair that was pinned over her face. "Dane was out at the ranch all night. Gerald was assisting in a calf birth, and the forceps they used hit him in the face."

Nichole instinctively brought her hand to her mouth. There was an instant moment of concern, but then laughter hit her chest before she reeled it back.

"That's horrible," she said lowering her hand. "Is he okay?"

"Six stitches and his eye is swollen shut today, Dane said. He is going to be milking this injury for a few weeks."

Audrey turned Gia back around in the chair and shifted a glance to Nichole. "Ben didn't mention it to you?"

Nichole sipped her coffee. "I didn't talk to him after he left the house. Nor have I talked to him this morning."

"He was at your house last night?" Gia asked as Audrey adjusted the clips in her hair. "So things are heating up?"

Nichole took another long sip of her coffee and considered what was being asked. "I can't say they're heating to anything. He brought over dinner and helped the boys out with their homework."

"Ah-ha, so he just happened to be in town when he lives forty-five minutes away?"

Nichole felt the warmth rise in her cheeks. Right now she could hold them off of the conversation because there wasn't any heat. But what would happen when there was?

"We're feeling it out. I have a lot of..."

"Baggage," Audrey said. "We got that. But he still showed up."

"Yes," Nichole expelled the word realizing that he had shown up, and of course knew that nothing would have happened because her kids were there—but he'd brought dinner and stayed even after she'd accused him.

She had more baggage than just her family, she thought.

"I have always liked him," Gia offered. "In fact, I got very lucky to marry into such a gracious family. He's a good find." Gia managed a look and smile in Nichole's direction.

Nichole sipped her coffee and thought about the argument she'd had with Ben—or more like the argument she'd started with Ben. Gia was right. He was a good find, and these women were her friends and knew more about him than anyone.

"I accused him of moving in on my kids to get to me," she

admitted and watched as both women turned to look at her. "It was stupid. I know."

Gia spun her chair to face her, and Audrey set her scissors down and propped her hands on her hips. Obviously, Nichole had just started something, she decided.

"He'd never do that," Audrey argued. "I can't believe you..."

"I know," Nichole cut her off. "I know it was stupid, but my kids come first."

"He'd understand that. How did he react?"

Nichole set her mug on her station sat back in her chair. "He told me that wasn't what he was doing. He was offended, as he should have been. And then he helped them with their homework. Before dinner, he offered to leave and to give me time with my kids."

"So he left?" Gia asked.

Nichole shook her head. "No. I asked him to stay."

Audrey picked up her comb and gestured toward her. "First argument out of the way. I think it's time you moved this relationship forward and see what's in store."

"What is forward?" Nichole snickered as she picked up her mug.

"I'm going to watch your kids tonight, and you're going to go out and see Ben. No timeline to get back home."

Nichole looked at her over the top of her mug before she took a long, thoughtful sip of her chilling coffee. "You're going to stay the night with my kids so I can go get..."

"Yep!" Audrey agreed. "They love my dog, Black Sabbath, and he needs some kids to run around after. I'm much too tired to run after him myself." She turned Gia back to the mirror and continued to cut her hair.

So, now his family was in on making sure they hooked up. She sipped her coffee, which was now stone cold. Maybe she should consider Audrey's offer. Maybe.

26

Gerald looked like crap, Ben thought as he left his parents' house and headed out to the barn to help Eric get the horses ready for the group of riders that were coming out for a guided ride.

His list was long today with all of the jobs he had to do. Added to the list were Gerald's items, which somehow had become his items. There was a little irritation that his brothers hadn't taken on any of the additional jobs. Eric was taking out the riding group. Russell was working on remodeling their mother's bathroom, and Dane was out fixing fences.

Ben blew out a breath as he moved to the next job on his list.

It was nearly seven o'clock when he headed back to his house for the night. He was muddy, smelly, and more tired than he'd been in years. All he wanted was a beer, some ESPN, and hot shower.

Taking the last turn to his house, he slowed as he noticed a car parked out front of his house. Nichole sat on the front step and rose as he drove up.

She was in a sundress covered in big yellow flowers, and the sight of her lit up his day. The breeze blew the skirt around her toned and beautiful legs, and she pushed back her hair as it blew over her face.

Until that moment, he'd wanted to be alone for the night, but now he was very happy to see her standing there.

Ben parked his truck and climbed out as Nichole walked toward him.

"You're a sight for sore eyes," he said as he closed the door to his truck and watched as she continued to walk to him.

Nichole said nothing as she moved to him and slid her arms up around his neck. Instinctively, his hands came to her hips as she moved in and pressed her soft, warm lips to his.

She rose up on her toes, pushing her body firmly to Ben's, and forcing him back against his truck for support.

Ben slid his hands up her back and into her hair as her mouth opened and he took. The air around them grew thicker and hotter. The taste of her sent pulses through his veins that ignited everything inside of him.

When she pulled back, she lingered close, those dark eyes burning into his, her breath heavy as she fought for air.

Sucking in his own breath, he pushed a strand of hair from her forehead. "What brought you out here, and where are your kids?" he asked and she eased back further on a laugh.

"Your cousin is spending the evening with them, at her request."

For a moment he studied her, those long lashes batting behind the lenses of her sophisticated glasses. "Audrey is babysitting? I guess that's not a good term, is it. None of them are babies."

"It's more like kids are wearing out the dog."

He chuckled with that. "So you decided to come out here?"

A line formed between her brows. "Let's say I was convinced, to come out. I don't know if her motives are true, but your cousin decided," she sucked in another breath, "well, I think she just wants some new gossip."

The sexy smile that crossed her mouth had Ben willing his hands to rest on her shoulders and remain there. "And you made the long trip out here just because she wants gossip?"

Nichole inched closer to him again, wrapping her arms around his neck, and pressing her body to his. "All of that stuff I said the other night, I didn't mean it. I want you to know that I am genuinely interested in you, and I know you feel the same way."

Ben wasn't sure *interested* cut it anymore. It was so much more than interest. His heart had tumbled past interest into infatuation, and it was drifting awfully close to love.

"If you want to reconsider..."

Ben cut off her words with his mouth on hers. They could go rounds and rounds with this, he decided. He could decide she had too much baggage, and that the kids were a lot to take on. She could decide his motives were not genuine, even if she didn't believe it. The only logical thing was to move to the next stage, and she wouldn't have come out to his house looking like she did, tasting like she did, feeling like she did, if she wasn't game.

But first, he was going to take her inside and explore the wonders of her a little more. There was no timeframe tonight, and she'd come to him looking and smelling so sweet that he wouldn't be able to keep his hands to himself much longer.

Taking her hand, he tugged her into the house before he spun her to him in the living room. There was no time to make it all the way to the bedroom.

Running his hand up her back, he took hold of the zipper and eased it down as he feasted on her delicate neck.

"Don't you want to..." she muttered under his kisses and he silenced her again with his mouth.

"Right here. I don't want to wait to touch you one more moment," he said as he slipped the dress from her shoulders and it pooled around her feet.

IN THE STILLNESS of the night, Nichole laid in Ben's arms. The only sounds were of their breath combining. Her sweat-slick skin still pressed to his, and his scent surrounded her.

For only a moment, she thought a breeze would be nice. The heat from the end of June mixed with the passion that they had endured. But she wouldn't move, not for anything.

"I'm starving," Ben panted. "Thank God Susan always brings me food."

Nichole laughed. "What do you have?"

He hummed as he thought. "She was trying out a new recipe for a chicken dish. I have no idea. I know there's a tray of brownies. Or half a tray of brownies," he corrected. "There's a bag full of muffins, from a brunch meeting she had catered. And I do believe she brought me a whole lot of lunchmeat. I'm going to guess my mother put her up to that one."

"Once a mother, always..."

"I get it. And you're probably laying here wondering when I'm gonna let you go."

"I'm trying to think about it. The truth is, I don't want to go anywhere."

"But you're worried. And something tells me you're just a little conflicted."

Nichole shifted and propped herself up on her elbow to look at him. "Did I say anything that would make you think that?"

He ran a finger over her cheek and down her throat. "No. You look satisfied. I just know your heart."

Sitting up, Nichole reached for the sheet and covered her body. "That's a lofty statement, Mr. Walker."

"I'd be disappointed if you weren't thinking about them."

Would she always put her children in her own way? She knew they were fine. Audrey would never let anything happen to them. Not only that, if something did happen to them, she would call. She knew where Nichole was. She was fairly sure Audrey knew exactly what Nichole was doing. if she didn't stop making her children an excuse, she would never find happiness. And dammit, she wanted happiness. She wanted it with Ben.

Deciding at that moment to take a stand against herself, she lowered the sheet, and laid back against him.

"Don't give up on me."

Ben adjusted so he could look at her. "What made you think I was giving up on you?"

She pressed her hands to her belly. "Nothing. I just realized I keep getting in my own way. I keep thinking you're going to think less of me, because of my family. I know better. I know that's not the truth. I know that's not who you are. So, don't give up on me while I try to put that in my head and cement it there."

Ben ran a finger over the curve of her shoulder, down her arm, and back up again. "I promise to never give up on you."

She let that reassure her. She truly wanted a new start. She needed to let herself have a new start.

"I'm starving for a chicken experiment. Can we please go eat?"

Ben chuckled as he sat up and pulled her up to him. "I can guarantee you anything Susan makes as an experiment is phenomenal."

"I would expect no less."

"And I have no problem with dessert before and dessert after," he admitted. "And by dessert, I mean brownies."

Splaying a hand across his chest, Nichole gave him a wicked smile. "Brownies are nice."

Ben took a long deep breath and let it out slowly. "Do I get to keep you until morning?"

She hadn't completely thought about it. Audrey said that it was fine, but honestly, Nichole hadn't anticipated it.

Ben held up a finger. "I'm going to go start the chicken. You call my cousin, and see how things are going. Get back to me on the all-night. But, I would love to hold you while you sleep in my bed."

He pressed a quick kiss to her lips, reached for his jeans, and pulled them on. Without worrying about a shirt, or shoes, he left without his jeans even buttoned and headed to the kitchen.

Nichole took a few more moments before she pulled on her dress. She would go into the bathroom and clean herself up. For some reason that made her feel better about calling home.

Pressing her hand to her chest again, she felt the beating of her heart. At one time she thought it was broken and could never be repaired. But right now, standing in Ben's bedroom, she knew that he was exactly what she needed. It was the right thing to do. Something deep inside her told her that Ben Walker was going to make them all very happy.

BEN READ Susan's instructions three times before putting the tray of chicken in the oven. Perhaps it took three times to read because he was focused on the conversation Nichole was having on the phone in the other room.

His mother would be mortified to think he was eavesdropping, however he was doing a horrible job. To his credit, he was trying not to listen.

In all honesty, he shouldn't have asked her to stay the night. It was putting a lot of pressure on her, and he knew it. What if the boys didn't like that? What if the boys had questions of their own? Was he ready to face them, and was he man enough to face them with that?

He ran his hands over his face. Dear God, he had just taken someone's mother to bed.

The thought made him chuckle as he opened the tray of brownies and cut them into squares.

It wasn't as if he thought of her as just some woman to have. Sure, he'd had his share of hookups, short-term, good and bad relationships. For some reason, deep in his heart, he knew this wasn't one of them. He cared about those kids that she was talking to on the phone in the other room. When the time was right, he decided, he would have a talk with those boys. They needed to know his intentions. Of course, he didn't know his intentions quite yet. All he knew was that his heart had never felt like it did when he was with Nichole. And that had nothing to do with the amazing sex they had just had, that was simply a bonus. If he didn't think it was so awkward, he would've thanked his cousin for setting that up.

When he turned, Nichole was standing in the doorway, leaned against the door jamb, her arms folded in front of her. Never in his life had he known anyone so beautiful.

"Dinner should be ready in about a half-hour," he offered. Can I get you a glass of wine? A beer?"

"I'll take a small glass of wine," she said as she sauntered toward him. "In fact, I'll take a full glass. It seems as though my children want their babysitter and her dog to stay all night."

"Is that so?"

"That's so. I didn't bring an overnight bag. I have to admit, I hadn't planned to stay."

"Then why don't we get you one of my T-shirts. Wouldn't want to see you get anything on that dress."

And without another word, Nichole turned and walked toward the bedroom, letting the dress fall from her again.

Ben waited a moment before he followed her. After more consideration, he absolutely was going to thank his cousin.

27

---

*P*erhaps the sunrise was more brilliant through the windshield of Nichole's car because she was so relaxed from her night in Ben's arms.

The smile that formed on her lips was hard to push back, but who cared? For the first time in a year, she was ecstatically happy.

It wasn't the earth-shaking sex she'd had with the most handsome man she'd ever known. It wasn't the fact that they'd walked hand in hand in the fields under the moonlight in a romantic moment that made her heart squeeze in her chest. Nichole knew full well the smile radiated from the inside because deep within her she was falling in love with the man.

He was a breath of fresh air in her complicated life. Ben Walker was a hard worker and a fantastic looker. Oh, and what a gentle lover.

Her lover.

Just the thought of it made her skin flush with heat. They were lovers—intimate friends, she supposed. Actually, what were they? That was going to need a serious conversation.

As she pulled off the dirt road and onto the highway, she laughed at the fact that she had to be so serious about it.

Who cared if they were just lovers? She deserved a lover, and so did he. Not only that, he cared about her children, and that meant everything to her. And didn't she have their blessing to marry the man?

Nerves began to push their way through the contentment, and she realized that she had to face her sons when they looked at her now. Wasn't that why she'd left at the crack of dawn? If she were sitting there when they woke, perhaps there would be fewer questions.

Although, those two boys were awfully smart. She wouldn't put it past them to somehow know what she'd been up to, even if they didn't have a clue about what really went on.

After the last time when they'd asked her about him being her boyfriend and all, what were they going to ask if they knew she'd slept there?

Should she tell them she'd been with Ben? Had Audrey already told them?

The heat that simmered on her skin began to make her question what she'd done all night.

Nichole was shaken from her thoughts when the chiming alert from her car told her that she was in need of gas.

She let out a laugh. Even the simple day to day things were slipping from her.

As she drove into town, she pulled over to the nearest gas station. With the early morning breeze in her hair, she opened her gas tank and slid her credit card into the reader. Transaction denied.

"What in the world?"

Nichole completed the process again and rescanned the card. Again, she was met with the same response. She tried her backup credit card, with the same results, and then her debit.

Frustrated with the situation, she walked into the building and straight to the counter.

"I think the reader on the pump is broken. I'm not able to scan any of my cards," she said to the attendant on duty, who looked as if he'd been there since early the previous morning.

"Let me see," the young man said reaching out for her card.

"I'd like to fill up on this card." When he stared blankly at her, she replied, "Please put twenty on pump two."

The man ran the card, swiping it over and over. Then he shook his head. "Nope. It won't take it."

A groan gurgled from her throat. "Here, try this one." She handed him the other card, and the same process played out.

"Nope. You'll have to pay cash," he told her as he blew the greasy clump of blond hair from his eyes.

Nichole pulled a twenty from her wallet and handed it to the man. "Here. Twenty dollars on pump two, please."

He snapped the bill out of her hand and gave her a nod after he thoroughly checked the bill.

Nichole hurried back out to her car and pumped the gas.

The sunrise was no longer so brilliant, Nichole thought as she drove through the town she loved and toward the house that held her loved ones. Now her mind was filled with doubt and irritation. What the hell was wrong with that gas station?

Pulling into the driveway, Nichole forced herself to be calm. So, one thing went wrong in her day. This was no reason to walk into the house upset. She needed to remember where she had come from. The warm, romantic night, the man she shared it with. Just remembering it made her skin warm again.

As she stepped out of her car, the front door opened and Audrey stepped out onto the porch.

"I thought maybe you'd sleep in longer," she said with a wide grin on her mouth.

Nichole shut the car door. "I decided it would be better if I were home when they woke up."

"Lucky for you they stayed up late." Audrey gave her a wink. "I won't indulge you with what they ate, or what they watched," she said as Black Sabbath poised himself between the doorjamb and her leg.

"Considering the evening I had, I won't divulge any of that either."

Audrey chuckled as she stepped back and nudged the dog back as well. "I take it it was a night well spent?"

"Indeed." She walked into her own house, which was tidier than she had left it. Setting her purse on the chair, she knelt down to pet the dog who had come to greet her. "Did you take good care of my kiddos?"

"That might be a conversation your boys can have with you. One night with the dog and, well you know, now they want one."

"I know how to field that conversation," she said standing up. "Thank you again, I don't know how to repay you."

"Well, when I have kids, and I need a good night with my husband, I'll call in the favor."

Nichole laughed. "I promise I'll be available."

Audrey stretched her arms over her head and twisted her neck from side to side. "I guess I will take my beloved dog and head home. I slept on that beanbag in Laura's bedroom. Not so comfortable."

With those words guilt bubble in Nichole's chest. "Was she having a hard time going to sleep without me?"

"Actually, I was dressing her doll. We put her in every outfit we could create. Laura gave up before I did," she said with a laugh. "I kind of just fell asleep there. All three of them were fantastic, Nichole. You have good kids. They're a joy to watch. So, any time you need some time to yourself, or with my cousin, give me a call."

Nichole pulled her in and gave her a tight hug. "Thank you. You don't know how much I appreciate it," she said stepping back.

"I can see it in your eyes. You look happy."

"I am."

They heard the undeniable sound of Laura talking to her dolls.

"I guess my mini-vacation is over," Nichole said.

"I'll see you on Tuesday," Audrey said as she gathered her bag and her dog and headed out the door.

As Nichole listen to her daughter talk to her dolls on the baby monitor, she went to her room and changed her clothes. Pulling her hair atop her head in a ponytail, she decided this was the perfect look for a Sunday. She would let herself relax, enjoy her children, and in the back of her mind, relive the night she had.

28

*I*t seemed as though the entire town was getting married. Nichole had booked three wedding parties for the next two weekends. Usually, she thoroughly enjoyed the hustle and bustle of the wedding crowds, but this time she found they were simply making her depressed.

That was two weekends where she would be on her feet nonstop. Extra hours would be put in at the salon. And honestly, all she wanted to do was see Ben.

She could tell there was equal frustration on his side. Gerald was taking longer getting back to work, Eric and Susan had planned to take their daughter on a mini vacation, and that left him with a lot more work. Even though he had wanted to come into town and see her and the kids, he just couldn't make time for it. And now with the bridal parties, she couldn't get out of town.

It didn't matter much, she decided. The relationship she had with Ben was new. Perhaps it was a test. If they could make it through this next month, they have a better understanding of each other's lives. Besides, the boys had been invited to two birthday parties, and somewhere she had decided signing them up for flag football was a good idea, and they had their first game coming up. Such was the life of a single parent.

Gia walked into the salon as Nichole finished putting the last bridal party into the computer.

"Hey, Nichole, that candle you ordered just came in."

"Fantastic. I can't wait to smell it. I am absolutely scheduling myself a bubble bath tonight when everyone is in bed."

Gia smiled. "I just got in some new bath salts too. I could add them to your order."

Nichole wasn't sure if it was the thought of the bath salts or Gia's beautiful accent that had her sold. "Let me get my credit card."

She retrieved her purse from the back room, pulled out the credit card, and walked back up front and handed it to Gia.

"I will go run this and bring back your order. You are going to love those salts," she said as she walked out of the salon waving Nichole's credit card.

It was good to have friends that understood you, Nichole thought as she continued to type away on the computer. Audrey had been there to give her a night off. Lydia had all but done some spiritual dance to get her and Ben together. Gia, though it still helped her business, always knew what would lift Nichole's spirits. Then there was Pearl, she simply made Nichole feel sophisticated just hanging around her. Together, they made a circle that Nichole fit into. They had accepted her as family, and she hadn't known how much she needed that.

Gia walked back into the salon with Nichole's credit card in her hand. "It wouldn't let me run it. It said declined, but didn't tell me why."

Nichole let out a breath. "Oh shit! I forgot to check into that. I tried to run it for gas the other day, and it wouldn't work either. None of my cards would work. I thought something was wrong with the gas station."

"Give me another one. Let me try it."

Nichole walked into the back room and dug out her other credit card and handed it to Gia.

"I'll be right back."

Gia was back in under two minutes.

"This one says declined too."

Nichole took the card from her. "I don't keep balances on my credit cards."

"I would get on the computer and check. Identity fraud is huge."

Nichole gritted her teeth together. "I'll come over before you close. I'll bring you cash for my items."

"No hurry," Gia said as she placed a hand over Nichole's. "It is not the first time I have seen somebody's credit card get stolen. The companies are usually pretty good about it. Hopefully, they will not give you any trouble."

As Gia turned to leave, Nichole hoped they wouldn't give her any hassle either. The last thing she needed was stolen credit cards.

An hour later, Nichole sat in the back room, her head in her hands and her cheeks damp with tears.

"Hey, beautiful," the familiar voice broke the silence.

When Nichole looked up she saw Ben standing in the door-way, a bouquet of flowers tucked in the crevice of his elbow. His eyes went wide when he saw her.

"Hey, what's wrong?" he asked as he moved quickly to her.

She held up a hand as if to ward him away. "Nothing. Not a damned thing."

Carefully, he set the flowers on the table and pulled out the chair next to her. "You want to tell me about it?"

"No, I don't want to tell you about it." She got to her feet and slammed the chair into the table.

Ben didn't move or say another word. That would seriously

work to his credit. Nichole scrubbed her hands over her face and wiped away the tears that continued to fall. None of this was his fault, so why was she yelling at him?

With her back turned to him, she dropped her hands from her face. "I'm sorry. I had no right to yell at you."

He stayed in the chair. "You've got something on your mind, feel free to let it out."

Nichole chuckled. "You're not even fazed by that?"

"Are you mad at me?"

She turned and looked at him through tear hazed eyes. "Are you currently the one in Cabo buying tequila?"

His eyes narrowed and studied her. "Last time I checked, it'd been a couple of days since I even had a beer. Mostly because I ran out. What are you talking about?"

Nichole tossed her hands up in the air and then sat back down with a humph. "Somebody stole my credit cards and have run up fifteen-thousand dollars."

"Just one credit card?"

"No. I have two, and they did it to both."

"They don't make you pay for fraudulent charges."

She buried her hands in her face again. "I know. I know. It just makes me sick."

Ben reached across the table and took one of her hands in his. "Hey, if you need some money..."

As if she'd been burned, she pulled back her hand and shook her head. "Oh, no. There is no way I'm borrowing money from you, or anyone else. I'll have this taken care of by tomorrow. Right now, it's just weighing me down."

"Tell me how I can help."

She studied him for a moment, and then the flowers on the table. "Did you bring those for me?"

He acknowledged the flowers. "My mother raised me to bring flowers to a woman who has been on my mind nonstop.

That woman is you. I can't get you out of my head," he said as he raised her fingers to his lips and brushed a gentle kiss across her knuckles.

Suddenly the mess that faced her melted away for the moment. "Can you come to the house for dinner?"

"I was hoping I could scam an invite."

"It's not much. I have beef stew in the crockpot. The boys have a flag football game tonight. So it's kind of a rush dinner."

"Flag football? I haven't played flag football since I was twelve."

The smile came genuinely as their fingers interlaced. "If you're not busy, maybe you could go with us. You could share your knowledge with the boys. They're only starting to learn what it's all about."

"And I thought the night was going to be lonely," he said moving into to press a kiss to her lips.

She felt that tumble as his lips moved against hers. Every moment she was with the man she fell deeper in love with him. It was much too soon to tell him. Something like that would make a man freak out and run away. She was enjoying him too much to scare him off.

FOR THE TIME BEING, Nichole forgot about the hassles of canceling her credit cards as she loaded the boys into the car, and buckled Laura into her seat. Zane and Wyatt hadn't stopped talking since she'd walked through the front door with Ben right behind her.

It warmed her to see how their eyes widened and lit when he was around because she knew seeing him did the same for her.

Ben helped them all wash up before dinner as Nichole got the table set and stew into each of the bowls. She was more than prepared for Wyatt's nose to turn up at the sight of what she had to offer for dinner but maybe seeing Ben eat it would help.

She could hear the water running in the bathroom, and the laughter put a smile on her face. When there was a knock at the front door, she set the serving spoon down in a bowl and went to answer it.

"Hello, Mr. Cowell," she said as she opened the door to her landlord who stood on her front step. His short stature and silver cap of hair made him look much older than she knew him to be. Usually, he wore a warm smile, but tonight his brows were furrowed and his lips drawn down. "How are you this evening?"

"Nichole, I hate this part of my job." He handed her an envelope. "Your rent check bounced. Twice. I'm afraid I'm going to need your payment by the end of the week."

She took the envelope from him and opened it. Inside was the bank paper saying that her check had indeed bounced twice. That wasn't possible. She kept enough money in that account to pay for multiple months. How was it possible that her credit cards were compromised and so was her bank account? She had her wallet in her possession. No one had stolen it.

"Mr. Cowell, I'm so sorry about this. I don't know what happened. I have plenty of money in that account. In fact, I only use that account for rent, and I have three months of rent saved in it at any time."

"Perhaps it was a mistake on the part of the bank, honey. If you have the money in there, it shouldn't be a problem to have it to me by Friday then."

"Of course not. Again, I'm so very sorry this happened. I'll look into it. But I'll bring over the money before Friday," she promised.

He gave her a warm smile, and it lit in his eyes which had been dark and clouded with worry. "I'll see you then."

Looking at the piece of paper, Nichole closed the door and turned to see Ben leaned against the wall.

"It's not polite to eavesdrop," she said through gritted teeth.

"Didn't mean to." He stood and walked to her. "How can I help you?"

She set her jaw and raised her eyes to meet his. "Clever. You think that I'll just tell you I need money if you word it that way?"

He shrugged. "I think maybe you could fill me in on what's going on."

"I did fill you in. And you overheard this. It looks like I'm walking through some shit storm and it's about to get really bad."

Ben stepped in closer, invading her personal space, but she didn't take a step back.

"Then let me ask you again. How can I help you?" He raised a finger before she could lash out at him. "I want to help you. I have no doubt something is going on, and this isn't just you losing track of things. I've been around you enough to know you don't work like that."

"Just because we're sleeping together doesn't mean you need to just step in and save me," she whispered so that the words didn't carry to the ears of the children laughing in the kitchen.

"A little crass, but okay. Let me say that since we are sleeping together, I don't take what's between us lightly. In fact, I usually am very involved with a woman if I'm sleeping with her. I take her interests to heart, and it's usually because I care a great deal about her. So if you want to belittle what we have by labeling it the way you do, then I suppose I'll be a bit heartbroken in the end. But now you know where I stand."

She felt her mouth open, and tears clogged her throat, but she wouldn't let them pass. For a moment she considered his words against hers. There was no way in hell she was taking money from him, but she'd consciously take a step back and let him into her troubles.

"Ben, I don't know what to do. I only have two credit cards and two checking accounts. I had three full months of rent set aside just for emergencies in that account. There is no way this could have bounced."

"Why don't I go get the kids settled and feed them. You go look at your accounts, and we can talk about it all when we get home from football."

The words *when we get home* resonated with her. Perhaps it was because she was in a moment of shock and feeling weak, but she needed to accept the gracious words.

With a nod, she moved in and rested her head on his shoulder. "Thank you. I owe you."

"You don't owe me anything. This is what I can do for you right this moment." He gently pressed a kiss to the side of her head before she walked down the hallway to her bedroom and shut the door.

29

Nichole was quiet through dinner and on the drive to the football field. Ben wasn't sure the kids even noticed, but he had.

Something was processing inside that beautiful head of hers. When they got back to her house, and everyone was settled for the evening, they would talk. And damnit, she was going to open up. He wasn't sure what was happening, but Ben was damn sure not going to let her go it alone.

On the drive to the football field, Wyatt and Zane had been asking questions about Ben's time playing. He answered questions about the flags and the game itself. Zane was at a loss as to how it was possible to grab for flags, but not tackle the other player. The coach had made him sit a few times during practice since he hadn't understood it, he confessed.

Ben found it amusing, and he wondered how many of those same questions he and his brothers had asked his parents as they were driven into town for their first game.

He hoped he was being helpful by keeping the kids engaged in conversation as Nichole drove to the field. Did she even realize she wasn't present?

He'd seen the same look on his mother's face more than once, and now he wondered what took his mother into those dark places. Had there been times that something worried her enough to force her into silence? Surely if one of them were to speak to Nichole at that moment, she'd never even notice.

When they reached the football field, Nichole had mustered up a smile. She greeted the other mothers who had gathered, and with some space between them, she introduced Ben as a family friend.

Acknowledging the state of mind she was currently in, he didn't find any reason to get upset at the introduction.

She cheered and high-fived the boys when they made a good play or simply got excited about running out on the field. There was joy in her eyes again, and when Wyatt ran in for his first touchdown, she grabbed hold of Ben and planted a noisy kiss right on his cheek.

The simple gesture lit a fire in his belly. Then, when Laura tugged on his pant leg and put her arms up for him to pick her up, he did so only to have her give him a noisy kiss on the cheek as well, and that lit a fire in his heart. Keeping her arms wrapped tightly around his neck, Ben held her on his hip and continued to watch the game.

They waited after the victory for the boys to enjoy their orange slices and bottles of water, which the coach had brought before they headed back to the car.

Laura, exhausted from cheering, had rested her head on Ben's shoulder as he carried her to the car. The boys walked ahead of them, each of them talking over the other about the game.

Nichole slipped her hand into Ben's. When he looked over at her, he saw the softness in her eyes now. He was sure the worry hadn't disappeared, but for the moment she resonated calm.

An hour later, Laura had been bathed and put to bed, and

the boys were splashing about in the tub. Nichole dealt with them as, under protest from her, Ben tended to the dinner dishes which they'd left in order to get to the game on time.

He had started the dishwasher when Nichole came back into the kitchen, her shirt wet and her hair now piled on top of her head.

"I'm not condemning your upbringing, but something tells me your mother didn't teach you to clean a kitchen like this," she said looking around.

"What's wrong with how I cleaned the kitchen?" he asked leaning up against the counter.

"Nothing. Your mother just doesn't seem like the kind of woman who would have tolerated young boys underfoot in the kitchen."

He chuckled. "You're right. But I lived in a tiny apartment when I went to college. One of the girls in the apartment was more than a little bitchy and persnickety, so we all did our part to ensure she didn't stab us in our sleep."

A smile slid across her beautiful mouth as she moved to him. Running a finger over his chest, she shifted her eyes to his. "You lived with a girl?"

Ben gave her a slow nod. "Two of them."

"Man about town." Leaning her body against his, she raised her arms around his neck, and his hands came to her hips. "And which one did you share a room with?"

Okay, he thought, he could be playful too. "Neither, but certainly not the bitchy one."

"So, no sleeping with your roommates?"

"Mate. Singular." He pulled back to judge her mood. "And because I want to be totally honest, I'll admit it."

Nichole's fingers curled up into his hair. "That's a college boy's conquest dream, right? The roommate?"

"I suppose. Drunken night. No one else at home. But I didn't share a room with her. It just was a thing that happened a few times."

"So as per our earlier conversation, if you slept with her, it meant that she meant something to you and you cared a great deal for her."

In a moment the conversation could flip on him if he wasn't careful.

"That's what I told you, and I mean it. We didn't date, not in the conventional sense. We both had a lot on our plate. But I did care for her, and if someone were bothering her or hurting her, I would help her as well."

Nichole took a step back from him and wrapped her arms around herself.

"I guess there's no skimming over this."

"Just want to know what's going on."

She turned from him and walked to the refrigerator. Pulling out two bottles of beer, she handed one to Ben. He took it, twisted off the top, and took a long deep pull as he watched her do the same. Obviously still working on what she wanted to tell him, Nichole took the caps and threw them away.

"All of my credit cards have been maxed out, and my bank accounts drained."

Just as Ben was about to take another pull from his beer, he stopped. Setting it on the counter he reached for her and drew her closer. "Drained?"

"My car payment was returned. My rent. The check that I wrote the organization for football, they'll be reaching out very soon, too. I have nothing," she said, her voice shaking as she did so.

He took her beer from her hand and set it on the counter next to his, then pulled her to him and held her as she began to sob.

Running his hand over her hair he spoke softly in her ear,

"We'll take care of this." When he felt her try to pull away, he held her tighter. "I said we, and I mean we. I'm here for you. For all of you."

He'd never meant the words more than he did right at that moment. No one was going to mess with this little family, and at that moment, he was part of that family. The woman sobbing in his arms held his heart like no other woman ever had. He'd use everything he had to fight for her.

When her sobbing had eased, she pulled back to look at him with red-rimmed eyes. "You don't have to do this for me. You owe my kids and me nothing."

Resting his palm against her cheek, he kept his gaze on her. "You're all very important to me. I'm feeling things I didn't expect to feel, but they're there. Will you trust me with this? Show me the details, let me see for myself."

He watched as her mouth opened slightly and she took a breath as if to argue, then released.

"Ben, I'm scared. Everything I've worked for is gone."

"And we're going to figure that out."

"I can't pay off the debts that are going to accumulate. And the kids..."

"They don't need to know what's going on right now. You're going to hate this, and you're going to try to turn me down, but I'm going to help you, Nichole. I'm going to lend you the money..." he lifted his finger to her lips as she began to speak. "I'm going to do it whether you like it or not. Tomorrow we're going to go to the bank and the police and let them know what is happening. Someone is stealing from you and making you and your kids suffer. Well, not on my watch."

"You make it very hard to argue with you."

He smiled down at her, wiping a tear from her cheek. "Good. There aren't going to be any arguments." As if to seal the deal, he pressed his lips to hers and lingered a kiss there, warm and soft.

It hadn't been a lie. He'd never felt so much for one person ever in his life. If someone were just taking advantage of her, he could deal with that. There were things in place to take care of people like that. But what if someone was trying to hurt her? That he couldn't tolerate, nor would he.

As her arms linked around his neck, and she sunk deeper into his kiss, he steered away from the money and the onslaught of legal problems she was about to face. Clearly, the one thing that began to dance around in his head was how he was going to gather enough courage to tell this woman, the mother of three fantastic children, that he loved her, especially when it seemed like her world was crashing down around her.

30

*P*hone calls, emails, and a mailbox full of notices had started Nichole's morning. She couldn't keep her mood intact. One representative would scream at her while the next would nearly offer to send her money to help the cause.

The credit card companies had been understanding, as that was what they dealt with every day. She had learned that the card was a duplicate of her card, the physical card had been used, and they were going to use their sources to track the person who had charged up new clothes, Uber rides, and was having a nice vacation at her expense.

The bank wasn't going to be able to do anything about getting her money back, but since checks had been written on the accounts, they were turning them over as fraud and they would be investigated. However, she was dirt poor, and owed fees and money to everyone.

What she did have was a spreadsheet on her computer filled out with every account she'd paid money to, and whom she needed to contact to find out what fees were going to go along with her bounced checks.

It was enough to plant a near migraine in her head before Ben arrived.

Picking up her coffee, she took a long sip only to find it had gone stone cold. As she stood to refresh it, the doorbell rang. Glad to finally have Ben there, she walked to the door and pulled it open.

He stood there with a box of bagels in his hand and a tray of coffees. "Might be late for breakfast, but bagels are good all day," he offered with a bright smile.

"I certainly could use that." She stepped back to let him through.

"Looks like you're already drinking coffee. Guess that was overkill."

"This is cold. I could use another cup."

They walked to the kitchen, and she saw him scan a look over her makeshift desk on the table. For the moment, he refrained from saying anything.

Taking a few moments, they each chose a bagel and a cream cheese flavor, then eased against the counter as they ate standing in the kitchen.

"It looks like you've been plenty busy this morning," Ben said as he looked back over at her pile of papers on the table.

"I've been at it all night. I couldn't sleep."

"I can imagine."

"I don't understand why someone would do this. Nor do I understand how they were able to. It's not like I'm not safe with my personal data."

Ben set his bagel on the counter and took a sip of his coffee. "I had a thought. And maybe I'm way off course, but you did once tell me that your ex-husband had a gambling problem?"

Nichole took a thoughtful bite of her bagel and stared at him. "He gambled. He didn't do things like this. Besides, he doesn't know where I am, so he couldn't have gotten hold of anything here."

She watched his eyes narrow on her. "He doesn't know where you are? Where his kids are?"

Nichole pushed back her shoulders and set her jaw. "Don't judge me. You don't really know anything about me or my situation."

"Not judging."

"Sure you are. You should see your face right now." She left her bagel on the counter and went back to her seat in front of her computer. "I don't need your help, Ben. I'll get this all handled."

He took another sip of his coffee. His eyes remained coolly on her. "Are you done riding my ass? Your life is your life, but I'm here to help you deal with this."

"You have no idea about my life before I came here," she said looking at the screen of her computer.

Ben moved to her, reached for her hand, and pulled her to her feet. "Tell me about your life. Let me be a part of all of this."

"Why?"

She watched as his eyes hardened. His grip didn't tighten on her as if he were angry, but she prepared for it. "You mean something to me. Don't you get that? You all mean something to me."

"You don't need the hassle of my life, Ben."

"I guess that's my decision." He pulled her against him, and she could feel her tough exterior begin to crumble.

"I'm overwhelmed, and I'm taking it out on you. I'm sorry."

"People who mean something to one another do that."

She nodded against his shoulder. "You do mean something to me."

Ben lifted her chin with his finger and looked into her eyes. "I'm glad to hear that. And I'm not going to let our conversation go, we'll just revisit it when you're ready to talk," he said before nipping her lips with a gentle kiss. "Now let's finish our breakfast and then you can show me what you have going on here. Then, together, we will decide how to get this all fixed."

She loved him, completely and undeniably. What man would take all of her problems on like this, and behave calmly even when she didn't? She'd tell him what she did—about leaving with the kids. But first, she would try to piece back together her life, because when she told him, it'd undoubtedly change how he felt about her.

NICHOLE HAD TAKEN the next hour to walk Ben through everything she had on her accounts. Whoever had done this to her was thorough.

Leaning back in his chair, Ben cupped his hands behind his head and stretched. "I can't help but think this feels like a personal vendetta. How did they get a copy of your credit card? Have you spoken to your family about this?"

She shook her head. "My mother would be out here in a minute if I did that. There's no need to worry her over this. She's blissfully unaware that anything has disrupted my life."

He supposed he understood that. The wrath of his own mother would have people shaking in their boots. Just the thought of it had him chuckling and Nichole raising her brow to him.

"I was just thinking about my mother's reaction if I told her I was in this situation. Oh, she'd hunt them down and hurt them."

Nichole nodded. "You understand my secondary dilemma." She flipped through a few more papers and then sat back in her chair. "So now I need to start over. Really, I guess that's what this comes to."

Ben sat forward and scooted his chair closer. "I'm going to financially help you," he said raising his hand as she took a breath to interrupt. "I am. The credit card companies will help you on that end, but I'm going to pay off what you have with everyone else."

"Why would you do this?"

Covering her hand with his, he spoke softly, "Don't you get it? I'm in love with you. This is what you do for people you love."

Her eyes had grown wide, and he knew that he'd taken her by surprise. Well, if she was going to be pissed about it then fine. She needed to know where he stood, even if this wasn't quite the setting he'd hoped to tell her his feelings in.

"Ben..."

"That's how I feel. And before you bring the kids into it, I love them, too."

Tears pooled in her eyes, and she raised her hand to her mouth. "You do?"

"I would have thought it was obvious."

IT WAS stupid for her to sit there and stare at him, but Nichole couldn't help it. He loved her. Ben Walker loved her, and not only that, he'd said so, aloud, in her kitchen.

Her heart hammered in her chest as she watched his cool blue eyes stare back into hers.

Not only that, he loved her kids, too.

"It is obvious. And I can tell you, you've earned a lot of points for how you handle and take care of my kids," she admitted.

"I wasn't doing it to earn points."

Now she held up her hand to cut off his explanations. "I know. It was a compliment. I promise."

Easing back into her chair at the kitchen table, she let the warmth of his words continue to resonate through her. Looking at her computer screen, she hoped they were enough to get her through the mess that splayed out in multi-color panels on her computer.

"I guess we'd better get back to this." She nodded to the computer.

Ben scooted his chair around next to hers and looked at everything she'd inputted. "I can't believe they're using your card in Mexico. Wouldn't they have alerted you?"

"Sure, if I hadn't called them and told them I was in Mexico."

"Someone is impersonating you?"

She shrugged. "Sort of. The card is in my name, but the signer doesn't sign the whole name. Just N. Lewis. What I've learned so far is the person who was in Mexico, registered at the hotel is a Nathan Lewis."

"So they have him?"

She shook her head. "No sign of him at all. And from what I gathered when they were trying to talk around it, you know not saying anything to protect themselves, N. Lewis is a woman, just not the N. Lewis that belongs to the card or Nathan Lewis under whom the room is checked out to."

"So maybe it's not personal. Do we know if Nathan Lewis' credit or identity was stolen?"

Nichole leaned in and rested her elbow on the table and rested her head in her hand. "I'll let you know when he calls me back."

Ben's eyes widened. "You got a hold of Nathan Lewis? You should be a detective. How did you do that?"

"He happens to be my father."

She watched his face contort from shock to anger as he sat back in his chair. "So it is personal."

"It is now."

"And you don't think your ex-husband has anything to do with this?"

She chewed on that for a moment, let it process, let it filter through her thoughts before it came out her mouth. "The person of interest is a woman."

"Could be someone involved with him."

"Could be."

"If they're opening cards in your name, they have to know where you are."

"Scary thought."

"Because he doesn't know where you are?"

"That's how I wanted it."

Ben pressed his fingers to his eyes before he lifted them to meet hers. "You ran away with your kids, didn't you?"

"Well, at least you didn't ask me if I kidnapped them," she said with a bite before standing up and walking over to the sink.

Resting her hands against the counter, she braced herself and told herself to be calm even if everything in her raged and burned. Didn't he say he loved her kids too and wouldn't that mean he'd want what was best for them? He deserved to know.

"He didn't have any custody rights. He was allowed to see them if he wanted to, but he had no custody. He fought to have all of what I had, which was nothing, because he'd lost it all. In the end all he got was the divorce."

"If he had no custody rights, then what's the problem?"

"Like I said, his rights were to see them when he wanted, and I wasn't to leave the state without his consent."

"Nichole..."

"Don't lecture me. And if you don't want anything to do with this, then you should go now. If he knows where I am, it means I need to pick up and leave again."

She didn't have to turn around to see his face. When she heard the chair kick back, and the footsteps, she knew he was walking out the door forever.

A moment later the door clicked closed, and Nichole slid to the floor and let the wrenching sob take over.

31

_I_t wasn't his place, and he knew it, but Ben wasn't going to risk Nichole loading up her kids and driving out of Georgia in the middle of the night to hide somewhere else.

He didn't want to risk her going to jail either. With that in mind, he was sitting in Phillip Smythe's office waiting for him to process what Ben had just told him.

"Shit, Ben." Phillip leaned his arms on the top of his desk and let out a breath. "This isn't good."

"That's why I'm here. It's not as if she's hiding too well. She's living in the open under her maiden name, working, with her kids in public school. If she was concerned that she'd be arrested or something, wouldn't she have changed her name or something?"

Phillip leaned back in his chair. "There has to be more to it than just packing up the kids and leaving. I'm going to have to do some investigation and see what the parameters of the divorce agreement were."

"Right. But what about her accounts being breached?"

Phillip leaned forward again. "That's criminal. You seem to think that this has something to do with her ex-husband?"

"C'mon. The man gambled away their savings, their car, and the money for rent. Phil, he left his kids homeless because of his gambling debt. Then her credit cards are stolen, her bank account emptied, and they're using her father's identity? I'm no detective, but doesn't it seem too neat and tidy?"

Phillip nodded, his eyes coolly focused on Ben's. "Let me look for some data on her ex-husband. If he's running a straight and narrow life, she could be in a heap of trouble."

"That's what I'm afraid of, but I don't think that's what you'll find."

Phillip ran a finger over his temple and chewed his lower lip. "How involved are you with her?"

"Very involved."

"More than just acquaintances, I take it?"

Now Ben leaned in resting his forearms on his desk. "I love her. I love those kids. Listen, I know she could be in a world of trouble, but she did what was right by all of them. There has to be more, right? I mean if they got divorced, and he could see the kids, but didn't have custody, there would be no reason to run unless there were more to it. And why mess with her parents?"

"Don't get too far ahead of yourself. Let me see what I can find. I need to talk to Nichole."

"Yeah, well get your keys, because I'm sure that the way my conversation with her just ended, she'll be packing up her shit right now."

BEN PULLED up in front of Nichole's house with Phillip in his cruiser right behind him. Both men got out of their vehicles and went straight to the door. She must have seen them coming because she opened the door and stepped out onto the porch.

Her eyes narrowed on Ben before shifting to Phillip. "Gentlemen, what can I do for you?"

Phillip stepped in closer before Ben could speak.

"Nichole, Ben says you've had some fraudulent charges made to your accounts."

He saw the relief blanket her face as she looked at him and then back to Phillip. "Yes."

"Bank accounts have been emptied and cards run up?"

"Yes."

"Also, your father's identity compromised."

"Yes."

Phillip removed his sunglasses. "Can we come in and talk about this? I want to help you take the next step in getting charges pressed when they find the party responsible."

There was some hesitation, but she eventually opened the door for them to walk inside.

Ben had been right. He noticed right away that Laura's toys were not in the living room where they always were, and there were a few duffle bags in the hallway that hadn't been there an hour earlier.

"All of my notes are on my computer in the kitchen," she said, steering them through the house. "Have a seat. Can I get you something to drink?"

"I'd love a glass of water," Phillip said.

"I'll get it," Ben offered, moving past her. Guilt twisted in his gut when he noticed how red her eyes and cheeks were from the crying jag she must have had when he'd left.

He watched as Nichole nervously sat down across from Phillip. As he pulled down a glass from the cupboard, he decided she'd need a glass of water too. He filled them both and walked them to the table.

"So, Nichole, tell me what's going on," Phillip began as he gave Ben a nod of thanks for the waters..

Ben then stepped back to lean against the counter and watched her fold her hands tightly in her lap before taking a deep breath.

He listened as she relayed the story, just as he had. The tale of debts that had been created and the charges that had been charged.

Phillip took a notebook from his pocket and made notes. "Your father, has he had his accounts compromised as well?"

"I haven't talked to him quite yet. I'm waiting for him to return my calls." Her voice shook as she relayed the information and Ben saw tears well in her eyes.

Since Phillip was there, and chances were she wouldn't attack him in front of Phillip, he moved in and placed his hand on her shoulder.

To his amazement, she placed her hand on his but didn't shift her eyes in his direction. It wasn't until Phillip mentioned her taking the kids that he felt her tense up beneath him.

"I did what was best for my family and me. I don't regret that."

Phillip nodded slowly. "I understand that. By the parameters of your divorce agreement, what does it state about you moving away with the kids?"

Nichole chewed her bottom lip, and he watched as she picked at the skin around her thumbnail. "Phillip, I'll move on with them if I have to. I'll do anything to keep them safe."

"And why do you think you're not safe?"

She shrugged off Ben's hand and leaned her elbows on the table. It hurt to watch her shoulders rise and fall because she was crying, and all he wanted to do was scoop her up and hold her.

Phillip reached out a hand and rested it on hers. "You take your time. This isn't easy."

After a few moments, Nichole's tears eased, and she sucked in a breath. "He didn't want a divorce," she said sniffing and wiping at her eyes. "He didn't understand why I wanted it, even after everything I had was gone."

"You had him served?"

Ben stood against the counter again, and now he could see the corner of her mouth twitch into a slight smile. "Had him served in the middle of a poker game with his friends. He was up a grand and lost it all in the next hand after they handed him the papers. I'm not above some humiliation when I'm hurt," she said sharply.

Phillip sat back in his chair. "I'd like to ask you not to run off to anywhere. I'm going to follow up on this and see if I can get some leads. I might want to ask you more questions."

Nichole nodded in agreement. "I'll stay, as long as my kids and I are safe."

"And I'll do everything in my power to make sure you are. You're heading into work today?"

Nichole shook her head. "It's my day off. Usually, Laura and I do our housekeeping on Mondays, but I sent her to the sitter so that I could work on all of this."

"I want you to keep living your normal life," he instructed. "But I would like to request that you consider letting Ben stay here with you, or even better, maybe the two of you could hole up at his place for a bit."

Ben shoved his hands into his pockets because he was readying himself for a fight with her. Instead, she turned, teary-eyed and faced him. "Would you consider it?" she asked as she knuckled away tears from her cheeks.

"Staying here? Of course."

Smiling, she said, "No. Can my children and I move out to your place?"

His heart slammed in his chest. God, she hadn't given up on him after he got Phillip involved. That was love, he figured. Trust and true love had a woman asking to uproot her family and move in when she could run again, just as she'd planned to.

"I can't think of anything I'd like more than to have you there with me for as long as you'd like to be."

32

*L*aura had been picked up from the sitter's, and Ben called in a few favors from his brothers to do his part of the work on the ranch for the day, and then to meet him at his house when school was out to settle in the family.

True to the Walker family ways, not one person asked why or what was wrong. They all simply stepped up and agreed to help.

Nichole worked to pack up clothes, toys, and necessities that would get them through a few nights. Glenda had a couple of blow-up mattresses that she offered for the kids to sleep on, until Ben and his brothers would come back and get the beds.

Ben paid Nichole's rent and took care of the fees the landlord had been charged from the bank. She had five more months on her lease, but Ben would be happy to pay for it if it meant keeping her with him, he thought. It was something to bring up after they'd all piled into his small home and tried to live as a family. It was going to be an experiment of epic proportions.

As Nichole made phone calls to the few people she'd written checks to over the past few weeks, Ben took Laura out back and pushed her on the swing. He knew his nephew Lucas loved to swing high and fast, but Laura enjoyed a softer touch. She just wanted to go back and forth, slightly.

There was great comfort in enjoying the moment with her. Her giggles and that infectious smile had him grinning at the little girl who looked so much like her mother. Would his daughter look like Laura, he wondered, and then the thought smacked back at him. He'd never thought much about having children, nor had there ever been a woman in his life that made him even consider it. But looking at Laura, and the joy it gave him to see her eyes light up when he pushed her on that swing, well, suddenly it meant something to him. It meant a great deal to him.

Ben watched as Nichole moved to the back door. The reality was that Nichole had a lot on her plate right now, and sure, he was the knight in shining armor—the superhero. But her mind was probably a million miles away from where his had just gone.

She had three kids to think of already. Even hypothetically introducing the topic would be inconsiderate of him. Then the jolt that kicked him right in the gut popped into his head. And what if things didn't work out between them after they had gotten married and had their own children? Would she steal them away from him too, just as she'd done to their father?

"Go inside," Laura looked up at him as the swing slowed.

Her small voice snapped him from his thoughts, and he scooped up the little girl who had wound her way around his heart so tightly it ached.

"It looks like you two were having a great time," Nichole said as Laura reached for her.

"Ben push."

"He sure did," Nichole said laughing as she kissed Laura on the top of the head and then set her down to run into the house. But she didn't move from the doorway. Instead, she lifted her eyes to Ben's and watched. "What's wrong? You have worry all over you."

He was sure he did. He'd worked up quite the freak-out in his head. "I'm fine. Just a lot on my mind I guess."

She nodded as she lifted her hand to his chest. "If at any time you decide that this is too much you just..."

Ben took her hand and kissed her fingers. "I'll say the word. But it's not going to be too much. I love you, and I love your kids. It's all going to be just fine," he assured her, and himself, as he pulled her to him and kissed her gently on the top of the head.

GERALD WORKED with Ben to unload his truck while Nichole stayed in town to pick up the boys from school.

"Aren't they almost done with school for the summer?" Gerald asked as he carried in a box of toys, some of which were shooting or whirring in the box.

"Soon, I'd think."

"Then what? She has to put them all into daycare?" Gerald asked as he walked into the house and deposited the box into the bedroom they had marked for the boys. "That's got to be expensive."

Ben set his box in the living room and listened to his brother. He hadn't considered the burden to her when the kids were out of school. Did she make enough money to feed, clothe, and shelter her kids as well as find care for them all summer while she worked?

Some things never crossed his mind, and why would they have? When school was out for him and his brothers, they enjoyed the lazy summer on the ranch. Sure, they had their jobs, and the older they became, the more intense the jobs became. But their mother never had to worry about their care. They had their grandparents in the main house and plenty of ranch hands to keep an eye on them.

As they headed back out to his truck for another load, he figured Nichole had faced this dilemma every year. The boys were seven after all. A year ago, she would have had her family nearby, but by the sounds of it, her ex-husband wouldn't have been any help.

"Hey, heads up," Gerald yelled as he threw out a box from the back of the truck. "You're in la-la land. What's up?"

"Just thinking about all the things Nichole has to deal with. That's all."

He saw the grin on his brother's face, and the barrage of questions was bound to follow if he didn't turn and hurry that box back into the house.

As he climbed the steps to the porch, he heard another truck coming up the road. A moment later Dane and Russell pulled in next to his pickup.

"Mom sent these mattresses over, and boxes of food," Russell said as he climbed out of the passenger side of the truck. "I guess she figured you would starve out here."

Ben chuckled. His family would never cease to amaze him. Perhaps they were precisely what Nichole and her family needed. A good dose of Walker family values.

Dane picked up a box out of the back of his truck. "I have a hammock. Where do you want it?"

Ben stopped and looked at him with wonder. "I don't even know why you have a hammock."

"The boys are going to be cramped in that little room. They're going to want to be outside. What better way to do that than to swing on a tree. Seriously, you have nothing out here to entertain kids."

"It's a temporary situation," Ben reminded him. "No need to build a tree house and a swing set."

When Dane and Russell both looked up at him with wide eyes, he knew that there would be a treehouse above that hammock by the end of the weekend.

Dane passed by him and shouldered him as he did. "You're screwed, man. My wife is in on the pool that says you'll be married in a month."

Ben turned and called after Dane who was now walking around the side of the house. "Who has a pool on that?"

"Lydia," Dane called back as he disappeared around the back of the house.

"Tori is at least giving you through the summer. She figures Nichole will want a big wedding," Russell added.

Ben watched as Russell carried the rolled-up mattresses into the house.

Well, he had a lot to think about, he decided, as he picked up a box of Laura's toys and carried them into the house. Perhaps they'd see where things went when everyone was living under one roof.

33

From behind the house, sitting in the hammock that Dane had hung, Ben heard Nichole's car pull up and the sound of the boys as they slammed doors and ran up onto the porch and around to the back.

"That's cool!" Wyatt called out as Zane ran up next to him. "When did you get that?"

Ben grinned up at them as Nichole, with Laura on her hip, walked around the back of the house. "Dane thought you guys needed a place to hang out."

Zane started toward him. "Can I sit in it?"

"I want to sit in it," Wyatt called after him as he followed.

Ben laughed as he struggled to climb out. "There's enough room for all of us, so I know the two of you can be in it together."

Laura wiggled down from her mother's arms and toddled down the steps and toward her brothers. Ben helped to load both boys in and squeezed Laura in between them.

The three of them giggled as they gently swung in the hammock and looked up into the trees. As Ben walked toward Nichole, he heard Zane calling out that one of the clouds looked like a butt, and that started the laughter that rolled from them.

"They might be in there all night," Nichole said as Ben moved toward her and pulled her into him.

"Dane was damn sure that was what they needed. How do you feel about tree houses?"

Nichole eased back and looked at him. "You don't need to uproot everything for my kids."

"Oh, that wasn't me. Dane and Russell got it into their heads that it needs to happen," he offered to pull her to him again. "I think this weekend Russell is going to bring Lucas out and they're going to plan it."

Nichole rested her head on his shoulder. "I can't believe you'd take us all in and take care of us."

"Believe it. I'll always take care of you. I want you safe, Nichole. I want all of you to be safe."

"I don't think my life is in any danger."

"No, but someone is messing with you, and I feel better having you close. Let me be manly and protect you."

He felt her laugh against his chest as she rested her head there. "They have a pool going at the *Mecca* you know."

"I heard. I'll give you fifty to add to it, you choose the date."

She stiffened but didn't move. "Let's not discuss that right now. If their gleeful giggles cease in a few days because they've been uprooted again..."

"You'll move back to town. I know."

He held her there, both of them understanding that what was between them was only a small part of the puzzle. The kids and their feelings would always come first, even if it caused the demise of what they had for each other.

When the kids finally tired of the hammock, they climbed out, and both boys took care to carry Laura to the porch, where she finally wiggled away from them.

"Mom said we're going to be staying here," Zane said shooting a stare at Ben. "Are we really?"

"We were going to try that out. Do you think that'll be okay?"

Zane exchanged looks with Wyatt. "You live really far away from our school and our friends."

"I do. But you only have a few more weeks of school. Summers are pretty fun out here."

"How long are we going to stay?"

Ben noticed Nichole ready herself to jump into the conversation. "Well, I'm not really sure," Ben began. "You boys feeling up to a manly talk? Both of you and me?"

Now they all looked toward Nichole, whose lips had pursed.

"Why don't you girls get settled. The boys and I are going to take a walk," Ben decided before she could say no.

"Ben..."

He knew the next words she was going to speak. That said a lot, didn't it? When a man had that power, then they'd moved past casual and falling in love. They'd dived into it whole-heartedly.

He gave her a nod that told her he'd protect them. He knew talking man to man would ease some of their fears as well.

Ben started off the porch, and eventually, Zane and Wyatt caught up to him, one on each side. He kept walking in silence for a few more moments gathering his thoughts, but Wyatt helped pave the way for his conversation.

"Mom said she's your girlfriend. Is that why we're staying out here?"

Well, that would give them a place to start, Ben thought. "It's one of the reasons I offered. Do you know what identity theft is?"

Zane shrugged. "They say it on TV."

"They do. It's a serious crime."

Wyatt picked up a rock and threw it out into the pasture. "Did Mom do a crime?"

Ben smiled easily. "No. I can't imagine your mother committing a crime. But someone is using her name and all of her money. So right now, we thought it would be best if you all came out here until things get sorted out."

Zane stopped. "Someone stole all of Mom's money? She said she'd take us to Disney World someday."

"I can see where that would be worrisome," Ben agreed. "That part is all temporary. She'll get her credit cards back, they just had to freeze them for a bit until they can issue her new ones. But she will have to save money again, and if you're all out here, that'll help."

They stopped at the fence overlooking the pasture. Each boy climbed up a rung until they were as tall as Ben, and the three of them stood there looking out over the cattle.

He noticed the boys exchanging glances as if they had something to say too.

A moment later, Zane turned toward Ben. "We told Mom it was okay if you marry her."

Ben froze at that moment, staring out over the land he loved so dearly and taking in what the boys were saying to him. He absolutely hadn't expected them to say that at all.

"She didn't mention that to me."

"We wanted her to know it was okay. We like you, Ben."

The smile was instantaneous. "I like you guys too. I guess we'll see how things go, and if I do decide, well, if your mom and I decide that getting married sounds like the right thing to do, I'll talk to you guys first."

He watched as they both took in that information and let it process.

"You know, my brothers Dane and Russell think we need a treehouse out here. What do you guys think?"

A unison, "Yeah!" was the answer.

"They'll be happy to hear that. I really think they want a tree house. Ours came down years ago." Ben stepped away from the fence. "I suppose we should go back to the house. We brought most of your things out here. We'll go back and get your beds tomorrow. For tonight, we have blow-up beds that my mom sent."

"It'll be like camping," Wyatt said, kicking up dirt.

"Sort of," he agreed as they walked back toward the house. He supposed the next part of the evening would deal with where Nichole would sleep. He'd have to not be disappointed when she resigned to sleep somewhere else.

The boys ran up the back steps of the house and pushed open the back door. He heard the delighted squeals from Laura before he ever saw her face. She reached for her brothers and pulled them into the house.

He took a moment to appreciate the scene from outside the house. A mother and her three children with their faces smiling. There was hope there. There was love there.

It looked much different than the scene in her kitchen that morning when she looked mad with delusions of running away with her children.

Ben walked to the back door and leaned against the jamb. He thought about his talk with the boys, and their talk with him. Warmth spread in his chest when he thought about them telling Nichole she could marry him. A smile formed on his mouth as he watched the boys run in and out of their new bedroom. They liked him. They'd take him on as a part of this close union. It was something to be proud of, that was for sure.

It would certainly change the dynamics of the little house out in the country.

"What are you doing out here?" Nichole walked into the kitchen and looked at him standing there watching.

"I'm just taking it all in."

"It's overwhelming, isn't it? It's too much for you?" she asked as concern masked her face.

Holding his hand to her, she took it, and he pulled her to him. "Your boys said I could marry you."

Her eyes went wide and then quickly softened as she placed her hands on his chest. "They told you that?"

"They did. And I suppose I just broke the cardinal rule of not sharing man talk."

She eyed him carefully. "They told me that too. But don't get anything into your head, Ben Walker. You just took on a whole family, and they haven't melted down yet. But they will."

"I've thrown a few temper tantrums in my life. I know it's not a permanent thing. But I won't rush into anything. I'm just enjoying the moment. They trust me with their best girl. It means a lot to me."

Nichole rested her head on his chest. "It means a lot to me too. I love you, Ben. Had I ended up on the road tonight taking them away, I'd have missed you like crazy."

He lifted her chin with his finger, and her eyes rose to meet his. "There is never a reason to take them away or to run. I will be here to help you with anything. I love you."

34

As the sun rose, and the light filtered through the curtains, Ben reached for Nichole, only to find her side of the bed cold and empty. He sat up and searched for his phone to check the time. It was only five-thirty.

He laid there a moment longer and listened to the silent house. It didn't seem as if anyone else was up, so where had she gone?

Pulling on his pajama bottoms, he ran his fingers through his tousled hair and walked toward the living room. There he found the most precious of sights. Nichole lay sleeping on the couch with Laura sprawled out on her chest. On the floor was one of the mattresses, and both boys.

Had he missed their cries in the night? Did they come for her while she was sleeping in his arms? He knew that had been a touchy subject for her, as he'd have expected it to be. Ben was a single guy. He didn't have to think about what was in the heads or hearts of others, but she did. No matter that they had given their permission for her to marry him, it still had to be strange waking in a different house and having their mother sleeping with a man that wasn't their father.

The thoughts in his head swirling around that topic were making him dizzy.

Tiptoeing around the family, he walked to the kitchen to start a pot of coffee. He'd wanted to take the boys to the chicken coop and let them gather the eggs and feed the chickens. Would they want to see how a day on the ranch started? Was it of any interest?

Picking up the coffee pot, he carried it to the sink and filled it with water. As he poured the water into the maker, he noticed movement in the doorway. When he looked up, Nichole stood there in a tank top and shorts with her hair piled up on her head. How was it she could be so sexy looking just like that.

"You're up early," she whispered.

"Not out here I'm not." He pulled a filter from the cabinet and placed it in the maker before spooning ample heaps of coffee in. "Looks like you all had a slumber party."

Nichole looked back at the sleeping children. "Laura usually wakes around one. I had gotten up to check on her, and she wanted to sleep with me, so we slept on the couch. About two, Wyatt had to go to the bathroom, so he dragged his bed out to where we were. I don't think Zane joined us until about four."

He laughed as he pressed the brew button. "I can't believe I didn't hear any of that."

"I was hoping you wouldn't. We didn't want to wake you."

"I wouldn't have minded." He held out his hand to her, and she moved to him, wrapping her arms around him. "I want to take them to my parents' house when they wake up and feed the chickens and gather eggs. Do you think they would want to do that?"

"I'm sure they would. I'll get ready so that..."

"No. Let me take them. Just me."

She leaned back and looked up at him. "You don't want me to go?"

"I think it would be good for us. Let's see how Laura does."

He watched as she worried her bottom lip. "I guess I won't be too far away. Are you sure?"

"I am. You take the little bit of time and enjoy yourself on the patio, or in the hammock. I have some books on the shelf in my bedroom if you want to read something." The look of hesitation in her eyes stung, but if her kids were going to be part of his life, he wanted to spend some time with them—alone. He lifted his hand to her cheek. "Why are you so worried?"

"I'm worried about everything, Ben."

"Don't be. Day by day and we'll get through it. All of us —together."

She sank into him, resting her head on his shoulder. "How is your bathtub?" she asked, and he chuckled as he ran his hands over her back.

"Neglected."

"I think I'll give it some attention while you're all gone."

Ben pressed a kiss to the top of her head.

"That sounds like a plan."

IT DIDN'T TAKE much effort to get the kids up to help with chores. Ben was sure the newness of that would wear off by the following weekend. But for now, he'd enjoy the chatter in the back of Nichole's car as he drove toward his parents' house. His mother had texted him that she'd made fresh cinnamon rolls. Gathering eggs and feeding chickens had never been so enticing.

Growing up, the chores would have had to have been done before cinnamon rolls were consumed, but Ben found it inter-esting that the kids could eat, have orange juice, and run through the yard before the chores were started. What had happened to his mother, he wondered over the brim of his coffee mug. How had she gone so soft?

He knew the answer, of course. Grandmothers were always softer when it came to the rules than they were when they were mothers raising kids. Even his own grandmother would bend a rule once in a while, he humored as he sipped from his mug.

"Egg basket," Laura said as she ran up to him with an old Easter basket in her hands. In the bottom was a towel, and she pointed to it.

"Are you ready to go get eggs?"

She nodded and reached for his hand. The gesture tugged at his heart and when he watched those dark eyes bat long lashes up at him, he felt his insides melt. Oh, taking on these kids was going to be harder than he thought. He was going to be as soft as his mother.

Zane was fearless when it came to the chickens. He had no problem sticking his hand under a hen and coming out with the egg. Wyatt, on the other hand, would much rather have the coop empty before he touched one of those smelly, sticky, dirty eggs. Laura had screamed for Ben to pick her up and hold her the moment his mother opened the door to the coop. She was mixed between screaming when a chicken would come near Ben, and laughing when he handed her an egg for her basket.

In the end, there had only been one egg fatality, and that had been his own doing. The boys asked to go again, and Laura nodded in agreement as they drove back out to his place.

He laughed as he listened to the boys talk about how easy the chore had been. Oh, maybe he'd make them country kids after all.

As he turned up the road to his house, he noticed a car in the driveway. A moment later, Zane was unbuckled and hanging over the back of his seat.

"Why are the police at your house?" Zane asked.

He recognized Phillip's car, so it shouldn't worry him that a friend had stopped by. But something in his gut said this wasn't a friendly visitation.

35

*B*ecause Ben knew it was Phillip that would be sitting at his kitchen table with Nichole, he didn't feel the need to protect the kids. Phillip would use discretion in anything that he said or did.

As he pushed open the door to the kitchen, from the patio, he saw Phillip raise his coffee mug to his lips, give him a nod, then sip. The boys hesitated, looking at the police officer sitting at the kitchen table.

"Hello, boys," Phillip said.

"Hi," they muttered in unison.

"Is that a real badge?" Zane asked.

"Sure is. Want to touch it?"

Zane nodded and moved right to Phillip reaching out his finger to put it on the badge. Once he'd done it, then Wyatt followed.

"You didn't have this on at the wedding," Wyatt said.

"No, it was in my pocket that night. I was a guest, even if I was watching out for everyone," Phillip said, smiling at the curious boys.

They turned their attention to their mother to relay their

stories about their morning with the chickens and the cinnamon rolls. Though her shoulders were tense, Ben admired how she gave the kids her full attention.

"You sound like you had a very busy morning," she said as she lifted Laura onto her lap. "You know what. I think you guys deserve some Disney Channel for being so good. Did you know Ben had that?"

Zane looked up at Ben. "You watch the Disney Channel?"

He chuckled. "I just love me some Mickey Mouse," he said as Nichole maneuvered the kids to the other room. Then the mood grew serious as he looked at Phillip. "What's going on?"

"Let's wait till she gets back in here. We need to talk."

Ben clenched his jaw and walked to the cabinet for a mug and poured himself some coffee. He stood leaning against the counter until Nichole came back into the kitchen and sat at the table.

She looked over her shoulder and nodded for Ben to join them at the table. Slowly, he moved to them and took the open chair.

Phillip leaned in over the table, his mug between the palms of his hands. "I've already talked to Nichole, and she knows what's going on. For the sake of the kids, we need to talk low, and be calm."

Ben wasn't sure that was even possible at this point. "Something's going on with the identity theft, right? You found out who's doing it?"

Phillip ran his fingers over the top of his mug. "They arrested her father yesterday on fraud charges."

Ben looked at Nichole who wiped tears from her eyes.

"I don't understand. I thought they stole his identity too."

Phillip nodded. "They did. But not before they caused a lot more problems. Whoever they are. And that's why I'm here now. I'm taking Nichole in."

He felt the rage rise from the pit of his stomach and burst in his head. Had Nichole not sent him a look of warning, he'd have flipped the table with that rage.

"I don't understand. Is this because of the kids?"

Nichole rested her hand on Ben's. "No. Whoever stole my identity has defrauded a company my father was once part of. He retired years ago, but somehow it all leads back to him —and me."

"But you didn't do this," he said it with a hint of questioning, though he knew deep down in his heart she would never do anything to deceive anyone—except to take her kids.

Sweat beaded on his brow and he wiped it away with the back of his hand.

Nichole gave his hand a squeeze. "Phillip is going to take care of all this. Gerald knows a lawyer, and he's going to call her for me."

"Ella Mills?" he asked knowing full well that if Gerald was involved, he'd call Ella even if Ben didn't understand why Gerald would even give her a chance. Perhaps Ben felt more jaded that she'd once turned down his brother's marriage proposal than Gerald did himself.

Phillip sipped his coffee. "Yeah, Ella has some background in all of this. I have to process her, and we'll get her back. But she's going to have to post bail."

"She didn't do anything."

"I know that, and you know that, but the trail ahead of her doesn't say that at all," Phillip argued.

Ben glanced at Nichole, who looked out into the living room where all three kids sat on the couch watching some show he'd never seen before. Why didn't she look worried? If she was wrongly accused, wouldn't she be freaking out? He was.

When she turned back to him, her eyes settled on his. "I need your help with them. I have nowhere else to turn. They need to stay with you," she pleaded and then he heard her voice break under it all.

"They live here now. That isn't going to change." Turning back to Phillip, he bore a stare into his friend. "How much is bail?"

"Two thousand."

"We'll get it together. What about her dad's?"

"Her mother already posted his. He's out. Now we just need to find the S.O.B. who's behind all of this," Phillip said.

"And where is your ex-husband?" He'd turned his attention back to Nichole, but her eyes filled and she didn't answer before Phillip did.

"M.I.A. We're looking for him."

"That's a little sketchy," Ben offered. "He just disappears when all of this happens?"

"We're looking at it from all angles." Phillip finished off his coffee. "We need to go."

Nichole wiped her eyes. "You're not going to handcuff me, are you?"

"No need for that. Just tell the kids you're going to ride with me into town. When y'all get everything together, you can come get her. I won't let her out of my sight until then," Phillip promised.

"It will be better if I tell them I'm leaving than to just sneak out the back," Nichole said as she stood, pushing her chair back.

They watched as she went to them, kissing each of them on the top of the head. "I have to run into town, and Officer Smythe is going to drive me. You all come with Ben later and pick me up, okay?"

Laura stood on the couch and gave her mother a tight hug before plopping right back down between her brothers to continue watching TV.

Wyatt looked up at her. "Why do you have to go to town?"

"Always something to do in town, right? You guys stay here with Ben."

Wyatt studied his mother for a moment and then agreed with a nod.

She walked back to the kitchen. "I have to get my purse from the car, and then I'm ready," she said.

Phillip walked out of the kitchen through the back door, and Ben reached for Nichole's arm before she followed.

"I don't like this," he whispered.

"I don't like it much either. But it is what it is, and I can't fight it. I didn't do anything wrong, Ben. You have to believe that."

"I do. But now I'm worried about you."

She pressed her cheek to his. "So am I. Come get me," she said as she slipped by him and out to her car. She pulled her purse from the back seat and then climbed into the front seat of Phillip's car.

36

*B*en had quickly learned the art of being stealthy around children. Even though they'd had plenty of cinnamon rolls, they'd wanted a snack. Laura had wanted to use the potty, and that was a lesson in itself. Thank goodness his mother had talked to Gerald and headed straight out to his house.

It did something to his heart to see the kids jump up and run to her, even though they had only seen her a few hours earlier. They loved her, and it was evident in how they circled her and talked all at once.

"You know Lucas and his sister are coming over to the house. Would you all like to come?" she asked and Laura held up her arms for his mother to pick her up.

"Mom, are you sure?" Ben asked, and she nodded.

"We are going to use the chalk on the driveway. Lucas called me to tell me he got a new box," she said in a calm tone, which he had to assume was for his own benefit. "Then Lucas' grandpa said we could make hotdogs on the grill for lunch."

Zane shot up a finger. "I like lots of ketchup."

"I remember," she said.

Wyatt moved in closer to her. "When Ben marries our mommy, can we call you Grandma and Lucas' grandpa can be our grandpa?"

Ben felt his heart stop for a moment, and noticed that his mother's eyes had quickly gone wide and then gentle again. "Well, I suppose that would be the way of it if that's how things happened. Let's see what plays out. C'mon, you can all climb into my car and I'll take you to my house."

He watched her walk out to the car without another word to him and load up the kids into her car.

She was wise and sneaky, that mother of his. He'd put a reminder in his phone to ask Gia to find something nice for him to give her as a thank you gift. It seemed as if his mother was there to save his ass.

As soon as his mother's car was out of sight, he sat down at his kitchen table and began making calls.

The bail money wasn't going to be a problem. They could secure that, and he'd started the process of making that happen first. Next, he called Gerald.

"I hear you put in a phone call to Ella for us. That's mighty big of you to do," Ben said as he rubbed the tension from his forehead.

"Just because a woman turns down your marriage proposal and starts dating your best friend the next week, it doesn't mean you can't give her credit for being a great lawyer. She can help, Ben."

"I appreciate it. Mom just took the kids to her house and I'm headed into town to post Nichole's bail."

He heard the sigh from his brother. "This is a messed-up situation. I've never heard of someone getting arrested because their identity was stolen. I guess it happens, but..."

"Yeah, well someone is going to pay for this," Ben promised

as he finished his phone call with his brother, gathered his checkbook, and his keys before heading into town.

His phone rang as he passed from the gravel to the paved road. Pulling his phone from his pocket, he noticed Audrey's face on the screen.

"What's up, cuz?"

"My manager was arrested? What the hell is going on, Ben?" Her voice echoed in his head.

"Yes, but it's all a big mistake. Someone stole her identity and her father's identity. It's gotten out of hand. We have a lawyer, and Phillip had to take her in, but he's on her side, Audrey. She didn't do anything wrong."

"Her ex-husband gambles. Does this have anything to do with him?"

"I thought that too. But it doesn't seem to be leading to him, yet anyway. I'm headed into the station now. I'll have her touch base with you when everything is taken care of."

Ben pulled into the parking lot of the police station next to the familiar silver BMW of Ella Mills. Gerald was right, she'd be able to help, however, Ben still held tight to the anger he had for the woman. Ben knew it was stupid to feel the way he did about her. After all, his brother was the one that had been miserably dumped, but Ben held that grudge. He figured this was as good a time as any to get over it. If the woman could help clear Nichole's name, then Ben could certainly let go of any resentment.

When he walked into the station, he could see Ella sitting in the conference room with Nichole. She'd been crying, and that tore him to bits.

"Ben."

He turned when he heard his name called and walked toward Phillip, who stood in the doorway to his office.

"I have her bail," Ben said as he walked toward Phillip.

Phillip only nodded. "Yeah, well, we will talk about that in a bit. Come sit down."

Ben tucked his hands into the front pockets of his jeans when he realized they were shaking.

Phillip walked around to the back of his desk, motioning to Ben to shut the door before taking a seat.

"What's going on?" Ben asked as he sat down across from Phillip in the tiny office that had him sucking in a breath because it was claustrophobic with its tiny window and wood paneling.

"You haven't had any calls or visitors, have you?"

Ben stared at him, not able to piece together his question. "No. Why?"

Pushing a piece of paper across the desk, Phillip leaned in and steepled his fingers. "This is an invoice from Gia's store."

Ben picked it up and looked it over. It was for a set of custom made glasses, and the name on the order was Nichole Lewis. On the receipt was a copy of the signed credit card slip with Nichole's signature.

"What is this? This is dated yesterday."

Phillip nodded. "Yeah."

"Nichole was at my house all day yesterday. Well, after she got off work." He looked at the receipt again. "This receipt was made at one o'clock in the afternoon. Nichole was at work."

"Yeah, well, I have it on good authority that she had a client in her chair at one o'clock," he said running his fingers over his newly cropped hair. "Our identity thief was in Gia's store while I was sitting in Nichole's chair."

"Why didn't Gia catch this?"

"Sunshine was helping her out for the day. Nichole Lewis is a common enough name. Gia caught it this morning."

"Video. Gia's store has cameras."

"And the woman had on a large hat. You can't see her face,"

Phillip said as he sat back in his chair. "I'm going to let Nichole go, but as long as she's with you the whole time. Keep the bail money. Who knows, you might need it later for something else."

"Why is she talking to Ella then?"

"Because when they find out who this person is, they're going to go after her."

That brought some joy to him. It seemed as if they were closer to cracking down on this maniac. But the fact that she was in town, and as close as she was didn't sit well with him. If this woman who was impersonating Nichole was bold enough to follow her within a few feet, what was she capable of?

Phillip stood and Ben followed. "I want you to keep her in your sights. When she goes into work, Audrey will keep an eye on her. I've already talked to her."

"I'm not very comfortable with her in this situation."

"The two of you can work it out then. But I don't want her alone."

"What about her ex-husband. I'm still worried about him finding her."

Phillip ran the back of his hand under his chin, brushing it against the stubble that had been obviously unshaven for days. "He's M.I.A. right now."

"Well, crap. If this woman found her, he could find her too."

"We've got ears to the ground and we're not going to let him get to her or the kids. Ben, nothing is going to happen to her."

"You can't promise that."

"No, I can't. But I sure as hell will do everything in my power to make sure that's the case."

What more could he ask for? Phillip was a man of his word, and Ben knew that. But no one was going to hurt the woman Ben loved, or the children he loved. If it came down to it, he'd pack up his own life and hit the road too. Nichole would never be without him, and that he could promise her, and he would.

37

*B*en waited for Nichole in the hallway. Not letting her out of his sight started right now, he thought. He'd called his mother as well and let her know about the woman at Gia's store. She promised to keep the kids within reach at all times, and his father and his brothers were going to be very vigilant against anyone on the property.

It was another twenty minutes before he watched Nichole stand and hug Ella. Even from out in the hallway, Ben could see how red her eyes were from the tears she'd shed.

When she opened the door and saw him there, she smiled. "What are you doing here? Where are the kids?"

"My mom and dad have them. They're okay, I just talked to her. I came in to get you, and it seems as if you're off the hook."

She fidgeted with the wadded-up tissue in her hand. "Well, they don't think I've been defrauding anyone. But I don't see that I'm off the hook. The woman was in Gia's store. That means she's here, Ben."

He moved to her now and took her hand. "I know. And I can guarantee you that there are enough Walkers around town that are on the lookout, she won't get very far."

That was met with a smile as Ella walked out of the conference room and stopped. "Hello, Ben. It's been a long time."

He bit back his resentment because now wasn't the time for it. "Hello, Ella. Thank you for helping Nichole out. I really appreciate it."

"Anything for the Walkers. I was glad that Gerald called. I've promised Nichole that when we find this woman and any accomplices, we will prosecute and we won't be soft."

And that was the Ella he remembered. The small frame and sunny blonde hair was a false exterior, he'd always thought. She was ruthless and downright mean when she needed to be. Luckily, that was usually saved for those she was prosecuting, and for that he was grateful. This woman and anyone else involved would pay greatly.

"I appreciate that," Ben said and realized it might not have been his place to say it, but he meant it. He turned his attention back to Nichole. "Are you ready to go?"

She nodded. "Yes. I need to call my parents."

He took her hand, and they headed for the front door as Ella walked back to the conference room and gathered her things.

Ben could feel her shaking as he held her hand and they walked toward his truck. What could possibly be going on in that head of hers, he wondered and worried. He sure as hell hoped she wasn't even thinking about running again. But considering he didn't plan to leave her side until all of this was done, there was no way she'd be able to run without him.

He opened the door for her to climb into the truck, but they both stopped as Phillip ran down the steps of the station and toward them.

"You two better get back inside. We just got some news," he said quickly before waving them back toward the building and running inside.

NICHOLE EXCHANGED looks with Ben before taking his hand and following him back into the building. She wasn't sure she could handle much more. Her body ached, and her heart was sick with the thought that she and her parents were part of all of this. All she wanted to do was get back home to her babies. And if she needed to, they would leave in the middle of the night. No one was going to take her away from them again.

As they entered the building, Ella was walking from the conference room and heading toward Phillip's office.

Phillip sat behind his desk hitting keys on his computer.

"What's going on?" Ben asked as he and Nichole crossed into the office. "What news do you have?"

Phillip raised his eyes to Nichole. "Jerome Whittaker."

She felt the sweat bead up on her brow. "What about him?"

"Ex-husband?"

Ben squeezed her hand, and she exchanged a quick look with him before focusing back on Phillip. "Yes."

"He was arrested last night on embezzlement charges at the casino where he worked."

She wasn't sure what she was supposed to feel because the mad and elated were mixing in a fight that had her stomach tied up in knots. If he were locked away, where he belonged as far as she was concerned, then she was free to have her babies anywhere with her.

"So he's not the one who's been doing this to me, or at least he wasn't involved?"

Phillip turned the monitor of his computer to face them, and for the first time in a year, she saw the face of the man she'd once thought she'd loved. And at that moment, she knew she'd always been mistaken.

"That's him."

Phillip nodded and clicked the mouse to open another

screen. Another photo popped up, and Nichole sucked in a hard breath.

"Justine Meyers," she said as she studied the still shot that had been taken from a surveillance video of Jerome and Justine walking with their arms around each other.

Phillip sat back in his chair. "She turned him over to the police. She had all the evidence on him."

Nichole reached for the back of the chair in front of her, and then broke free from Ben's hand and sat down when her knees threatened to give out.

Ben moved in behind her and rested his hands on her shoulders. "And who is Justine Meyers? That picture doesn't look as if they're enemies."

Phillip ran his tongue over his teeth as he watched Nichole. Perhaps he was looking for her reaction, but she wasn't going to give him one. Justine Meyers was a thorn in her side and had been since she'd first left Jerome. She shouldn't have been surprised to see them together. Perhaps she was surprised that she'd rolled over on him and turned him in.

Phillip rested his arms on his desk and eased in. "You've had run-ins with Justine in the past, haven't you?" he asked, and she felt her skin break out in a cold sweat.

"Yes," she said flatly.

"She's the reason you didn't take your husband's last name."

Now she couldn't hold back the tears that were choking her. "How do you know that?"

"She's been involved with Jerome Whittaker since before you were married."

"So?"

"So, you knew that."

"And because my husband was never loyal to me and gambled everything away, this is my fault?"

"I didn't say that. I'm confirming that she's been around for a long time. She turned him in for the embezzlement, but records trace back to her as well. I think that's why she's on the run and I think she's running under your identity."

Nichole brushed away the tears that had fallen over her cheek as the mad broke through and she gritted her teeth.

"You think she's the one behind all of this?"

"It makes sense. You had what she wanted, right? Jerome Whittaker and his family. But you didn't want it enough to even take his name or give it to his children. That sounds like a solid reason to me."

Nichole turned and looked at Ben. With a nod he pulled his phone from his pocket. "I'll call Mom again and check on the kids," he said as he turned and stepped out into the hallway.

Nichole looked at Phillip. "But you don't know that it's her."

"I called Sunshine and asked her to come in and look at the picture. The cameras in the store might not have a good shot of her face, but she might be able to identify her. And if it is her, then we know who we're looking for."

Nichole placed her hand on her chest and took in a long, slow breath. Could it be possible that the woman who had caused her so much pain through the years was the one causing it now? If she'd somehow framed Jerome for the embezzlement at the casino, then why did she need to go after the measly savings of a single mother? And how in the hell had she found her?

Then again, that last question was probably easy enough to determine. If she'd been able to get into her parents' accounts, then she probably could have easily learned where Nichole had landed.

Ben placed his hand on her shoulder again when he entered the room. "Mom says they are all together and fine. The house is full of people, she said. My brothers won't let anyone get near them."

Phillip reached his hand across the desk and placed it on hers. "Why don't the two of you head home. I'll let you know what I find out from Sunshine."

Nichole nodded and stood. "Thank you all for everything you're doing to help me. I don't know how all of this followed me here or why someone would want to do this to me and my family."

Ella reached her hand out and touched her arm. "They're criminals for a reason. They don't have a conscience. And if it is her, she won't get away with it," she promised.

Nichole took Ben's hand and let him lead her back to the truck.

"Are you okay?" he asked as he opened the door for her.

"None of this makes sense, Ben. I know he wasn't on the up and up, ever, but this is beyond him."

"It seems as if he could be easily persuaded then. Let's not worry about it for the rest of the day. Let's get the kids and get home."

Turning, she wrapped her arms around him and pressed her cheek to his chest. "I love you, Ben. You need to know that no matter what happens with all of this, I love you."

He pressed a kiss to the top of her head. "Oh, Nichole, I love you too. And all of this doesn't mean anything, and you know that. It's a bump in the road of the rest of our lives."

Looking up at him she could read that truth in his eyes. "Do you really mean it? The rest of our lives?"

Brushing his thumb over her cheek, he pressed a gentle kiss to her lips. "I have permission, you know. When seven-year-olds give you permission to spend the rest of your life with their mother, you take that very seriously."

Nichole smiled. "The sooner we can make this go away, the better then. It sounds like there's so much more out there for us."

"You can guarantee it."

Nichole climbed into the truck and Ben closed the door before walking around to the other side and jumping in.

As they stopped at the stop sign, Nichole looked out the window to see Ella get into her car, and another car pulled out of a space and followed them through the stop. Sunday afternoon at the police department was a busy time, she thought as she closed her eyes and rested her head back against the seat.

38

*S*leep didn't come that night. Nichole found herself sitting in the hallway outside her children's bedroom while they slept. Her mind raced in a million different directions. Jerome was in jail, and it wasn't just going to be for a night or two. This was a big-time felony now, but it eased the worry from her taking the kids. Ella said they'd work to get the wording in the divorce agreement changed so that she not only had full custody, but she could go anywhere at any time with them, and he couldn't say a word.

Of course, had that been all she'd learned that day, she'd be sleeping like a baby. But the fact that Phillip had called to inform them that Sunshine confirmed the woman's identity, that had her up wandering the house and sitting in the hallway.

There was no doubt in her mind that Justine Meyers was the person who had stolen her identity. With the help of Jerome, she'd have had a lot of information to go on. But again, why? Of all the people Justine could have stolen from, why chose someone who didn't have anything?

It wasn't worth arguing that in her head. She knew exactly why Justine would do such a thing. Oh, she might have always been in the picture, even when Jerome and Nichole were married, but she'd never been the one Jerome chose over anyone else. Justine was always the other woman.

Nichole might not have much, but she had more than Justine Meyers ever would. She had a life she had built all by herself. She had three incredible kids and a family that loved and supported her. And, if she was really in town and had been for any length of time, then she knew Nichole also had the love of a good man from a good family. That had to drive Justine insane with jealousy.

"What are you doing sitting out here?" Ben's sleep-filled voice stirred her from her thoughts.

She looked up to see him standing in the doorway in a pair of shorts. They'd become so comfortable together, and she found that kind of comfort extremely sexy.

"I couldn't sleep. I have a lot on my mind," she offered as he moved toward her and sat next to her on the floor. "Go back to bed. You don't have to sit here with me."

"I told you that you'd never be alone. I'm keeping my word," he said as he gathered her hand in his. "Are you nervous about this woman being in town? The kids could all sleep in our room with us, or we can pack up and go. Your call."

Nichole rested her head on his shoulder. "You're too good to me."

"You deserve it."

But she wasn't so sure. "That woman always wanted my husband. And she had him, so I'm not sure why she's got to do this to me. I worked hard for everything I had. Why would she want to take that from me?"

Ben rubbed his hand down her bare arm. "People like that don't understand what you've accomplished. They want everything easy."

"What I don't understand is why she wasn't arrested when she turned over Jerome. They know she was part of it."

Ben kissed her temple. "She'll get what she has coming to her. And you'll get what you deserve too."

Nichole turned her head to gaze into Ben's sleepy eyes. "And what's that?"

"A man who loves you and your children."

She was sure she'd never tire of hearing such a thing.

NICHOLE FIGURED it would take a lot of getting used to, leaving her child at the ranch, even if it was with Ben and his mother.

Tuesday morning, she drove the boys into town to school. They only had one week left, and she'd be happy when that was over. She'd walked them into the school and proceeded to the office where she let them know what had been going on recently.

In her heart, she wondered if taking them to school was the right thing, but if she didn't, they'd miss a field day, and assembly, and all the special events that kids had on the last days of school. Moving to Georgia was supposed to give them a normal life. She could never have imagined that it would have her scared and wanting to run again.

The school staff gave their word that they would keep the boys safe. There was no reason to assume otherwise. She'd arranged to pick them up at the end of the day and take them back to work with her. She'd be more comfortable when they were all back together.

The salon buzzed with hair dryers and gossip as Nichole walked through the door. Each of the girls waved as she walked toward the back to store her bag, but Audrey's eyes were cool on her.

Nichole stored her bag in her locker, poured herself a mug of coffee, and pulled the towels out of the dryer and began to fold them.

"What the hell is going on in your life?" Audrey asked as she walked into the room.

"Some crap followed me to Georgia I guess. It won't interfere with my work. I promise."

She saw the quick flash of anger in Audrey's eyes before she noticed how dark they looked as if she hadn't slept in days. "I'm not worried about your work. I'm worried about you. I think we've well moved past the boss/employee relationship. I'm worried about you as a friend and a potential family member. So, what's going on?"

Nichole piled towels on the table. "I just have had crap luck with a man in my past, and it just so happens that the woman he had on the side has a psycho streak."

"A psycho streak is damn right. I mean stealing all your money and taking an expensive vacation is one thing. But showing up here, that's where she goes psycho."

"Sunshine confirmed it was her. Now we have to keep an eye open."

"I won't lie. I'm a little freaked out. We had three walk-ins this morning alone, right after we opened. Don't think I wasn't comparing faces to the picture that Phillip sent over."

A smile tugged at the corners of Nichole's mouth when she thought about Phillip sending out a picture of Justine to ensure everyone kept their eyes open. How had Nichole gotten so lucky to fall into a town where everyone looked out for one another, and treated her like family.

"I can't imagine she'll stick around."

"You remember that Gregory had a stalker? Yeah, you assume they'll just go away, but they don't. Just watch your step. I don't want anything to happen to you. I need you."

"I'm not going anywhere." Nichole folded another towel and kept her eyes steady on Audrey. "Are you feeling okay? You look as if you haven't been sleeping."

Audrey smiled as she walked to the table, pulled out a chair, and sat down. "I'm not kidding when I say I need you. I'm going to need your word that you'll be around for the long haul."

"That's the plan."

"I'm going to need to take some time off," Audrey said as she took a towel from the pile and folded it.

Nichole didn't like the way that sounded. She pulled out the chair in front of her and sat down. "What's going on? Are you sick? God, you don't have some disease, do you?"

That had Audrey laughing. "I feel sick. I feel horrible, but it's not a disease."

"Don't leave me in suspense. What's going on?"

Audrey leaned her arms on the table and eased in closer to Nichole. "I'm going to need to take a maternity leave."

Nichole heard her, but it took a moment to register. When it did register, Nichole was to her feet and pulling Audrey up and out of her chair.

"Oh my God! You're pregnant!"

"Shhhh." Audrey laughed. "I'm not telling the girls yet."

"I should have known. I should have seen the signs."

"Your mind has been occupied with sleeping with my cousin and losing all your money."

For the first time, Nichole could laugh at her situation. "If you promise not to have an intervention again, I'll tell you all about my relationship with your cousin now."

Audrey smiled. "You're in love, that's all I need to know. It's written all over your face."

Nichole stepped back and placed her hands on her cheeks. "All over?"

"All over."

"I do love him. I can't say I wanted to. I just liked the attention he was giving me, and there was something to how it flustered him to do so. But he makes me feel like no other man ever has. He'd take care of me, and my children. He loves my children."

"He's a good man. I've told you that."

"He is, and I know how fortunate I am that he loves me."

Audrey's smile grew wider. "He's told you that?"

"He has."

"Well, don't go thinking that you can have time off for maternity leave until I get back from mine," she joked, and Nichole let out a long breath.

"That's not in my plans right now."

"Oh, it will be. Especially if it involves a Walker man from that side of the family. They're tight."

"I know."

"And Glenda loves her grandkids."

That statement warmed Nichole from head to toe. "She loves my kids too. She's watching Laura today."

"They make her happy, Nichole."

Both women turned when the bell over the door rang. "I'll bet that's the start of my day," Nichole said gathering the folded stack of towels from the table. "I won't say anything about your condition," she whispered as she walked out of the room and heard Audrey's laugh carry on the air behind her.

39

*H*e was grateful that his mother had wanted to take Laura because Ben had an itch to go into town. Nichole would probably be furious to know that he wanted to check up on her, but he couldn't help it. He didn't like the thought of the boys being at school, or Nichole being at work.

There was no need for her to work, he thought as he crossed from the gravel road to the paved one. Nichole could stay home with her children and raise them. Wasn't that what every mother wanted? It was what his father had wanted for his mother.

Maybe that was old-fashioned thinking. Of course, it was. When he thought of the women in his family, he was sure that even if Nichole didn't argue the fact, they would.

He was surrounded by strong-minded, and willed women who forged their own paths. His cousins were business owners and investors in the community. All of them. And the women his brothers and cousins had married were equally strong-minded and willed.

Perhaps that was why he fell so hard and so quickly for

Nichole. She was as strong as all the women in his family combined.

As he came to the end of the long road that would lead him to town, he saw a car on the shoulder with the hood up. Ben slowed and noticed a woman standing over the engine studying it.

Deciding it was the neighborly thing to do, he pulled up behind her, put his truck into park, and stepped out.

The woman, small in stature with dark hair pulled back in a ponytail, looked up at him through large dark glasses. "Hello," she said, her voice relaxed and a bit carefree.

"Hi. You having some engine problems?"

"Yep," she said with a thick southern accent. "I don't know the first thing about cars."

Ben looked at the engine, the woman leaning up against the car next to him. "I'll tell you what. I can give you a ride into town. My cousin owns a garage, and he could come out and get you back on the road."

"Really? You'd drive me in?"

"Sure," he offered as he stepped back from the car. He studied the woman who looked familiar, but he knew he'd never met her before. "Are you from nearby?"

"Just passing through. Checking out the lay of the land so that I can relocate."

Ben started back toward the truck. "Where are you from originally?"

"Here and there," the woman said as she opened the passenger door and climbed in. "You local?"

Ben slid in behind the wheel, closed his door, and nodded. "Lived here all my life."

As he started down the road toward Jake's, he watched the woman take a compact from her purse and apply lipstick. Her nails were painted pastel pink, and peeking out of her purse were a pair of pink and black eyeglasses.

He bit down firmly on his bottom lip. "You look as though you might have been on vacation recently. You have a sunny glow."

The woman smiled wide and licked her freshly glossed lips. "Just got back from a resort vacation. You're very observant."

Yeah, he thought. Not observant enough quickly enough, he cursed himself. He had just picked up Justine Meyers, he was sure of it. Her hair was colored the same color as Nichole's. The color on her nails matched the same color Nichole had on hers. And when he'd seen the glasses in her purse, he'd known who she was.

She didn't look like the photo Phillip had shown them anymore. It was quite obvious that she'd taken the stolen identity a bit too far.

He realized she'd asked him a question while his mind wandered to what he was going to do with her.

"I'm sorry, what?"

She smiled easily as she tucked everything back into her purse and set it at her feet. "Jake, that's your cousin, right?"

Ben shifted her a cautious look. "Did I tell you his name was Jake?"

Easily on a laugh, she tipped her head back. "Oh, Ben. I know everyone in your family."

The use of his name had his heart pounding in his chest. "And I didn't tell you my name either."

"You didn't have to." She reached her hand over to his thigh and pressed it there. "Don't act like you don't know who I am, Ben."

"I'm very sure we haven't met," he argued as he focused on the turn ahead.

Her hand lingered for another moment before she pulled it

back and crossed her arms in front of her. "I'll be very disappointed if you act like I'm not the woman you're sleeping with every night. I won't have you blowing me off."

"Listen, honey, I don't..." Those were the only words he got out before his vision blurred as something cracked him across the head.

He'd felt the jarring of the truck and the impact, but everything went black.

NICHOLE SITUATED the boys in the back room of the salon with after school snacks and her iPad with a new movie on it. She felt horrible that they were going to have to be there until seven o'clock.

When she had called Glenda, to check up on Laura, she had told Nichole that Ben was heading into town. He wasn't comfortable not being with her. Though she thought that was extremely romantic, she wondered where he really ended up. According to Glenda, that had been hours ago, and she hadn't seen him.

Then again, she'd been busy with clients one right after the other. She'd even managed to work in a haircut for Jake while another client was processing.

She had just started her next client when Phillip walked through the door and grabbed Audrey by the arm, escorting her out of the salon through the back door when he'd noticed the boys.

What on earth would have made him do that?

She kept an eye on the back room and listened, but she never heard another word. But when Audrey reappeared, all of the color had drained from her face.

Nichole excused herself from her client and hurried to her.

"You should sit down. What's wrong? You're pale." She tried

to move her to the back room, but Audrey shook her head. "I'm fine. I have Patty coming in. I just called her."

"Okay, what's going on? Are you sick?" She moved in closer to whisper. "Is the baby okay?"

A tear streaked down Audrey's cheek. "Phillip is out back waiting for you. He needs to talk to you. I'm going to work on your client and Patty will finish up for you tonight."

Now it was Nichole's turn to go flush. She felt the blood drain from her head and the room began to spin. Audrey took her by the arms and pulled her into the back room and dropping her into a chair. She looked at Wyatt. "Get your mom a glass of water," she demanded and then looked at Zane. "Open the back door and tell Officer Smythe to come in."

Nichole sipped the water when Wyatt handed it to her. She despised that his eyes were wide and she could see the worry in them.

"I'm okay, honey. I am," she assured him as she heard the door open and Phillip walk though.

"Nichole, are you okay?" She heard his voice before she saw his face as he knelt down in front of her.

"I'm fine. Audrey says you need to talk to me."

He nodded slowly looking at both of the boys.

Audrey smiled. "Boys, why don't you grab your iPad and come out in the salon with me. You can sit in the dryer chairs for a few minutes while your mom and Officer Smythe talk."

They hesitated until Nichole gave them a reassuring nod.

When they had left the room, Nichole lifted her head and looked Phillip in the eye. "Something bad happened. What's going on?"

"Let's take it one step at a time." He held her hand as he shifted to sit in the seat next to her. "You're okay?"

"I'm fine."

"I need to know if you've been here all day."

She could feel the tears stinging her eyes. "Yes. I took the boys to school and then came in. I only left to pick them back up from school and bring them here."

"I would assume that your schedule will verify that."

"My schedule. My clients. Audrey. Even Pearl and Lydia know I've been here."

He patted her hand before he sat back in his chair. "Then I can assume you weren't the woman who robbed the liquor store and shot the clerk in the stomach."

Nichole's hand came to her mouth and the tears that had only threatened, spilled. "She hurt someone?"

Phillip leaned in over the table. "More than just the clerk. The photo I showed you of her, well, she looks totally different."

"What does that mean?"

He pulled his phone from his pocket and scrolled. When he turned the phone around Nichole felt her head spin again. "Oh, God."

"I've talked to a few witnesses who claim you're the one they saw leaving the scene."

"That's not me."

Phillip tucked his phone back into his pocket. "I know. There is one more thing." Now he took her hands and held them in his. "We found a stolen car abandoned outside of town on the same road you would take to get to the Walker's ranch."

Nichole's pulse quickened and her breath caught in her lungs.

"My baby."

"She's fine. But we have reason to believe that Ben might have picked her up assuming she was having car problems."

At that Nichole fell toward him and gripped his shirt as she sobbed. "God, where is he? What did she do?"

"He's at the hospital. He was in an accident. It wasn't bad, but his truck went into the ditch. He has some head trauma, but the doctors say it's not life-threatening."

"I have to go to him. I have to see him."

"You need to be calm for your boys. Ben's dad is headed into town. He's going to meet us at the hospital and take the boys back to his house. Gerald and Eric are with Glenda and Laura. No one is going to leave the kids or you alone."

She was torn. No one should have her children but her, but then again, she'd trust no one but the Walkers to keep them safe. And of course, she wanted to be by Ben's side. That horrible, home-wrecking woman from her past had hurt the man she loved. And for what?

"He's okay?" she mumbled again against his chest.

"He's going to be just fine."

40

The boys were humored by the fact that they were riding in the back of a police car, but Nichole couldn't enjoy their banter. Why Phillip didn't have his sirens on was beyond her. This was an emergency. She needed to get to Ben.

When they arrived at the hospital, Phillip opened the locked back doors to let the boys out, and Nichole quickly grabbed hold of their hands.

"Now the two of you need to simmer down. Hospitals aren't for silliness."

Both sets of eyes were on her.

"Mom, is Ben okay?" Wyatt asked, and she couldn't even answer.

Phillip placed his hand on Wyatt's shoulder. "He's going to be fine. He lost control of his truck, and it crashed into a ditch. He's a little banged up. If the nurses let you see him, I'm sure he'd like to say hi. Then, his dad is going to take you back to his house to be with Laura."

Nichole exchanged a grateful glance with him.

"We get dessert when we eat dinner at their house," Zane informed him.

Phillip smiled as they began to walk into the hospital. "I know. I've eaten over there a few times. You're lucky boys."

They took the elevator to the floor that Phillip had said Ben was on. It made Nichole sick to think he'd been there for hours and she hadn't known what had happened.

Phillip checked in with the nurses and turned toward the boys. "She says you can have five minutes. His dad is in there now so you can go home with Mr. Walker after that."

She saw the fear in the boys' eyes now. They didn't know what to expect, and they loved the man they knew was just beyond the door. Maybe it wasn't a good thing for them to see him. What if he was worse than Phillip had said? Perhaps it was she that wasn't prepared, she thought as her knees threatened to buckle under her.

Phillip pushed open the door, and the two hands that Nichole held in hers squeezed hard when they saw Ben on the bed.

His face was cut up, and there was a bandage that covered his right eye.

Nichole sucked in the pain from seeing him. She willed herself to be brave, but she wasn't sure she had it in her.

Ben turned his head cautiously. "Hey there," he said, his voice raspy and weak. "It's my best guys."

The boys stopped their forward motion into the room as they both stood and stared at him.

"I look bad, huh?" he asked.

"Did you really wreck your truck?" Wyatt asked.

"I guess I did. I got a little beat up, but I'm okay. Actually, I'm better now that you guys are here," he said as he looked up at Nichole.

He studied her as if he were trying to read her, but she couldn't even imagine how she looked at him in that bed. He looked like that because of her—because her past followed her where she thought no one knew where she was.

"Are you boys hungry? I've heard that Susan and Mrs. Walker have been cooking dinner. And you know what that means?" Everett asked.

Zane smiled wide. "Dessert."

Everett laughed. "Mostly. But it means we eat like kings tonight. Are you both ready to head home?"

The words he chose squeezed at Nichole's heart. She couldn't deny that home was with the Walkers, no matter where that was.

The boys both agreed and took Everett's hands as they walked out of the room.

Phillip rested his hand on Nichole's shoulder. "I'll let you two have some time. I'll be back in shortly."

She kept her eyes on Ben as Phillip left the room and shut the door.

"You can come over here and touch me. I'm not that fragile," Ben offered holding his hand upward for her to take it.

She hesitated before taking the next step toward him. He looked horrible, but he was so brave, and she only wished she could be brave too. But the tears came, and they wouldn't stop.

How could she break down in front of him now? How childish and simple minded was it of her to be thinking of herself and not of him?

Nichole sat in the chair next to the bed and laid her head against him, and he placed his hand on her head. She sobbed until she thought the tears would run out, but they continued.

"This isn't your fault," he said. "I know that's what you're thinking."

Nichole lifted her head and wiped at her cheeks. "It is my fault. That woman was after me, and here she is hurting you."

"You didn't make her do this. You did nothing to provoke any of this. She's not right in the head, Nichole. Did you see what she did to her appearance? I think the reason she stole your identity is that she thinks she is you."

"She hurt you. She shot another person. Even Jerome is in jail because of her, but okay, he deserves that," she said and then let the small chuckle escape that followed. "I'm afraid she'll come after my babies and me next."

"No one, and I mean no one, will let her do that."

She knew that to be true. She'd let Everett Walker take her boys and leave, and her heart said it was the right thing to do.

"What did she do to you?" Nichole asked lifting her fingers to the bandage on his head and then retracting.

"I was giving her a ride to Jake's so he could go out and fix her car. She had big sunglasses on, and her hair pulled back. She didn't look like the woman in the picture Phillip had, nor did she look like you. But when she opened her purse, and I saw the glasses like yours, I knew who she was. I just knew. Then she started talking about being the woman I slept with at night and then she hit me with something. I think it was a gun." He winced. "Did you say she shot someone?"

"She robbed a liquor store and shot the clerk in the stomach. Witnesses thought it was me."

"No doubt."

"Ben, I didn't expect anything like this to happen. If I would have thought it was possible I wouldn't have gotten involved..."

"With me? Nichole, there were so many forces pushing us together, there was no way we wouldn't have ended up together. And let's add in there that fate played a big role in that. Why else would you have ended up at my cousin's?"

His optimism had her smiling. "She's not gone yet, Ben. I don't know what to do."

"Go on and live as normally as you possibly can."

She let out a snort. "Have you seen yourself? This isn't normal, Ben. Some man got shot today, and he thinks I did it."

"The world is a little crazy, Nichole. Trust me. My family has seen crazy in all forms. This is not something to stop us from living. In fact, it's only more proof that we need to keep on living and loving."

"She's still out there."

"But she won't be for long. She's already risked too much. And now she has all of these other charges to go with her embezzlement charges. Once Phillip gets his hands on her, she's not going to be a problem ever again."

Nichole rested her head against Ben again, and he stroked her hair. "When do you get out of here?"

"Maybe tomorrow. They said my wife could stay with me," he told her, and she lifted her head. "I'm just telling you what they told me. I didn't correct them. What they don't know won't hurt them."

"The kids..."

"Are fine with my parents. I'd really like you to stay."

Nichole contemplated the offer for only a moment and then rose to press a gentle kiss on Ben's lips. "I want to stay too."

41

*T*he phone call from Audrey filled Nichole with a million different emotions. She was angry, hurt, spiteful, gracious, thrilled. It all stirred in her belly until she was nearly sick.

Audrey laid it out and told her that until Justine Meyers was behind bars, Nichole was to stay away from the salon. She'd even make sure she was paid in advance if she needed it. But she wanted her to stay clear.

And the sentiment hadn't only come from Audrey. She'd received texts from Pearl, Bethany, Gia, and Lydia too. She realized she could be angry that everyone was pushing her out of her own life, or she could be grateful that everyone loved her enough to have her back.

Ben sat on the couch with Laura tucked up against him and the boys seated in the floor watching the Cars movie. Nichole had decided that there was no need for them to finish out the last week of school if it meant they had to be away from her.

Susan had stocked the refrigerator, and even though she claimed it was leftovers from a catering she'd done, Nichole was sure she'd cooked just for them. Either way she was grateful.

Phillip had sent word that the liquor store clerk was fine. He'd be released from the hospital soon. Unfortunately, when shown two photos, one of Nichole and one of Justine, he couldn't differentiate which one was the woman who had robbed him and shot him.

For the rest of the week, Nichole bided her time as a house-wife, Ben had joked. She'd cleaned every inch of the house and weeded his garden. She and the kids had gone over to Glenda's every morning and gathered eggs and fed the chickens. There was plenty to keep her busy, but she could feel the need to be around people buzzing through her veins and it was driving her mad. How much longer did they expect her to hide from that crazy woman? She'd go berserk first.

Luckily Ben had a doctor's appointment. It would be an excuse to go into town, maybe stop by the *Bridal Mecca* and say hello. Lucas was supposed to spend the day with his grandpar-ents, so naturally they invited Nichole's kids to join them.

She wasn't sure how she'd ever repay Ben's entire family for everything they did for her.

Once the kids were dropped off at his parents' house, Nichole and Ben started toward town. She'd been in her own world the entire morning. She hadn't realized she hadn't spoken at all until Ben took her hand and pressed his lips to her fingers.

"You're off somewhere else," he said, and she glanced at him before looking back toward the road.

"I guess I am. I'm a little out of my element just hanging out at the ranch."

"I could tell."

His voice carried a disappointment that knotted in her gut. "I'm not belittling it, I'm just..."

"Bored. I know. Your need to be around the general public is much different need than mine. But I get it."

Nichole let her shoulders ease. "I thought I'd like to stop in and say hello to everyone if that's okay."

"I thought they told you to keep away."

"I'm not going to work. I just want to say hello. I feel isolated, Ben."

He gave her hand a squeeze. "Then we will stop. I told Phillip we'd stop in there as well."

Unless he had more news, Nichole wasn't sure why they needed to do that, but he was going to humor her by stopping at the *Bridal Mecca.* She could take time to stop by the police station too.

AT LEAST THE bitch hadn't left any permanent marks on Ben, he thought gratefully as he walked out of the doctor's office. The lump on his head from where she'd hit him would take a while to go down, but he could deal with that. He wasn't dead on the side of the road, and that was what mattered.

Their next stop had been by the reception hall to see Lydia who had nearly broken into tears when she saw him. Then they said hello to everyone else before walking into the salon.

Audrey's glare in his direction was understood, but it had softened when she wrapped her arms around each of them and held them tightly.

"You guys are a sight for sore eyes." She turned to Ben. "How are you feeling?"

"I'm fine. I have a good nurse, and no lasting harm was done."

"Your truck is totaled. Jake told me."

"It is. But that's immaterial."

As they walked back to Nichole's car, Ben thought about the conversation they'd had with Audrey. His truck didn't matter. Nothing mattered except Nichole and her kids, and his family. It had broken his heart when he'd seen the boys walk into the hospital room and stop, afraid of what had happened to him. Laura, on the other hand, took one look at his cuts and bandages and took his hand to sit with him on the couch. They loved him too, he realized at that moment.

Nichole pushed the button on her keys and unlocked the doors. He felt her fingers begin to pull from his so that she could walk around to the driver's side and climb in, but he pulled her back.

Eyes wide, Nichole smiled, but it quickly slid away. "What's wrong?"

"Nothing. In fact, everything is right in the world." He said gazing at her, her dark hair catching the sunlight. "I just wanted to look at you for a moment."

Now she laughed. "You can look at me all you want when we get home," she said pulling back, but he tugged against her.

"We are home."

She narrowed her eyes at him. "Are you feeling okay?"

"Home is where you are. I just realized everything else is material. I'm home with you and the kids." He pulled her closer. "I know you're an in-town kind of girl and I'm a country kind of guy, but none of that matters. What matters is waking up each morning with you next to me and having breakfast with the kids."

"What are you getting at?"

"Marry me." The words flew from his mouth. "No, wait. Don't say anything to that."

She burst into laughter as she wrapped her arms around him. "Did they give you something at the doctor's office?"

"Nothing. But I can't just blurt that out. I have some other people to talk about this before I say that again." He rested his hands on her hips. "I love you. Let's leave it at that."

Nichole brushed a kiss to his lips. "I love you, too." She

pulled back and headed around to the other side of the car. "I want to stop by my house and grab a few things."

"Sure." Ben opened his door and slid inside. "I can say, I'd love to have you all stay with me at my house. Permanently."

"I still have five more months on my lease."

"Right. Offer stands. I don't want you moving back until Justine is locked up, but honestly, I don't want you to move out. Any of you."

Nichole started the car and pulled into traffic as she headed toward her house. "I suppose I could sublet it."

He watched her lips curl into a beautiful smile, but her eyes stayed on the road.

He wasn't going to say another word. For the moment, he felt as if he had his answer. Now he needed to talk to her boys. He'd promised them he'd ask first, even if they'd given their permission.

But he absolutely knew he wanted to marry her. He'd never been more sure about anything in his life.

Nichole had chosen that neighborhood specifically for the homey feel it gave her when she drove down the street. Luck had been on her side when the house, as cute as it was, had been available for rent.

It tugged at her heart when she thought about not living there anymore, but warmth and joy filled the rest of her when she thought of living out in the country with Ben.

She tucked her lips between her teeth to keep the growing smile from surfacing. He'd asked her to marry him. God, she hadn't wanted him to do that, but at the moment that he had she'd nearly jumped into his arms and screamed yes. What had given her such a change of heart? She loved him, but jumping into marriage, that just had seemed counterproductive to the life she'd been building. But now, it was exactly what she wanted.

The thought of taking his name and being part of the Walker family thrilled her nearly as much as being Ben's wife. And when she thought of the kids, she no longer worried that a decision like marriage would confuse them. She knew they wanted it as much as she did. And she did want it.

Pulling up in front of the little house she'd shared with her children, she realized it no longer held the appeal it had even a few weeks earlier. Now it was just a house. A house with good memories, but only a house.

She pulled into the driveway and put the car in park. "I'm going to walk down to Mr. Cowell's house and see what he thinks about me subletting the house."

"I'll walk down with you," Ben offered as he opened his door.

"You go inside and sit down. You're still in recovery," she demanded in a sweet, but direct tone. "I'll be five minutes."

"Fine, Mother. I'll go inside and wait," he joked as he shut the door and started up the steps. "I need a key."

Nichole laughed as she tossed him her keys and then headed down the street toward Mr. Cowell's house.

BEN WALKED up the front steps and put the key in the lock, but the door pushed open.

"What the hell?" he whispered to himself. Pushing the door open, he carefully walked inside.

The TV was on the Disney Channel, just as it had been when he'd last sat there with Laura. He could smell something cooking, and someone was humming in the kitchen.

Wasn't it his luck Mr. Cowell rented out the house and hadn't told Nichole. But, Ben had paid the rent for that month, and her things were still in the house.

Pictures of her and the kids still hung on the walls, and her furniture still sat in the same places it had when they'd rushed Nichole out of there.

He took a breath to call out to whoever was in the house but stopped when he caught a glimpse of the redhead in the kitchen.

Contemplating on whether he should turn around or say

something, he decided to retreat, but not before the woman turned to see him standing there.

When he saw her, he froze.

"Lover, you've arrived just in time. The kids are at their grandparents' house, and it's just you and me. I cooked supper for you, too."

Justine's look had changed, but no doubt it was her. He'd remember that voice anywhere.

"You cooked supper?" he asked noting that it was only lunchtime. "That was nice of you."

He thought if he bided his time he could come up with a plan.

Concern worried Justine's face as she walked across the room toward him. "What happened to you? You're all cut up. Were you in an accident?"

Ben studied her, but it was clear that she didn't know why he looked like he did. The woman wasn't right in her mind at all. How could someone so gone have masterminded the takeover of Nichole's identity? Perhaps that was how she'd done it, she thought she was Nichole. It hadn't been malicious—not really.

Ben set his jaw and watched the woman near him, raising her hand to caress cuts and bruises on his face. A tear rolled down her cheek.

"Who did this to you? Why? Why would they do this?" She asked, her voice wavering.

Ben gripped her wrist and held it before she could touch him. "You don't remember this? You and I were in a car accident."

Justine took a step back. "You're lying. I wasn't in an accident."

He tugged on her arm and looked down at it. "What are those cuts from?"

She looked down at them as if it were the first time she'd

seen them. Her skin went pale, and her breathing became labored. "What did you do to me?"

When her eyes met his, they were no longer sad but crazy with anger.

"Let's go in the kitchen and sit down a moment. Let's talk."

"You hurt me!" She pulled from him and lashed out with her nails as he stepped back.

"Stop! Justine, stop!" His own voice was filled with anger now.

"Don't call me that! You know my name. You know my body. Never call me that name again!" Her cheeks had gone bright red with anger, and she leapt at him knocking him back to the wall as she raked her nails across his face.

As he went to push her back, she rammed her shoulder into his throat causing him to drop to his knees.

"You can't come into my house and attack me. That low-life husband of mine did the same thing, and now he's locked away. You stay away from me," she screamed as she moved toward the wall and took down a picture of Nichole and the kids. She held it up over her head as if she planned to bring it down over his. "I'm going to leave here and get my kids and run. Just as I did before. I'll run from you now. Don't follow us."

As she lifted the frame up higher, Ben sucked in as much air as he could. His lungs burned, his vision blurred, but he would take her out before he'd let her hurt another person he loved.

Just as he attempted to get his balance, he heard her scream as he saw Nichole grab hold of Justine's hair and pull her back from him.

The frame crashed to the floor next to him as Nichole punched and pushed Justine until she too was backed up against the wall and slithering to the ground, her mouth bloodied now.

Nichole moved in again to land another blow, but she pulled

back and stopped, noticing Justine had collapsed where she had fallen.

Panicked, she exchanged a look with Ben. "Oh, God, did I kill her?"

Ben crawled to her and touched her neck. "No. She's alive." He sat back against the wall. "I think she was on something. She was absolutely mad—crazy."

"She is crazy, and I could kill her right now!" Nichole's voice raged, and he wondered if she might try to attack her again, but she eased back and covered her face with shaking hands.

"Oh, God! Oh, God!" she repeated.

Ben worked to find his balance and stand. He reached for her and pulled her in close. "Hey, breathe."

"Look what she did to you. And she was here, in my house." She pressed her face to his chest. "She's lost her mind."

"Yes. She truly believes she's you and that Jerome was her husband. He made her angry so she got him locked up. And when I called her Justine she threatened me, because she thought I was in love with her—you."

When Justine stirred, Nichole stepped forward, prepared to attack. "She's not going to get up, Nichole. Take it easy."

It was then he heard the front door open, and Phillip walked through the door with two other deputies, guns drawn.

"Nichole, step back easy," he said in warning.

"I didn't do anything wrong. She was attacking him," she shouted and Ben reached for her.

"Just ease back," he said, guiding her away from Justine.

One of the deputies moved in and knelt down beside the redhead on the floor. "This is her," he confirmed. "She might need an ambulance."

Phillip called for one on his radio and then holstered his gun. "What happened here?" he asked turning toward Nichole.

"I kicked her ass. Are you going to arrest me for that? She's in my house. She was cooking my food. And she attacked Ben. I'm just in what I did."

Ben wrapped his arm around her. "She came at me. Nichole happened to have gotten here just in time."

Phillip grinned. "I'm not calling you weak, Walker. But you were getting your ass kicked by a woman?"

Ben had to chuckle at that. "Yes. But drug screen her, I think you're going to find she's on something. She wasn't right, in the head, you know?"

"Yeah, we know. We've been looking for her once we realized she changed her look. We caught her dealer yesterday. Mr. Cowell called 911 when you left his house," he offered turning toward Nichole. "He said he realized it wasn't you that had been living in the house. Said he'd even spoke to the woman, thinking it was you just yesterday. Looks like he made the right call," Phillip said as he watched his deputy open the door for the paramedics.

"I want her taken down," Nichole spat out the words angrily. "She had no right to take from me or impersonate me. And she hurt Ben."

"We'll take care of her," Phillip promised. "Why don't you and Ben head back home and I'll come out later and talk to you."

Ben turned Nichole to face him. "Let's go get the kids. I think they'll make you feel better."

He watched as she breathed in and out trying to calm the anger that ran through her. He couldn't even imagine the satisfaction she felt knocking Justine Meyers to the ground after all the hell she'd put her though. Well, he could. He'd landed a few satisfying punches in his life.

"C'mon. Let's go home," Ben offered and her eyes went soft.

"Yeah. I want to hug my kids," she said with tears now welling in her eyes. "Thank you."

"You never have to thank me. We're a team." He pulled her in close before looking at Phillip. "Come by anytime. I'll have a beer waiting for you."

He shook Phillip's hand and escorted Nichole out of the home she'd once shared with her children and guided her toward the truck. Perhaps she'd never want to go back to that little house in the city after what happened. Maybe now she'd want to live with him in his little house in the country.

Nichole sat outside the ice-cream store on the bench she'd sat with Ben that night he'd first taken her out. God, she was glad she'd gone out with him even though he'd been so awkward. It humored her to think of it now in the August heat of late summer. The boys would be starting school in a few weeks, and Glenda had asked to watch Laura during the fall when Nichole was working.

She never would have thought that everything would have worked out so perfectly for her. She'd never thought she'd fall in love, but she had. She never thought she'd look forward to the forty-five-minute drive into town each day, but she did.

Not only was she happy in her life and in her job, but the kids were thriving living with Ben. They'd become a tight little family, she thought to herself as Laura came out of the ice cream parlor with an ice-cream cone which dripped over her hand.

Nichole pulled her up next to her and wiped Laura's hand with a napkin as she tried to lick the droplets quickly melting in the heat.

"Where are all of the boys?" she asked her.

"Machine." She took a lick. "Quarter in Ben's pocket."

Nichole laughed. She had no idea what that might mean, but watching her sweet daughter enjoy her treat brought her great joy. It didn't matter what it meant.

A moment later Zane and Wyatt walked out of the store with double dips of ice cream in their cones.

"Boys. That's too much sugar. I said one small one."

They laughed in unison.

"Ben said we could," Zane said as he licked his top scoop.

She supposed she could let it go. It was the end of summer after all.

Finally, Ben walked out of the shop with a shake in his hand with two straws. "I hope you don't mind sharing."

"I'd share anything with you," she said gazing up at the man who had stolen her heart the moment he'd walked in to get his hair cut for his cousin's wedding.

"I'm glad you said that." Ben handed her the shake and reached his hand into his front pocket. He pulled out a plastic container, one she recognized from the toy machines in the store. That must have been what Laura was telling her. He was buying toys with the quarters in his pocket.

Ben held the container in his hand and gave it a shake.

"What are you doing?" Nichole laughed as she sipped her drink.

"Laura picked this out. I had something else in mind, but she seems to think it's the right one."

Nichole noticed the boys giggle at the end of the bench as ice cream dripped off their chins.

"And what is it that my sweet Laura picked?" she asked, pressing a kiss to Laura's head.

Ben looked at the container again and then knelt down on the hot cement in front of her on one knee.

"What are you doing?" She laughed. "It's hot and dirty down there. We can scoot down."

Just as she was going to pick Laura up and put her on her lap, the boys stood next to Ben. She looked at the three of them with their matching grins.

"Mom, you should see what Ben brought you," Wyatt said. "But first you have to tell him your answer."

"My answer to what?" she asked.

Zane let out a huff. "Mom, we want Ben to be our dad. Is that okay?"

"Yeah," Wyatt agreed. "And we want to live out on the ranch forever. Okay?"

Laura tugged on Nichole's shirt. "I want ring."

With a grin on her lips, Nichole turned back to Ben who still held the plastic toy in his hand.

"Ben, what are my children trying to get at?"

With a twist of his wrist, Ben opened the little container and pulled out a large plastic pink ring. He held it up to the sun and examined it.

"I don't think I'll ever be able to top this. Laura did a great job," he said as he looked up at Nichole and reached for her hand. Pausing with the ring at the tip of her pinky he smiled. "Nichole, I want you all to live out on the ranch forever. I would love to be their dad and to give them my name. And more than anything, I'd love it if you'd be my wife and take my name too."

The chocolatey, ice cream grins surrounding her should have had her laughing, but she found that she was ready to burst into tears. Dear God, he was proposing to her. He'd asked for their blessing, and they had apparently given it to him. Her children wanted him as much as she did.

The first tear fell, and Laura sat up on her knees and wiped a sticky hand over Nichole's cheek.

"No cry, Mama. Nice ring."

She laughed through the tears. "You're right. It is a nice ring. I'd be honored to have it."

Ben narrowed his eyes at her. "Is that your way of saying yes?"

She nodded as she wiped away the tears. "Yes. Yes. I want to live on the ranch forever with boys and girls that have the Walker name. And I too would like the name. Above all else, I want to wear your pink ring forever."

Ben slid the ring on her pinky and then stood to kiss her, but not before Laura rose and kissed him on the cheek and wrapped her arms around his neck. He lifted her up and then took Nichole's hand to pull her to him.

"I'll love you forever. I promise you that," Ben said as the boys moved in around them. "I'll love all of you forever."

Nichole had never wanted anything more than to be Mrs. Walker. She wondered how it was going to be possible to wait to plan a wedding. She wanted to be Mrs. Walker at that very moment, and she knew that her children would be equally proud to be Walkers too.

EPILOGUE

*N*ichole had never seen any cuter boys than her own in the tuxes that they wore. Ben had chosen them as his Best Men, along with all of his brothers. Laura looked like a princess in her flowergirl dress. Pearl had pushed for the tiara, as she thought it was appropriate for a little girl whose mother was marrying into a family that would treat her like royalty.

Her mother had been crying tears of joy, she promised Nichole, all morning. And she was fairly sure she'd caught her father having a heart to heart with Ben.

Every moment leading up to the wedding had been memorable, even the bad stuff.

"Okay, I'm done nursing," Audrey said as she handed her son to Glenda." Give me ten minutes to shimmy into that dress."

Glenda rocked her great-nephew on her shoulder as she patted him on the back and Nichole watched. The woman was magnificent with children, and she supposed that was why she had five sons who were quickly being snatched up by women who loved them. They were kind, generous, and loving. And they all looked out for each other and took family very seriously.

"I have to admit, I've never seen anyone in a pink wedding

dress that looked more beautiful," Pearl said as she finished fussing with the bow at the back of Nichole's dress.

"I had to go with the theme," she offered, looking at the pink plastic ring Ben had given her which now was prominent on Laura's tiny hand.

Lydia stood next to her and looked in the mirror. Her short crop of hair was adorned with a ring of flowers. "You're a lucky girl."

"Don't I know it." Nichole smiled at her reflection. "We're all lucky to be marrying him." She looked at the boys who were standing with their grandfather.

"Everyone is ready," her father said as he took the hands of both boys. "I'm going to deliver these handsome men to the right people. I'll be back for you."

Nichole let out a nervous breath and giggled. She was about to become Nichole Walker. It was hard to believe.

BEN COULDN'T REMEMBER a time in his entire life when he'd ever been so nervous. His palms were wet and his stomach jumped. There had been a few moments that morning, when he'd seen the kids all dressed up, that he thought he might just pass out. Seriously, there was no reason to be so nervous.

He thought about the fact that a year ago he'd been sitting in his mother's garden watching his cousin marry the man of her dreams. Now Audrey was a mother, and Gregory was more smitten than ever with his wife and his new son. Ben remembered the casual looks behind him to always find Nichole looking back at him. They'd shared a promised dance at the reception, and had each caught the traditional bouquet and garter as well. Perhaps their union had always been destined.

Ben patted his tux pocket and felt the piece of paper inside.

Ella had worked some miracles for him, and he couldn't wait to share it with Nichole and the kids.

Gerald's hand gripped his shoulder and pulled him from his thoughts.

"You ready, man? Times up," he joked.

"Yeah, I think I am."

"Good, because I got a look at your bride, and you're one lucky man."

At that moment the music started, and Ben looked toward the house to see his cousins and Lydia walking toward them. Pearl held Laura's hand until she got to the garden, then she began to pour her flower basket out on the white runner Lydia had insisted they use. The guests chuckled, and both his mother and Nichole's mother wiped tears from their cheeks.

And then he saw her.

Her wedding dress was pink. The sight of her lit in his heart and a smile widened on his mouth. It was so much better than white, he thought. It was perfect, and it would go so well with the ring he'd bought for her.

When Laura made it to him, she tugged on his jacket and lifted her arms for him to pick her up. Nichole's mother moved in to take her, but Ben waved her off for the moment. He wanted to be holding Laura as they watched her mother come toward them. After all, this union wasn't just about him and Nichole. It was about all of them.

As Nichole's father walked her toward him, he stopped, whispered in her ear, and kissed her on the cheek. Then he shook Ben's hand before taking Laura from him and sitting with her on his lap.

"God, you're beautiful."

The smile on her face gave her a glow. "Thank you. I liked the pink dress."

"I like it too."

He took the hand of his wife-to-be, and they listened as the minister began the ceremony. They gave their vows and promised themselves to each other for eternity.

When the minister asked for the rings, Ben delighted in seeing Nichole's eyes widen as he slipped it on her finger.

"Ben, you got me a pink diamond?"

"It seemed right. Laura took your other one."

Once the ring was on her finger, she held it up to admire it. "I couldn't have picked out a better one." Looking up at him, she cupped his face in her hands and kissed him.

The guests laughed at her impromptu move.

The minister finished the ceremony and introduced the new Mr. and Mrs. Walker. When the guests applauded, Ben turned his wife toward him. He motioned to the boys to join them and Laura wiggled off her grandfather's lap and into her mother's waiting arms.

Ben pulled the piece of paper from his pocket and knelt down next to the boys. "My friend Ella helped me with something, and I want to give it to you now in front of all these people. It will be a new beginning for us all."

He watched as Wyatt wiped his eyes and Zane put his arm around his brother's shoulders.

Ben looked down at the legal document in his hands. "If you will all have me, I have permission to give you my name. You can all be Walkers too if you want to be."

Laura reached for him, and he pulled her to him.

"So my new name would be Wyatt Walker?"

"If you want it to be," he offered.

"Can I call you Dad?"

He felt the tears stinging his eyes, but he smiled through it. "That's up to you and your mom."

Wyatt and Zane both looked up at her, and she gave them a nod.

And with that, the boys wrapped their arms around Ben and Laura.

Laura looked up at him and placed her small hands on his cheeks, much like her mother had during the ceremony and said, "Daddy."

Now the tears spilled down his cheeks as all three of his children hugged him and his new wife joined them.

The minister laughed and announced, "It looks like I'm proud to introduce the new Walker family."

He would assume that there wasn't a dry eye in the crowd as they all stood and applauded, and a moment later his brothers circled around them engulfing his new family in an embrace. It was just the kind of beginning he'd been looking for, and he hadn't even known he wanted it.

PREVIEW OF WALKER DEFENSE

We hope that you liked this release from
Beginnings
by Bernadette Marie.

Please enjoy an excerpt from her next
Walker Family Series book
Walker Defense.

WALKER DEFENSE

BOOK NUMBER 9 IN THE WALKER FAMILY SERIES

by Bernadette Marie

Laughter and applause had enveloped all the guests at the wedding of Ben and Nichole.

Ella wiped the tears from her cheeks with a handkerchief as she watched the new family welcome their congratulations from Ben's brothers. She envied the relationship the Walker family had with one another. Ella came from a good family. Her mother and father had been married nearly thirty years and her sister was happily married with a growing family, but they didn't have the same bond the Walkers had.

Perhaps that made her a little weepy, and today wasn't a day to sob over her own life. It was a day to celebrate Ben and Nichole and their children.

She'd spent a lot of time with Nichole over the past nine months as they prosecuted the woman who had stolen her identity and attacked Ben. As far as Ella was concerned, Nichole and her family would never have to worry about her again.

Once that case was closed, Ben had approached her about

adopting the kids. In order for the adoption to take place, their father had to give up rights to his children. Considering he was in jail on embezzlement charges, he wasn't too worried about giving up his kids. In fact, Ella was sickened by how quickly he signed them away.

She watched as Ben and Nichole, and their little family, walked down the aisle headed back toward the house. They stopped when they came to her and both hugged her.

"Thank you for everything," Nichole whispered in her ear.

"My pleasure," she said as the new family moved on, followed by their attendants.

Swiping a thumb over her cheek, she wiped away a stray tear as Gerald Walker followed his brother down the aisle. His eyes automatically darted to her, and a nervous grin curled up the corner of his mouth before he quickly looked away.

Ella couldn't blame him for being nervous around her. She'd broken his heart, crushed his plans, and belittled him in front of his family. Angry with herself, she felt heat rise in her cheeks. She was lucky to even be welcomed into their home, she thought.

But as Glenda Walker passed by her too, she reached out her hand and gave Ella's a squeeze and a friendly smile. Perhaps she was being too hard on herself. The Walkers hadn't pushed her out of their lives, she'd stepped back away from them out of respect. However, when they'd needed her expertise, they'd called on her. For that she'd been grateful. It was the least she could do for a family that had once embraced her as one of their own.

The reception would follow at Lydia Morgan's hall in town. She wondered if they'd notice if she didn't attend.

As the guests began to stroll out of the garden, she caught the eye of Nichole, the bride, who waved with a smile. Well, maybe they'd notice.

She was heading back into town anyway, she might as well stop by the hall. Wedding cake was always a good reason to attend a reception, that and Susan Walker's catering.

It would be worth the slight discomfort to celebrate the marriage of Ben Walker, whom she'd always admired, though she knew he didn't think much of her. Perhaps his mind had changed after she helped his wife go after the woman who had stolen her identity.

As Ella started her BMW which was parked down the road, she heard her name called from behind her. When she turned, she saw Gerald hurrying toward her.

"Hey, it might sound crazy, but can I get a ride into town with you? Cars are full, with gifts and the wedding party. I seem to be the odd man out," he said as he reached her.

She knew she was staring, and for the first time in her life seemed to be out of words.

"If you have other plans I can..."

"No, no," she stammered. "I can give you a ride. No problem."

Her heart hitched when he smiled that smile she'd seen so many times years ago. She was sure she'd never see it again aimed in her direction, but here he was.

Unsure of what to say next, Ella opened her car door and climbed in. When Gerald didn't open his door right away, she looked toward it to see him standing there motioning to unlock it.

"I'm sorry," she said as he climbed in. "I'm a little nervous being around you and your family today."

"You've been around my family for nearly nine months working with Nichole on her case. What's making you nervous now?"

She started the engine and the car roared to life. "I've spent that time with Nichole, not with Ben, or you, or the rest of your family. Gerald, I know how they all feel about me. I know what I did and I know..."

"You don't know anything," he interrupted with a bite in his voice. "I've got every right to be mad at you for the rest of my life."

"Yes, you do," she agreed, and noted to herself that she'd interrupted.

"But you know my family damn well enough to know that angry or not, they wouldn't treat you badly."

As she put the car in drive, and began to follow the other cars down the dirt road to town, she wrapped up the pity party she'd been having. Gerald was right. His family, including him, would never treat her poorly for her decisions.

"I'm sorry for all of that. I'm just nervous."

"I get it. I'm nervous too, but I don't want to be. We were friends for years so why not start out again as friends now?"

Ella bit down on her glossed lip. "You're sure you want to be my friend?"

"Are you getting resettled in town and trying to build your career?"

"Yes."

"Have you been gone long enough that some things have changed?"

"Yes."

"Are you divorced and trying to work through that in your head and in your heart?"

That stung, she thought, but she answered honestly. "Yes."

"Then it sounds like you could use a friend, so why not me? And you don't have to worry. I don't get to town too often, so I won't be one of those drop by and stand on your porch kind of friends. You don't have to open up to me and confess all your sins or desires. You don't have to defend any decision you've ever made. We can just consider ourselves friends."

As she slowed behind the car in front of her to give herself visibility from the dust being kicked up, she considered his offer. She missed Gerald Walker in every way, but mostly as her friend. That had been a huge loss when she'd turned down his marriage proposal.

"I'd like to be friends," she admitted. "I had considered not going to the reception. I thought I'd feel out of place."

"That would be a shame if you missed it."

"It seems as though I've missed my share of Walker weddings in the past few years. I can't say I saw that coming," she humored as he fidgeted with the radio, a habit he had when he'd get into her car.

"I don't think any of them thought they'd all be getting married. And now there are kids too. Who'd have thought?"

Well, you and I had, she considered. *We'd talked about marriage. We'd made plans. Oh, we were stupid and young and foolish, but we'd thought about it.* And until the moment he'd asked her to marry him, she'd been right there with him making those plans. But she got spooked, and she landed in the arms of his best friend. Ex-best friend, she noted.

"They all seem very happy."

"They are. I guess there is someone for everyone," he offered as he found a song he liked, for the time being, and sat back in his seat. "So what about you? Are you dating anyone?"

Ella swallowed the lump in her throat. This drive was long enough without talking about dating with her ex.

"No. Not very interested in dating right now. My career is too important."

He nodded slowly, his gaze focused out the window. "It always was. You've done good for yourself."

Important enough that she'd given it as one of the reasons for not marrying him.

"What about you? As the only eligible Walker bachelor left, I'm guessing women are falling at your feet."

He gave her a shrug. "My cousin Todd hasn't gotten hooked yet. I think we're both safe. We enjoy our casual relationships with ladies. No need to go get all serious. We're young, successful men. We might as well enjoy our freedom."

The lump in her throat was back and it threatened to choke her. It was time to change the small talk to something that wasn't going to kill her. She knew he had no intention of hurting her with the conversation at hand. He was just being *friendly*. When the wedding was over, he'd go his way and she'd go hers. Just like it had been since she'd walked out of his life. Only now, she had a kind of permission to openly talk to him as if nothing had ever happened.

She focused on the turn in the road, and the silence between them.

"So, what do you think of the Braves this year?"

MEET THE AUTHOR

Bestselling Author Bernadette Marie is known for building families readers want to be part of. Her series *The Keller Family* has graced bestseller charts since its release in 2011. Since then she has authored and published over thirty books. The married mother of five sons promises romances with a *Happily Ever After always*...and says she can write it because she lives it.

Obsessed with writing since the age of 12, Bernadette Marie officially started her journey as an author in 2007 when she finalized a manuscript she'd been writing for 22 years, shelved it, and wrote 12 more books that year. In 2009 she was contracted with a small publisher in a deal that would eventually go bad. From that experience, she knew she could take control of her career and that's what she did.

A chronic entrepreneur since opening her first salon at the age of twenty, Bernadette Marie established her own publishing house in 2011, *5 Prince Publishing,* so that she could publish the books she liked to write and help make the dreams of other aspiring authors come true too. Believing there is a place for the fresh author's voice, she not only publishes but coaches others who wish to publish their work independently. Bernadette Marie is also the CEO of *Illumination Author Events and Services* offering smaller intimate author/reader events as well as author services.

OTHER TITLES FROM 5 PRINCE PUBLISHING

The Deja Vu House *Doug Simpson*
We Are From Atlantis *Doug Simpson*
Prez *Lissa Jay*
The Train Robbers *James P Hanley*
Walker Revenge *Bernadette Marie*
Lest We Aren't Forgiven *Railyn Stone*
Broken Hearts *M.O. Kenyan*
Goodnight Kisses *Wilhelmina Stolen*
The Three Stones of Bethany *April Marcom*
Wanderlust *Bernadette Marie*
Holiday Past *Jessica Dall*